SHIELD AND HUMBLED CROWN

THE ENERGY OF MAGIC
BOOK FOUR

J.E. NEAL

To the Anns — For their editing magic

CONTENTS

CHAPTER 1
WHAT YOU SHARE
~RAINER LAWSON~

Emily's speech at the press conference covered the papers the next day. When they returned to Arlington, Rainer informed Peterson that he and Emily would agree to drop the charges against Samantha if the press reported what really happened with Adeline's surgery and that Logan had never and would never use drugs of any kind.

Rainer spent the rest of the week refining his plans for Emily's birthday. He was growing more excited with each passing day. The Haydenshires were spending the weekend at home. They were thoroughly exhausted from their campaigning travels. Governor Haydenshire was hearing trials set for Friday. Saturday night was one of the debates between him and Peterson.

Mrs. Haydenshire was spending Friday and Saturday with the twins and cooking a meal for the entire family Sunday evening. Her security team, which consisted of eight Iodex officers, would be staying with her and the twins at the house, so Rainer and Logan were to be in the office Friday instead of babysitting.

After dropping Emily off at the arena and enduring Chloe and Garrett's rather heated rekindling of their relationship, which was playing out in the parking lot, Rainer fell into his desk across from Logan.

He tried to stop shuddering every time he recalled Garrett leaning Chloe out across the hood of her Thunderbird with his hands up her skirt and his tongue down her throat. Vindico had everyone catching up on paperwork as they'd all been out in the field trying to keep the Haydenshires safe.

With very little enthusiasm, Rainer set to work filling out paperwork on what he'd been doing the past few weeks and on taking down Malicai and LeCroy. His phone chirped just after he'd started in on the files on his computer. He smiled and pulled it from his pocket.

> Just changing for practice, and I missed you.

Emily had added a picture of her cleavage to accompany the text. He could see the very tops of her areolas and he caught himself trying to angle the phone in a futile effort to see more. He forced himself to close the text and get back to work. He worked steadily and tried not to think that if Emily was texting him pictures of her cleavage then she was definitely up for a little fun later. Rainer continued to slog laboriously through the budgetary reports on his Iodex gear.

A little while later, his phone chirped again, and Rainer snatched it off his desk. Logan gave him a quizzical glance. His brain was at war with his body. He'd hoped there would be another picture. Maybe this one would reveal a little more.

> Hey, remember when we were little?

Rainer was too intrigued to get much work done until the next part of the message came through. A minute later, clearly playing with him, she filled in.

> And I told you I wanted to touch it?

Rainer turned the phone face down on his desk. He clenched his jaw as he forced his way through another budget document he had to read and sign. He'd reread the same line four times when Emily completed the message with:

I still want to…

He momentarily debated booking a hotel room for lunch, picking Emily up from the arena, and doing all of the things racing through his mind.

Rainer's entire body pulled taut as he allowed himself a few minutes to fantasize. Just before he and Logan left to grab some lunch, another text came through. He quickly jerked his phone off his desk and read the words—

Hungry baby? I sure am.

Rainer stifled a groan and texted back:

You have no idea how badly I want you. You're driving me out of my mind.

With that, he shoved his phone in his pocket and followed Logan to the cafeteria. Emily texted a smiley face emoji back.

Vindico and Garrett joined the line in the Senate cafeteria behind Rainer.

"Hey, Bridgette really wants to see a Summation challenge and the arena and everything. She won't shut up about it. So, I was thinking about bringing her out to Angels Arena tonight. Maybe we could grab some dinner afterwards?"

Rainer noted that his boss seemed to have no interest in either Bridgette or touring Angels Arena. He assumed this was something else he was doing to keep Bridgette spying on Wretchkinsides and his men who were still frequenting the strip club where she worked.

"I have to pick Adeline up, but I could meet you somewhere after that?" Logan offered offhandedly. Rainer tried not to grimace.

He'd planned on picking Emily up from practice, feeding her something on the way home, and then carrying her to their bedroom and engaging her in things he sincerely hoped would drive her wild that evening.

He hadn't been planning to ask her to give Vindico's non-girlfriend a tour of Angels Arena and then to endure a dinner date with his boss. It did strike Rainer as odd that Garrett looked so concerned. Nothing shook Garrett.

"If Em's up for it, I guess it's good with me," Rainer answered.

He didn't particularly care that Vindico could tell he wasn't thrilled with the idea. Emily texted again while Rainer ate a bowl of chili with Logan and Vindico.

No joke, Chloe is throwing one of those lingerie and sex toy parties today, and she's giving us a two-hour lunch to attend. She's pretty jazzed about making up with Garrett, but what I need to know is if you prefer me in lace or satin and do you like black or purple better...

While imagining the sassy grin that was most definitely on Emily's face at that moment, Rainer stifled a groan. The following text a moment later added,

Oh, there are leather options as well, and what do you think about vibes? Fionna said we could play with it together.

Rainer accidentally dropped his spoon. It clanged loudly in his nearly empty chili bowl. Vindico and Logan gave him quizzical glares.

It took him a long moment to force his mind off Emily and Fionna Styler and a vibrator. He called himself several derogatory phrases as he realized that Emily had meant that Fionna had suggested that he and Emily could play with one together.

As Rainer followed a few steps behind Vindico and Logan back to the Iodex offices, another text came through.

He decided to wait until he was back at his desk to read it. He tried to listen to Logan and Vindico's conversation about the debate the following evening but found his mind full of images of Emily's body twisted in extremely lurid poses and making extremely dirty requests of Rainer. He added a vibrator into his imagery and suddenly his heart was flying. He'd been at half-mast long enough that he ached.

He fell into his chair. He didn't want to walk any farther in his current state. Rainer pulled out his phone and read.

So we got to try a few things on...

The attached picture was of just the top of Emily's thigh. It was covered in something that was hunter-green satin with a V hem that was covered in black lace. His heart raced. That was all he needed to see to make him ache for more.

He tried desperately to concentrate on everything he was supposed to be catching up on. He almost whimpered when the next message came through. After he picked up his phone, he furrowed his brow as he read:

TDTM.

He texted back question marks and moved on to the next form in his pile. Emily replied instantly.

Talk Dirty To Me.

She added another smiley face. With a slight headshake, Rainer texted back.

Are you enjoying driving me slowly out of my mind, Miss Haydenshire?

Yes!

was her immediate response.

She gave Rainer a little break, and he worked his way through several of the files on his desk before she texted again. He shook himself from the banality of the Interfeci accounts that Iodex watched constantly.

Kind of been a long week. I need you to help me unwind.

After deciding that if she could play he could as well, Rainer considered for a moment before responding. He recalled her earlier request.

Her response of,

only served to make Rainer ache more. At four thirty, she sent over another picture.

The words were under a shot of Emily standing just outside the Angels locker room. She was in her Angels short-shorts and a sports bra.

Rainer turned his slight groan into a cough, but he assumed he hadn't covered it well as Logan and several other officers shot him goading smirks.

By five, Rainer was thrumming. His entire body was poised and ready to take her and make her all his own. He signed his name on the last piece of paper on his desk and sprinted to his car.

CHAPTER 2
BRIDGETTE

After he whisked through the security detail at Angels Arena, he found the entire team standing outside the locker rooms glaring at the door.

The furious scowl on Emily's face wasn't at all what he'd been expecting when he'd flown there from the Senate.

"What's wrong?" He glanced around, wondering why the ladies weren't showering and changing.

"You don't know?" Emily spat.

"Uh, no."

He glanced up and down the line of scowling Angels all with their arms crossed over their chests. Rainer shook his head in utter confusion. He realized someone was missing. "Where's Fionna?"

"She went home in tears as soon as he got here," Emily huffed. "Vindico asked Chloe to give him and Bridgette a tour of the arena, but wait...there's more. Bridgette showed up in her Tantra uniform." Emily used finger quotes around the word uniform as Rainer's mouth fell open.

"Yeah,"—Emily scowled—"and apparently they're going out to dinner with us. Bridgette informed Chloe that she needed to use the shower and locker room to get ready. So, despite the fact that she doesn't seem to have any problem taking her clothes off in front of men all freaking day, she doesn't change clothes with women. We're all stuck out here until she finishes!" Emily's acrimony was rolling in enflamed red waves off her rhythms. She gave Rainer a hateful glare.

His mind raced. He wasn't certain where to begin, and he didn't really want to plead for forgiveness in front of the majority of the Arlington Angels. Rainer tried to think of something to say. Being incredibly turned on all day made him stupid.

He drew a deep breath and took in all of the irritated glares he was receiving. "I never told Vindico we would go out with them. He mentioned at lunch that he was thinking about bringing her out here tonight and asked if we wanted to get something to eat. I told him I'd see if you wanted to go, and that was it." Rainer glanced around to make certain his boss wasn't in the general vicinity. "I was planning on bowing out. I'm sorry, sweetheart. I had no idea he'd do this."

Emily edged away from the Angels slightly. "I've been texting you all day! You could've said something about dinner before Vindico got here and informed me that we're going out." Furious tears pricked her eyes. She wasn't just annoyed. She was visibly hurt, and he knew most of it was her hurt for Fionna. They'd become closer than any of the friends Emily'd had at the academy.

Rainer took her hand and pulled her to the other end of the hallway. "Please believe me. You've had me tied in knots all day. All I wanted to do was come pick you up and take you to bed. That's all I've thought about all day. I don't want to go out with my boss and his non-girlfriend. Honestly, I don't know which one of them is using the other one more, but it's awful all the way around. I want to go out with you and then do all of the things you've been texting me about all day long."

Emily couldn't quite hide her pleased grin, and Rainer knew he'd gotten to her.

"But we have to go out with them, don't we?" She sighed.

"He's my boss. I'm pretty sure I don't have a choice." He was thoroughly irritated with Vindico. He'd convinced her though, and she was on the verge of forgiving him right up until the moment Bridgette stepped out of the locker room.

Emily's eyes goggled, and Rainer turned to see Bridgette wearing a miniskirt so short Rainer had no idea how she would be able to sit down without showing off everything and a red halter top with a V-neck collar that dropped all the way to her navel. Her breasts were only marginally covered.

Rainer spun back to Emily. "I thought she was changing."

"She did." She stormed into the changing rooms to get her things. Rainer's head dropped in defeat. He stood there and stared after her for a moment, but then he made his way back onto the field to wait.

Vindico was doing something on his phone. He didn't seem to have noticed his date's lack of clothing. He nodded to Rainer as he stowed his phone in his pocket. "You've met Bridgette, right?"

"Uh, yeah. You introduced us at the office the day she came by." Rainer gave Bridgette a half-hearted smile. Vindico received another text and went back to his phone.

"There's a decent hibachi place near here. I just texted Logan and Garrett to see if they wanted to get one of the four-sides with us," Vindico informed Rainer a moment later.

"Great." Utter defeat washed over him as he tried to envision Emily, Adeline, and Chloe Sawyer, one of Fionna's best friends since the academy, having dinner with Bridgette.

Garrett appeared before the ladies finished changing. He gave Vindico a nod and slapped him on the back. He had a polite smile for Bridgette. Garrett and Rainer exchanged a knowing look. Their evening would be spent trying to keep peace between Chloe, Emily, and Bridgette. Negotiating permanent peace between war-torn countries would've been vastly easier.

Although Chloe was most definitely a live-and-let-live party girl, Rainer knew that she, just like Emily, could become quite vicious when it came to defending someone she adored as much as Fionna. Garrett edged Rainer away from Bridgette and Vindico.

"All right now, I've never steered you wrong, so listen up." Absolutely certain that was not true, Rainer nodded anyway. "Chloe and I are going to ride with you and Em. Let them get it out of their system before we get to the restaurant, or this is going to get ugly. Dan doesn't have any idea that Fionna has been pining for him for years, and for her sake, we need to keep it that way."

After deciding that this was one of Garrett's better ideas, Rainer agreed. "Even if they don't say anything about Fionna, they're not going to be nice to her."

"Yeah, well, Dan kept putting her off on meeting his friends, but she got insistent. Everything about this is fucked the hell up, but he won't listen to me. Why the hell did she want to come here?" Garrett shot Vindico a thoroughly annoyed glance.

Unable to believe what his evening was rapidly deteriorating into compared with what he'd been planning all day, Rainer's fantasies morphed from the things he so desperately wanted to be doing to Emily into images of him with his hands wrapped around Vindico's thick neck.

The girls emerged, scowled, and glared hatefully at Bridgette. Chloe was frantically texting, and Rainer didn't have to ask whom she might be talking to as his stomach churned.

"Hey, I'm on my bike, baby, since this was all kind of last minute. Why don't we just ride with Rainer and Em to the restaurant?" Garrett soothed.

"Whatever!" Chloe spat. Her eyes shot daggers at Bridgette. Garrett had a rather nice Harley Softail Fat Boy that he drove occasionally. He'd clearly been strategizing since he'd gotten the invite from Vindico at lunch. Rainer wished he'd had his brain above his belt line for more of the day and could've eased Emily into this a little more smoothly than he'd been able.

"Ready?" Vindico quizzed. Everyone nodded and followed Vindico and Bridgette out of the arena. Rainer tried to take Emily's hand, but she jerked it away defiantly. With a defeated sigh, Rainer whispered another apology as he opened the Mustang's door and pulled the seat forward to allow Chloe to climb in the back, beside Garrett.

Once Emily was seated, Rainer moved to the driver's side and watched Emily's eyes swirl with fury as Bridgette threw her leg over Vindico's Agusta and slid her arms around his chiseled chest.

Rainer cranked the Mustang. He started to rev the engine but decided against it. Emily was way beyond that being able to soothe her into smiling at him.

"Fionna Styler! He could have Fionna Styler, but no, the stupid, freaking idiot wants a skanky, Non-Gifted whore!" Chloe's voice rang with indignation.

Rainer grimaced. He didn't really think the point was that Bridgette wasn't Gifted and disliked the implication that Fionna was better only because she was. He also really didn't like the implication that just because she was a stripper that automatically indicated she was anything but a woman with a job.

"Come on," Garrett soothed. "You know Dan won't date Gifted women, and you know Fionna doesn't need to get involved in all of his shit. Bridgette's a distraction, and she's a means to an end he wants. That's all Dan will ever want. Fi deserves to be so much more than that." Garrett's voice was calming and quiet. Emily spun in her seat. She was still seething despite her big brother's attempts to soothe both her and Chloe.

"Why won't he date Gifted women?" Emily demanded.

With an audible huff, Garrett rolled his eyes. "You don't need me to explain this. Think about it."

"I'm too furious to think, so just tell me." Emily's entire body was braced to claw either her brother's hair out of his head or Rainer's.

"Em." Rainer rubbed her leg between switching gears. "Come on, baby. You're a Receiver. Think about what being with someone like Vindico would mean. Think of what she might feel from him. He'll never let anyone in that close."

"Yeah and Em, no offense, but Fi's way more powerful than you even," Garrett reminded her.

"I know that. I'm not offended at all." Emily's fury seemed to ebb as she thought about Vindico's reasoning. "She's amazing."

"What happened to Amelia fucked him up bad. I don't know that he'll ever get over it."

"I know," Chloe admitted as Rainer pulled into the restaurant parking lot. Vindico and Bridgette followed Chloe and Garrett in to secure the table as Logan and Adeline pulled in. Adeline looked almost as furious as Emily, a sight Rainer was stunned to see, and Logan looked defeated. Adeline and Emily instantly moved to one another like magnets. Logan hung back with Rainer.

"Yeah, so apparently, telling your fiancée that you're going to have dinner with your boss and his stripper girlfriend, after she's worked a twelve-hour shift and has nothing but scrubs to wear will get you yelled at all the way from DC to Alexandria."

Rainer sighed. "Join the club."

Logan held the door for Emily and Adeline who refused to even look at him as she went by.

"I don't know what I did wrong. I've apologized a million times, but I don't know what I'm apologizing for so that's not helping." Logan begged Rainer for his help.

"I don't really think there's anything we can do but endure this." He noted that the restaurant was very nice. The grills were located in the center of the tables, with each side seating two people. This left a small area for the chefs to enter to put on the show. It was relatively dark and decorated in tones of black, but there was an impressive fire pit in the center of the tables.

Bridgette sauntered up to Logan.

It took Vindico a rather long time to even notice she'd moved. Rainer was astonished at his ability to completely ignore her. He cleared his throat. "This is Logan Haydenshire. He wasn't there for the takedown at The Tantra."

While giving Logan a flirtatious grin, Bridgette offered him her hand. "I clearly need to get a job at Iodex if all of the officers are as cute as the four of you."

Vindico rolled his eyes, but no one else responded as Adeline and Emily glared at Bridgette. Logan quickly stepped back from Bridgette and turned his terrified, puppy dog eyes on Adeline.

In a show of petulant, female solidarity, Emily shoved Logan out of her way, and she and Adeline took one of the sides of the table leaving Logan and Rainer to sit by one another.

Garrett laughed. "You knew she was a spitfire when you gave her a ring," he goaded Rainer under his breath.

Logan threw his hands out in fury as he flung the chair back he'd pulled out for Adeline and seated himself.

Bridgette turned to Adeline with a spiteful glare. "So, are you one of those hospital candy striper thingies?" she drawled as she took an overly appraising look at Adeline's pink scrubs.

"Oh fuck." Logan let his head fall into his hands.

"I have a costume like that, but it's way cuter." Bridgette gestured to Adeline's scrubs.

"I'm an obstetrics medio." Adeline huffed, but upon seeing the confusion on Bridgette's face she edged. "That's a doctor. I'm finishing my fellowship to be an OB-GYN."

"That's a doctor for down there, right?" She scowled as she pointed to her own crotch.

Logan whimpered audibly as Adeline's mouth fell open, and Emily rolled her eyes. As Bridgette was awaiting an answer, Adeline ground her teeth and shot Logan a look that said he should consider himself very lucky if he got to see *down there* any time in the next decade or so.

"Down there?" Adeline huffed. Logan squeezed his eyes shut and turned to Rainer.

"Seriously, I had to ask her to stop using the medical terms for everything when we were in bed because it wigged me out. She's gonna blow."

Rainer tried to look sympathetic, but he'd never seen Adeline so irritated. It was so unusual it was fascinating. She was usually so passive and happy as long as Logan was nearby.

"If you're referring to your female reproductive organs including your uterus, ovaries, fallopian tubes, cervix, vulva, vaginal walls, along with a myriad of other things then yes, I suppose it is."

Bridgette didn't seem to notice Adeline's disdain. She stuck her tongue out and pretended to gag. "Those words are all so gross, but maybe once you're a real doctor, they'll let you wear cuter clothes."

Emily gasped as Logan stepped in to defend Adeline.

"I think she looks beautiful no matter what she's wearing, and the work she does is incredible. She is a real doctor. She's saving women's lives and bringing new lives into the world every day."

Adeline melted slightly. She was still irritated, but she did give Logan a smile.

The waiter appeared, and Logan and Rainer each ordered a beer immediately. They watched the chef prepare their meals in front of them. Things were relatively quiet, and Garrett began a conversation about the Crown debate the following evening.

"So, why isn't your dad running for king?" Bridgette pulled a piece of steak off her fork. Rainer and Logan shared a quick glance and waited to hear Vindico's explanation. After drawing a long sip of his own beer, Vindico shrugged.

"It's Crown Governor, and Dad's never wanted to be Crown. He became a governor when the Constitution was ratified almost thirty years ago. Even if he wanted to run, which he doesn't, if you'd ever met my sister Lindley, you'd know why he'd never stand a chance."

"How is Lindley?" Garrett motioned the waiter over to refill Chloe's drink.

"She's Lindley," was Vindico's remorseful quip. Garrett didn't seem to need any further explanation.

"Now you're brother and sister, right?" Bridgette quizzed Logan and Emily.

"Uh-huh." Logan was concentrating on his food.

"And you're his brother?" Bridgette pointed to Garrett.

"Yes," Emily spat. "I have lots of brothers."

Rainer shot her a pleading glance to be nice.

"How many?" Bridgette quizzed.

"Nine, and a sister on the way." Emily took the edge out of her tone slightly. Rainer glanced at Logan. None of them ever stated that they only had eight brothers living. Cal was always a part of them, no matter what.

"I would love to have a big family." Bridgette's entire face lit as she glanced at Vindico who adamantly refused to meet her gaze. "My mom left when I was a baby, and my stepmom threw me out. My dad's a guard at Felsink."

"Oh." Emily's face fell. "I'm so sorry."

Bridgette shrugged. "What can you do? But I always thought it would be so great to have tons of kids. You know, so you always have someone to be there for you."

Emily glanced from Garrett to Logan. "Yeah, I guess I do always have that."

"Yeah, Em, you do, and a lot of people aren't that lucky," Garrett eased. With one quick phrase, he'd pointed out all that she had and everything that Bridgette never would.

"Yeah, you're really lucky."

Visible guilt washed over Emily violently, and Rainer wished he could reach and hold her hand. He reminded himself that she had forced the seating arrangement, so he just smiled at her and gave her a reassuring wink.

"My dad got into some gambling debt after his fourth wife left him, so I'm trying to help him pay it off, and I make tons more money dancing than I did just waitressing. It's worked out great plus the extra cash for keeping up with Nic's boys." She rolled her eyes, and it took Rainer a minute to realize she was talking about Wretchkinsides. It struck him as odd that her father was in debt. Gifted prison guards were highly paid for their silence and were typically monitored to make certain none of them had any addictions that needed to be treated. The Senate would always pay for rehab and counseling. Everything about what she'd just said sounded fabricated.

"We really appreciate everything you've done for us," Vindico vowed in the longest sentence he'd spoken to Bridgette the entire evening. She looked thrilled to have his attention. After dessert was served, Vindico picked up the bill for the entire table despite Rainer, Logan, and Garrett's objections.

"So, thanks for showing me around the stadium thingy," Bridgette drawled to Chloe as Garrett offered her his arm. "I can't wait to see the game tomorrow."

"It's an arena, and we call them challenges. I didn't know you were coming tomorrow."

"My dad had a few extra tickets," Vindico commented.

"Great." Chloe forced a half smile. Rainer wondered how Bridgette would be able to tell what was happening at the challenge the next day against New York.

Non-Gifted people couldn't see the energy that would be in use or be able to see them release the iode. They couldn't see the energy that was constantly around them in any way at all. Why was Bridgette so interested in the Angels?

He moved to Emily, offered her his arm, and gave her a sweet smile, which she returned.

"Sorry, I was being a brat." She sighed.

Rainer shook his head. He knew perfectly well that Emily Anne Haydenshire could be a hot mess sometimes, but he'd never agree that she was being a brat. She was *his* hot mess, and he could never love anything more. He brushed a kiss across her cheek.

He recalled a few years ago, during the last few weeks of Mrs. Haydenshire's pregnancy with the twins. She'd been horrendously uncomfortable and in a horrible mood, very unlike her normal happy, caring self.

Logan, Patrick, and Connor had gone to Governor Haydenshire to complain about their mother's terrible mood. Rainer had been present for the conversation. With a wry grin, he recalled the governor's adamant vow, "Boys, take it from me—if you can't handle her at her worst, then you don't deserve to have your hands on her at her best."

He'd chuckled as the boys shuddered and groaned. They didn't want to think about their father having his hands on their mother, but Rainer had filed the advice away just as he always had.

He'd wanted a love and a marriage with Emily just like the Haydenshires had for his entire life. Maybe not with eleven kids, but definitely the love and commitment they'd always shown one another.

CHAPTER 3
THE WAY BACK HOME

After he'd returned Chloe and Garrett to the arena, Rainer drove Emily home. He found it odd that he didn't know what to say to her. He remained quiet for most of the drive.

"I wouldn't have flirted like that if I'd known we weren't going to be alone tonight." Her voice shook slightly.

Rainer chuckled. "I enjoyed your flirting. Believe me, your texts made an otherwise extremely boring day quite exciting. I'm sorry I didn't say anything about dinner with Vindico. I really thought I could get out of it. I was really hoping I could take you up on some of your requests." He reveled in her sweet giggle.

"If you still want to, I might could be persuaded to let you play down there?" She quoted Bridgette as Rainer joined in her laughter. His heart picked up pace as their bodies' magnetic need pulled them closer.

"And how would you like to be persuaded, Miss Haydenshire?" Rainer waggled his eyebrows at Emily. Her eyes danced and glimmered as she laughed. His heart beat disjointedly for a moment.

"I'm pretty sure you know most of the stuff I like."

"Most, huh? If there's something else I need to learn, I'm all ears."

"I like it better when you're all hands," Emily sassed as Rainer turned down their driveway.

"Oh, really?"

"Oh, yeah."

After pulling the Mustang into the garage, Rainer exited the car and rushed to her door. He pulled her out of her seat and then scooped her into his arms.

"Wanna see what I can do with my hands, baby?"

She shivered in anticipation. It drove him wild as he unlocked the door and took her to bed.

CHAPTER 4
DEBATE

"Are you enjoying playing house, sweetheart?" Rainer teased Emily the next evening as they put the twins to bed in the farmhouse and settled in to watch the debate. Emily had prepared a delicious dinner and seemed thrilled to cook in her mother's expansive kitchen complete with gourmet cookware.

Rainer had paid close attention to the smile she'd worn while he'd helped her prepare dinner for the boys. The debate wasn't set to start for another ten minutes, so Rainer decided to bring up something they hadn't really discussed yet.

"Where do you want to live after we get married?"

Emily looked like the question shocked her as she furrowed her brow. "I don't know. I've never lived anywhere but here," she offered as a hesitant explanation. Rainer gave her a sweet grin. This was going to be hard on her.

"I know, baby, but you know we have a little bit of money. If you keep playing like you did today, you'll soon be the highest paid Receiver in the league, so I thought if you wanted, we could eventually move out of your parents' guesthouse."

Emily always bristled slightly if Rainer pointed out the fact that they were quite wealthy.

A reluctant knock sounded on the door. Rainer sighed as he

answered. The Iodex team assigned as backup to Rainer for the evening was doing one of their random checks.

Rainer allowed them in and watched as they checked the twins and the house. By the time they'd finished, the debate was beginning, and Rainer and Emily watched as the cameras panned over Mrs. Haydenshire seated beside Will and Brooke on one side and Garrett on the other. Logan and Adeline had arrived early to address Peterson's accusations on Logan's drug use and then the redacting of the story.

Patrick and Lucy, Levi and Sarah, and Connor were seated on the same row as their mother. They were all wearing conservative suits and dresses. The camera moved to take in Yvette Peterson wearing a rather loud, neon green and black dress complete with a feathered fascinator.

"Did she get attacked by a peacock outside the arena?" Emily gasped.

Rainer laughed as he cuddled her close on the couch. Samantha was seated beside her mother and was wearing a dress that made her appear a good five or six years younger than she was.

"Oh, give me a break." Emily rolled her eyes.

With Peterson's numbers falling rapidly after his admission that the story about Logan and Adeline had been fabricated, he was obviously trying to play Samantha up as a cute, innocent, little girl in hopes of restoring his faltering image.

Rainer could feel Emily's nerves churning in her rhythms as he slid his hand under the edge of the T-shirt she was wearing so he could feel her stomach.

This was the first of two debates between Governor Haydenshire and Peterson and would be the first time the two men had been in each other's presence since declaring their candidacy.

"Your dad's gonna be great, baby. Don't be nervous."

Emily gave him his favorite mischievous grin and rolled her eyes. "Do you think you know everything about me, Officer Lawson?"

Rainer shook his head. "Most definitely not. I've been thoroughly committed to you since I learned to walk, but I still can't figure you out."

Emily giggled in her delight as she grabbed Rainer's hand from under her shirt and slid it to her bra.

"You might get a better reading here," she flirted as Rainer cocked his eyebrow upwards.

"I don't know." He feigned ignorance. "Might have to take this off. It's blocking your energy," he mocked as he tugged on her bra strap. She seemed to decide she liked her game so she reached back and unclasped her bra. Rainer shuddered and moaned.

"I think it might offend your dad if I did you on their couch, while we're supposed to be watching him on television." Rainer pulled the loosened bra forward and grasped her breast.

"Oh," Emily feigned concern. "Then maybe you should put that back on."

Rainer kissed her. He formed her lips around his own as he added to the intensity until she was gasping for breath.

"Unfortunately, baby..." he rasped as he pulled his mouth away from hers, "I only know how to take them off. I haven't ever tried to put one back on you."

She giggled.

With that, the first notes of the Senate Anthem were played by the house orchestra. Rainer tried not to be distracted by the fact that Emily wriggled beside him and pulled off her bra altogether. She declared that it had been pinching her anyway and threw it on the floor.

As the anthem played, Governor Haydenshire and Peterson shook hands and then took the podiums to a standing ovation from the crowd.

The Senate banner was unfurled. It displayed the Senate crest with the large falcon wings widespread and smaller versions of all of the animals of the family crests in the known Realm. On either side of the Senate banner, two smaller golden banners were lowered. These had Interim Crown Governor Vindico's crest on them.

The Vindico crest was a panther displayed with a fierce snarl. Its teeth were bared inside the falcon's widespread wings. A fearless, territorial protector, an aggressor who hunts alone—Rainer recalled the meaning of the panther from his Histories of the Realm classes.

According to the Gifted legends, the panther was the only predator capable of slaying a dragon.

That suited Dan Vindico perfectly. Rainer tried to pay attention to the debate as he considered whether or not Vindico's father lived up to the family crest the same way his son did.

As the moderators took their seats, Governor Haydenshire blew Mrs. Haydenshire a kiss and a wink, which made the crowd swoon. There were five moderators for the debate. Each could ask one question, and each man was given time for rebuttal. Then there would be a brief question and answer session with the audience.

Governor Willow stepped forward and posed a question about what the men had done as Realm governors that they felt would make them the best choice for Crown.

Peterson began in a long, drawn-out spiel about the things he'd done as a governor. None of them were very substantial. Emily shifted beside him, and Rainer tried desperately not to think about her bare breasts under the thin T-shirt, as she turned and the weight of them fell against his forearm. He cradled her back to his chest.

He wanted to lift their heavy weight, to massage them, to feel them pebble and then swell for him. He wanted to watch her nipples pucker as he built her desire. His breath quickened, but he forced his mind back to the debates as Governor Haydenshire began talking about working with Rainer's father to write and ratify the Constitution and all that he'd done in the past thirty years as a governor.

Guilt settled on Rainer as he reminded himself that his father had spent his life fighting and ultimately dying for the process he was watching take place. He scolded himself for the fact that he couldn't rein in his libido long enough to watch Emily's father debate his way to Crown Governor.

Emily scooted closer into Rainer's protective embrace as Governor Haydenshire elaborated on his friendship with Rainer's father and how he would fight to uphold everything that Joseph had set forth in his time as Crown.

Rainer's mind reeled again. The way her luscious curves wound around him, the way her backside was pressed against his length, with his hands inches from her breasts as he held her to him. His heart raced.

He attempted to draw a deep, steadying breath, but he inhaled the heady scent of her, mixed with the raspberry shampoo that she liked and the citrus scent of her perfume. It was the one he supplied her with on a regular basis. It was his favorite.

A commercial began, and Rainer reasoned that he could fantasize during the commercials as long as he paid attention during the debate.

Talk dirty to me. Her text from the day before seared through his mind. He let just a few of the phrases he knew she liked him to say form on his tongue. He bit his lip and refused to say the lurid phrases to her during the debate in her parents' home, on their couch, when they were supposed to be babysitting.

He reminded himself of all of their responsibilities, but that only served to make him want her all the more. He wanted to drown in her. The Realm seemed too much on this particular evening. He needed to fill her with all of him, to pump her full, and feel the sweet pulse of her release all around him.

She moved away from him. The motion shook him from his dizzying, lust-filled fantasies.

"I'm gonna go check on the boys. Do you wanna beer or something?" She stood and stretched. He watched the shirt she was wearing lift as she stretched her arms over her head. He stared unabashedly at the phoenix tattooed on her abdomen. The falcon's wings were hidden under her sweatpants, but his phoenix was there. Rainer longed to hoist the pants down and see all of his brand on her.

When he remembered that she'd asked him a question, Rainer shook his head.

"You go check on them. I'll get the drinks. Do you want a glass of wine or something?" He stood as well and slid his hand over her backside. He was simply unable to keep his hands off her luscious curves. Emily shook her head at him.

"Will you make me a cup of tea?"

"Sure, baby." Rainer moved to the kitchen, and she headed up the stairs. They met back in the living room. Rainer was carrying a Dr

Pepper and Emily's cup of tea. She beamed at him as she relieved him of the hot mug.

"They're out." She sighed peacefully as she curled up on the corner of the couch.

"We played with them outside for hours."

"Yeah, but I think they've been sleeping better because Mom and Dad have been here the past few days." She'd been worrying about the twins being without their parents so much lately.

The chorus of the Senate anthem rang again as the debate returned to the screen. As he thought about Emily's concerns over the twins and how amazing she was with them, Rainer pictured her pregnant with his baby.

He tried to imagine her body swollen, round, and full with their child that he'd put inside of her. He allowed himself to envision it. His hands on her, his mouth on her, feeling what they'd made together as it grew inside of her. His mind created vivid imagery of their future, of watching her hold his baby, and helping her take care of their child. His mind spun wildly with willful lust and abandon.

He reminded himself that it was largely chauvinistic and tried to quell the thoughts that he wanted to plant his seed, to claim her as his own, and to tie the two of them together with children they made together. Rainer shook himself and tried to focus on the television screen.

The rebuttals from the first question were taking place. Peterson was scowling over Governor Haydenshire's lengthy resume and quipped that he was shocked that he'd accomplished so much outside of his own bedroom.

Governor Haydenshire responded by asking Peterson to inform the Realm how many times he'd recused himself from a trial so that he could make his tee time.

Emily sighed as she drew long sips of her tea. They watched the debate turn ugly. As the grown men on television took part in the ancient practice of backhanded compliments and insulting another man with grace and panache, Rainer shook his head.

His father used to say that the mark of a true politician was the knife you pulled from your back after you'd shaken his hand. It appeared Peterson had the act down to an art form. After setting her empty teacup down on the table beside the couch, Emily laid her head in Rainer's lap and let him cradle her. This did nothing to quell Rainer's overly active libido.

She shifted and ran her fingers through her hair to brush it off of her face. Her long auburn tresses were now across him, and he tried not to groan. He knew how good it felt for her long, soft hair to caress over his length and his thighs as she took him in her mouth. The feeling was exquisite.

His breath caught as he pictured her on her knees staring up at him. Her eyes dark and hungry while she spun her tongue up his length and laved him in her mouth.

He needed to touch her. Rainer began to ease his fingers through her hair. A contented smile formed on her beautiful face. Her hair flowed through his fingers like spun silk, and the scent it released drove him wild. He shifted slightly and tried not to let Emily know what was pulsing through his mind and through his groin.

He chastised himself and tried to pay attention to what was happening on the television. Peterson had called Governor Haydenshire out for what he was calling misappropriation of funds and abuse of power because all of Iodex was being used to keep the Haydenshires safe.

Emily gasped and sat up as her mouth fell open. Outrage tensed in her rhythms. Governor Haydenshire just huffed as he shook his head and then informed the assembled audience and the Realm at large what Vasquez had done and who'd released him from prison.

As Mr. Buffett was the moderator who'd asked the question about financial reform in the Realm, Governor Haydenshire turned to Peterson and asked him to release the name of his largest campaign financier.

With his eyes goggling, Peterson seemed furious as the crowd waited with bated breath to hear the answer.

"I...I don't have to answer that!" Peterson spat, but the doubt had been seeded and an audible hiss rose from the crowd. As the camera panned, Rainer noted Dan seated in one of the VIP seats with a broad grin stretched across his face.

Governor Vindico quieted the tittering crowd and reminded Governor Haydenshire that it was up to the candidate if he wanted to reveal his campaign contributors.

Emily shook her head in disbelief. "Good grief."

Rainer wrapped his arm around her as she tucked herself back into his protective embrace. Things calmed as the governors were asked about their opinions on upping law enforcement and how they felt enhanced security should be funded.

As always, funding quickly turned to taxes. All Gifted people employed by the Senate or any Gifted facility paid a decent percentage of their income in taxes back to the Realm.

Emily grew bored with talk of finance reform and pulled a bridal magazine off the coffee table. Rainer gave a valiant effort to listen to Governor Haydenshire's plans to spend wisely.

He knew he should care. His inheritance and his and Emily's paychecks were taxed regularly, but thoughts of him and Emily between the sheets of their bed continued to pulse through his brain. He thought of taking her in her childhood bed, just one floor above where they were seated.

Dizzying fantasies of her asking for it, telling him to take her, to make her feel it, of her begging him to set her free and give her release, swirled in his mind and took up residence in his groin. His stomach clenched. His mouth watered as his shield hungered for her.

With a wry grin, Emily gave him a knowing glance. He'd gone too far this time, and she'd noticed his erotically charged energy.

"Is there something you want, Mr. Lawson?" she drawled flirtatiously. Rainer held her gaze, but he didn't reply. A storm of need tensed in his shield.

She trembled as he brushed his hand across her thigh and allowed the electricity to arc heatedly between their flesh. Her breath stuttered as she allowed his energy in.

"Tell me what you want," she whispered.

He gave her a greedy smile as he nodded. "I want to kiss you."

"Is that all you want?" She wanted to hear more, but he wasn't giving in. He was going to work her over slowly until she was begging him to set her free.

"For now." Her body pulled taut as her eyes flashed with desire. With that, Rainer placed his hand on her jaw and guided her face to his. He paused centimeters from their lips touching, until he could feel her breath coming in heated pants and their craving energy arced between their mouths.

He let the passion ignite in the moments that pulsed between them. He reveled in their energy beginning to spin and swirl as it permeated the air around them.

After a long drawn-out minute, he couldn't wait any longer. With his need to taste her driving him, he devoured her mouth as a low rumbling groan escaped his lungs and filled her mouth.

He cradled her face in his hand and guided her. He slipped his tongue between her lush lips. He moved it in heated cadence with hers. He pulled back and traced his tongue over her lips, while he sucked her bottom lip until he felt it swell as he dragged his teeth over it.

She arched her back and leaned into him. She hoisted her breasts in his face and showed him precisely where she wanted his attention.

"Do these need to be touched, baby?" Rainer let his index finger spin lightly around her nipples drawn pert and anxious.

Deep, desperate desire to control her, to make her feel his love, and his need to pleasure her to all new heights coursed through his veins.

He figured if he was going to have her in her parents' house again, this was the ideal time since he could see her father debating Peterson and the rest of her family seated in the audience.

He knew they wouldn't be interrupted, and he could draw this out until she didn't want anything as much as she wanted him deep inside of her. Rebellion mixed into the heady cocktail of love and lust that permeated his body as he awaited her answer.

Her energy was frantic. Her body fought with her mind. She wanted to let him have her and to let him instruct and direct her, but she was timid and nervous to give up control completely, no matter how many times they'd been together.

"Tell me, baby. Tell me you want me to touch them. Tell me you want me to suck them. Tell me you want me to bite them," he commanded, and she moaned as her body began to win out over her mind.

"Please!" she panted. "Rainer, please…" Her energy spiraled wildly as her body trembled for his touch. He forced himself to move slowly.

He edged her T-shirt off her and let her ample breasts fall into his hands as he began to massage and grope. He caught her nipples between his fingers and squeezed lightly as he handled her. He laid her back on the couch and huffed hot breath over her breasts as she arched her back.

"Suck me," she demanded in a desperate plea that drove him wild.

"That's it," he urged just as he pulled her left breast deep in his mouth and spun his tongue over her nipple. He sucked her hard, pulling the erotic energy from one of her storehouses, as she writhed and bucked under his embrace. He slid his teeth over the tender, fevered flesh and let his saliva soothe the exquisite pain he left. He moved to give the other equal attention.

Heated defiance set in her eyes as she grasped him, massaged him, and felt him throb for her. He wrapped his hand over hers and showed her exactly how to touch him. She went wild. Her eyes flashed in carnal craving as she kneaded him.

"You see, baby." He groaned from the heavenly sensation. "You see how hard you make me when you tell me what you want?" Her energy peaked in heady need. That wasn't at all what Rainer wanted. He clenched his jaw as he shoved her pants down and revealed thin, white, lace panties. He shuddered and growled as he grasped her waist and pulled her closer. He traced his fingers over the lace between her legs.

"You're so wet, baby. Now show me where you need me to touch you. Show me where you're needy." He dragged one finger tenderly along her slit and watched her lips clench in anticipation.

She decided to follow his commands on her terms, in true Emily Haydenshire fashion. She spun off the couch and stood before him. He sat up but was unable to take his eyes off the show before him.

"Show me," he ordered again. With a body-quaking shiver, she began to slide the panties down her legs until she tossed them in his face. Rainer grabbed them and inhaled before he grasped her backside. He pulled her to him, leaned, and dragged his tongue over her lips, swollen full and ripe from her desire to be opened.

He fell to his knees in front of her, between her legs, and kissed and licked up her inner thigh. He massaged her backside as he swirled his tongue around her clit. A loud, longing moan sang from her as her head fell back in the ecstasy of what he was doing.

"Come in my mouth, baby. I want to drink you. I want to feel how wet you get for me," he commanded fiercely, and he had her. She quaked and gave in to the sensation and let his words drive her over the edge as the liquid form of her energy flooded his mouth. He spun his tongue between her folds until the taste of her filled him.

He stood immediately to hold and steady her in her convulsions as she clung to him. A moment later, she was pushing him back on the couch in a seated position.

She pulled off his belt, and he helped her shed his shorts and boxers. She fell to her knees in front of him, and he moaned. She kept her eyes locked on his. She drew patterns with her tongue up his straining length. She cupped his sac in her hands as she kissed and licked him.

"Put it in your mouth. I want to watch you suck me," he ordered as another moan quaked through her body. She moved over him and drew him deep within her as she drowned him in her mouth and sucked him hard. His head fell back as his body thrust upwards of its own accord. Her moans reverberated through him. She was exquisite.

He tenderly caressed her face. He needed her to stop. Visions of exploding in her mouth did nothing to halt the imminent climax. She pulled away, and he quickly summoned from her erotic energy and sealed her closed.

He laid back on the couch, took her hand, and continued to guide and instruct her.

"I want you to ride me, baby. I want to watch you." He guided her legs until she was straddled over him. He wrapped his hands around her slender waist and guided her down.

She moaned her ardent approval as he bucked underneath her and drove himself in deep. She began to grind her body over him.

Their energy spiked as it joined in fevered waves all around them.

Rainer couldn't look away from her breasts. They bounced and swayed in an erotic dance as she moved. The sight threatened to end him instantly.

Her eyes flashed. He felt her swell around him. She drowned his length in her heated flesh and the liquid silk that flowed around him.

She slid her hands to her own breasts as a loud, echoing growl bellowed from deep within him. He grasped her waist again and flipped her underneath him. He couldn't stand it any longer.

"Take it," he demanded. "Take it all." He drove her hard, pounded into her, and pumped her full of him. He plunged her depths until she arched her back. Her temperature rose rapidly, and she screamed out his name as he set her free.

With one last ragged thrust, he filled her with all of him. He flooded her with everything he was as she writhed and tensed in his arms. He held her tight as they regained the ability to breathe normally.

"Are you okay?" he whispered in their afterglow.

"That was completely amazing." She continued to make Rainer feel like a king. He tried hard not to smirk.

"I'm glad you enjoyed it. I just hope your dad doesn't ask too many questions about the debate."

Emily giggled. "Even if he does, still worth it."

They redressed and cuddled on the couch until her parents and brothers arrived home. Rainer noticed that her cheeks were still flushed pink from her passion, and he hoped her parents wouldn't put two and two together.

Logan and Connor fell into the kitchen laughing.

"I cannot believe that guy asked that." Logan shook his head. Rainer and Emily shared a concerned glance. "Did you see that? I figured Peterson would have plants in the audience but wow."

Governor Haydenshire shook his head. "I don't think Lachland had that man ask that, son. Even he looked confused when the guy said it. Peterson's an extremely intelligent man, and that question was insane. Daniel said when he was escorted out he appeared to have been making electrical draws from his home. He's an addict. That will ultimately eat your brain,"

Emily pulled Adeline away from Logan and her parents. Rainer heard them whispering in the living room, and he prayed Emily would soon let him in on what had happened.

When they returned, Emily's flush had deepened to a crimson red, and Adeline was trying hard not to giggle. Rainer assumed Emily had confessed why they hadn't seen much of the debates. Still chuckling heartily, Logan slapped Rainer on the back with a sly grin.

"I really thought you'd be fuming that the entire Realm now thinks you're impotent."

"What!?" Rainer gasped. Emily's eyes goggled at him as she shook her head.

"You know…because that guy asked if our dads had betrothed us so that we'd have an heir. He thinks Dad is trying to take over the Realm and then the world. He accused Dad of trying to use the Lawson name to gain power, and…uh…then he wanted to know why I'm not pregnant yet." Her voice lowered with each word as she cringed. Rainer's mouth fell open in stunned disbelief.

"Didn't you see it? The entire arena was stunned. They called in Iodex. Garrett and I helped escort the nut job out. He kept screaming shit about how your dad had planned for you and Em to marry to try and create a stronger race or something, and that Mom and Dad have so many kids 'cause they're building an army." Logan laughed, but then his eyes lit instantly with understanding. Governor Haydenshire shuddered as he glared at Rainer.

"Uh," Emily grimaced under her father's glare. "We saw most of the debate. We had to walk the officers around, and we checked on the twins a lot."

Connor caught on immediately and began laughing with Logan. "I think you mean you checked on Rainer's twins…a lot."

Had Rainer not been so thoroughly mortified and worried that Emily was going to burst into tears, he would've laughed at Connor's quick wit.

"I'm going to bed," Governor Haydenshire fumed. He turned and pulled off his tie as he walked away, but he spun back instantly. His eyes goggled. "Oh, you better not have!" he demanded.

Logan, Connor, Emily, and Rainer all shuddered. They were horrified at the thought of having sex in the Haydenshires' bed.

"Ugh, Daddy, no!" Emily gagged.

When Governor Haydenshire made his hasty retreat with his head shaking in defeat, Connor leapt. "See, they should've had a camera here. Then the Realm would know your sack of surprises is fully loaded."

Certain his face was the color of Emily's hair, Rainer drew a steadying breath.

"Shut up, Connor." Emily sounded like she was ten years old again.

"So while you two were, uh…" Connor paused to try and come up with what he deemed as acceptable phrasing,

Logan stepped up to bat. "Churning butter?" They both cracked up again as Rainer glared at them with his jaw cocked to the side. He narrowed his eyes in on Logan.

"Are you jealous?" To his horror, Logan's entire expression changed in an instant as tears formed in Adeline's eyes. She turned and whisked to the bathroom.

"I'm so sorry. I didn't mean…" Rainer tripped over his words in his haste to get them out of his mouth.

"I know." Logan shook his head with a dejected sigh as he moved to try and extricate Adeline from the bathroom.

"What the hell?" Connor quizzed Rainer and Emily.

Emily made certain neither Logan nor Adeline could hear her. "She just had surgery. She can't…you know. She's convinced Logan's" —Emily hemmed and settled on—"wanting to and she can't yet. You know how she is about disappointing Logan."

"I have to go apologize." Rainer felt terrible as he turned and stalked toward Adeline who was emerging from the Haydenshires' half bathroom with red eyes.

"Adeline, I'm so sorry." Rainer felt his face flush again. "I didn't mean anything by that. I was just being stupid." Rainer wasn't certain what else to say as Logan was shooting him warning glares. Adeline gave him a kind smile.

"Don't worry. I don't know why I'm so sensitive lately," she dismissed.

"Well, that's probably all the same thing," Emily soothed. "And despite being a really great guy, he still says stupid, insensitive things without having any idea that he shouldn't until it's too late." She gave Adeline a hug. This brought a genuine giggle from Adeline.

"Let's go home. I'm sure Rainer and Em are tired out," Logan goaded.

"I'm not even saying anything else."

CHAPTER 5

HAPPY BIRTHDAY, EMILY

October dawned, cool and crisp, with the leaves turning brilliant colors of reds and orange. It was Emily's favorite time of year. She'd driven herself to distraction trying to figure out what Rainer was getting her for her birthday, so as the sun began its trek across the autumnal Virginia sky on her big day, she woke Rainer by bouncing on the bed. Without opening his eyes, he slid his hands to her waist and pinned her down.

"Hey there," he drawled. "Are you excited about something?"

While she tried to escape his grasp, she wriggled underneath him. "By the way, Happy Birthday, baby." He clasped her hands in his own as he planted a sweet kiss on her lips.

"Can I have my present now?"

"Uh no, you may not. You may have it tonight, when everyone else gives you their gifts at your parents' house." He thoroughly frustrated her. She poked her lip out in a delicious pout, and he chuckled.

"That won't work this time."

"But what if I want my present now before we go to my dinner tonight so that I can show you how much I like it?"

Rainer held her waist in his hands and positioned her seductively over him. She wiggled her hips to illustrate her point. The effect was evident immediately. She giggled as he shook his head at her.

"If you like it, you can show me when we get back home."

"What if you show me now, and then I'll take care of that little problem you've got there?" She gestured to his crotch with a mischievous smirk.

"Uh, excuse me, Miss Haydenshire, but it's not little, and trust me, baby, I'll have that problem as soon as I see you tonight so you can take care of it then." He feigned offense and reveled in her laughter.

She leaned forward so that her breasts fell onto his chest and pebbled against the thin T-shirt she'd slept in. He stared at them unabashedly as she grinned.

"I'm well aware that you're Gifted in more than just protective casts," she assured him.

After rolling his head to the side to take in the clock, Rainer turned back to her. "You have to go to work, and I have another day of defending the Realm against Keaton and Henry."

She laughed. "I thought you were supposed to be defending them against the Realm."

"Oh, that's right." Rainer gave her a wry smile just to hear her laugh again. With an audible huff, she extricated herself from his lap and moved to her dresser. She lifted the small, white, square box that her present was wrapped in and shook it for the hundredth time in the past two days.

"It's small like jewelry." Her eyes sparkled. Rainer pretended to consider her guess.

"Could definitely be jewelry," he hemmed. "Maybe."

"Ugh, you are making me crazy." She all but stamped her feet. Rainer sat up and laughed at her outright.

"I know, baby." He took her hand and pulled her back to him. "But trust me, I think it'll be worth it."

"Can I have a clue?" she begged.

"Okay, let me get a shower, and I'll see if I can come up with one clue. But only one."

He emerged from the shower several minutes later. Rainer chuckled as Emily handed him a towel, waiting expectantly on her clue.

"I thought of one."

"Tell me." She bounced on her tiptoes. Rainer ran the towel through his hair and over his body as he shook his head at her.

"Are you sure you're ready?" he teased.

"Yes, just tell me."

"Okay, your one and only clue, Miss Haydenshire, is…"—he paused and watched her titter frantically—"football." He had to fight hard not to laugh. Her hands immediately went to her hips as she glared at him.

"Football is my clue?

"Yes, football is your clue." He knew he shouldn't enjoy teasing her so much, and he wouldn't if she wasn't so adorable when he got her like this.

"What does my birthday present have to do with football?"

Rainer shook his head. "I said one clue."

Emily pulled on her practice uniform and marched into the kitchen. Logan and Adeline greeted her sweetly with Happy Birthdays.

She immediately cornered Logan. "What does football have to do with whatever it is Rainer got me?"

Rainer laughed as he poured himself a bowl of cereal. Logan furrowed his brow and studied Rainer. A moment later, he got it.

His eyes goggled appreciatively. "Oh, man. That was good."

"Thank you." Rainer took a mock bow. He handed Emily a cup of coffee. "Do you want me to put candles in your cereal?" he offered and watched her roll her eyes again.

"No, I want to know what you got me."

He planted a kiss on the top of her head. "Tonight. Just be patient."

"I'm very bad at being patient."

"Oh, we know," Logan assured her.

After dropping Emily and Adeline off, Logan and Rainer returned to the farmhouse. The Haydenshires were getting ready to do a press conference from the Senate. They'd be in town for the next weekend campaigning close to home. Emily texted several times throughout the day to ask for more clues, but Rainer refused her.

"Poor baby, if this wasn't so good, I think I'd tell her. I'm making her nuts."

Logan rolled his eyes. "She's not a baby. She can wait two more hours for her birthday present. She needs to chill."

They taught Keaton and Henry a very rudimentary form of football and even talked the additional security teams on the property into playing a game with the boys.

When the Haydenshires returned, Mrs. Haydenshire immediately began working on Emily's birthday dinner, spaghetti with meatballs with Nana's delicious sauce.

A little after four, Rainer went to the stadium to pick up Emily. The Angels had taken her out to lunch and supplied her with several birthday gifts, all of which she gushed about on the way back to the farmhouse.

Very pleased that she was having such a good day, Rainer escorted her into the kitchen. She was hugged and greeted heartily by all of her brothers and their significant others along with her parents and grandparents.

Emily seemed thrilled that everyone had turned out, and they had a wonderful family dinner. Mrs. Haydenshire retold the harrowing tale of how many hours she'd been in labor with Emily and how long she'd pushed.

"Sorry, Mom." Emily grimaced.

"You were worth it," her mother assured her as she served up strawberry shortcake with homemade whipped cream, another of Emily's favorites.

Brooke looked horrified throughout Mrs. Haydenshire's tale, and Rainer wondered if it should've been retold. Tradition was tradition though, he supposed.

"Aww, come on, Mom, aren't you going to tell us the story of Rainer's first word?" Logan sneered. Rainer rolled his eyes.

Mrs. Haydenshire beamed at him. "Not unless Rainer wants me to." Her tone was pleading.

Rainer would never deny his future mother-in-law the story. "It's fine, Mrs. Haydenshire."

Emily giggled as Mrs. Haydenshire began her well-rehearsed tale. "A few days after we brought Emily home from the hospital, Rainer was here. His parents had gone to New York for the day, I think, but anyway, he was sitting beside her little seat, patting her tummy, and he said baby. It was so sweet. I almost cried." All of Emily's brothers feigned swooning adoration, batted their eyelashes, and then promptly gagged.

"Yes, well, as I recall, a while after he called her baby for the first time he tried to lie on her in her seat. I should have known then what was coming. Not much has changed," Governor Haydenshire chided. A few minutes later, the laughter quieted down as everyone dug into their shortcake.

Logan raised his head, and his brow furrowed.

"Hey Mom, what was my first word? I don't think I've ever heard you tell anyone."

"Yes, well, there's a reason for that," she huffed as Will, Garrett, and Levi all hooted with laughter.

"What?" Logan studied his brothers incredulously.

Adeline looked very intrigued as she grinned at Mrs. Haydenshire. "What did he say?"

"Well..." Mrs. Haydenshire seemed uncertain about sharing the story.

Governor Haydenshire laughed and shook his head. "Panties," he informed the table as everyone cracked up.

"We gave him a cookie every time we got him to say it. So, he said it constantly," Garrett confessed. He was still cracking up. Logan was crimson in his embarrassment as Adeline tried hard not to laugh but couldn't quite manage it.

"And Emily's first word..." her father gave her a wink as he goaded Rainer.

"Was Daddy," Mrs. Haydenshire supplied. She shook her head at her husband's adoring pride.

After dessert, Emily was buzzing as she eagerly awaited her presents. Rainer had the small box tucked in his pocket. He was well aware that the gifts would be placed on the table, and that if he put it there, she would pick his first.

"I don't see yours on the table, Mr. Lawson," she sassed.

"I think you should open those first, Miss Haydenshire."

She got perfume from her grandparents. Will and Brooke went in with Garrett and Patrick and Lucy to get her a really nice luggage set, which she was thrilled over since she traveled a fair amount with the Angels.

Logan and Adeline got her a scarf and bracelet that Emily had admired when she'd gone shopping with Adeline recently. Levi and Sarah gave her gift cards to her favorite clothing stores, and Connor gave her one to Sephora, so she was thrilled.

Her parents' gift had her eyes dancing excitedly—more than any of the gifts so far, Rainer noted. She pulled the paper off several rather extensive cookbooks that were her mother and grandmother's favorites and a large, very expensive cookware set.

"Thank you!" She threw her arms around her father as he lifted her up in the exuberance of his embrace.

"I think there's one more, Em." Will winked at his baby sister. Her bottom lip slipped between her teeth as she nodded and turned toward Rainer. He was overwhelmed momentarily by the magnitude of his love for her.

She was absolute perfection. Rainer grinned as he pulled the small box from his pocket, while her family watched with bated breath. Emily pulled the tiny purple ribbon off as Rainer watched her nervously.

She opened the box, and Rainer realized he was holding his breath. She lifted the small pewter model of the Eiffel Tower out of the box and studied him quizzically.

"Thank you," she offered, but she was thoroughly confused. Rainer chuckled and kissed her cheek.

"You're welcome." After stepping back from her, he reached for the model. "See, I thought that we might eat here Friday night." He pointed to the center of the tower, watching as her eyes goggled. "And then I thought we'd hang out all around here"—he spun his finger around the tower—"until next Tuesday." She gasped as her mouth fell open in disbelief.

"Are you serious?" She squealed and threw her arms around him.

"I'm serious. I was told that Paris has the best wedding gowns, so I thought we'd make a trip. Logan and Adeline are coming with us, but they have to leave Sunday, so you have to find a dress either Friday or Saturday." She was beaming and bouncing up and down, making him chuckle.

"I can't believe this!"

Brooke stepped forward. "I made you a packing list, and my mom's expecting you for dinner Monday night." Brooke's mother had fallen head over heels for a Frenchman named Claude and had moved to Paris a few years before Brooke and Will had married.

They'd honeymooned in Paris for two full weeks and had been an excellent resource for Rainer in planning the trip.

"Wait, what does Paris have to do with football?" Emily asked.

Rainer and Logan cracked up. "Notre Dame, Notre Dame, get it?" Rainer laughed as she rolled her eyes.

Still chuckling, he pulled Emily to him and kissed her forehead. "The night Logan picked you up from work, I was at Will and Brooke's. They helped me plan the whole trip." Emily beamed at her big brother and sister-in-law. She wrapped her arms, as best as she could, around Brooke's large stomach.

"Thank you so much!"

Brooked squeezed her tight. "You're welcome. Now pack everything on the list. Rainer got you excellent reservations."

Emily turned back to Rainer and grinned. "Yeah, he's pretty much the best."

"Just promise to have fun, and bring me home a baguette," Will ordered.

"You got it!"

Brooke began regaling Emily and Adeline with things to do and places to eat in Paris. When she began elaborating on the many fabulous lingerie shops and where they could be located, Governor Haydenshire tinged green. He turned to Logan with a wry grin.

"I don't suppose there's any hoping that you and Rainer are sharing one hotel room while my baby girl and Adeline share the other?" He was teasing, but Rainer picked up on the slight note of hopefulness.

Logan laughed at his father outright and slapped him on the back. "Only if something goes horribly, horribly wrong, Dad." Everyone laughed.

"Paris, huh?" The governor sighed as he glanced Rainer's way.

He tried not to laugh. "I did tell you this was my plan for her birthday, sir."

"And we're certain the wedding dress is there?" he quizzed the room at large.

"If I can't find a dress in Paris, then I really am hopeless," Emily said.

Over the past several weeks, Rainer and Logan had taken her and Adeline, and often the twins, to cities all over the Northeast to look at gowns, but nothing had turned her head.

Rainer and Logan would find a nearby park or attraction to take the twins to while she and Adeline tried on gowns. Rainer and Logan were both very hopeful that Emily would find something in Paris, as they were growing weary of accompanying the girls on gown expeditions.

Emily had designed the bridesmaid's gowns with Fionna's help, and Mrs. Haydenshire promised to get them made after the election. Nana and Emily had many conversations about the perfect fabric for the dresses.

"You know...purple, but not pinky purple, but not dark purple, sort of a deep purple-purple," Emily had quoted to Rainer who'd nodded his complete lack of understanding.

Emily and Adeline listened to Brooke tell them all about where to shop in Paris. Adeline eventually pulled out her phone and began taking notes.

"At this point, I'm concerned," Logan whispered as he and Rainer laughed.

"Let her have a good time, son. She deserves it. If you need some money, I can help you out with that," Governor Haydenshire urged Logan quietly.

Logan shook his head with a wry smile. "You're letting us live here for free. I've got some money saved up, and she makes more than I do. She can shop as much as she wants."

"Jack told me what happened," Governor Haydenshire whispered.

"What happened?" Will and Rainer quizzed simultaneously. Logan shook his head and checked to make certain Adeline wasn't paying attention to him.

"She popped one of the drug tests a few weeks ago, and her mother's agreed to rehab in hopes of staying out of jail. She's been telling her counselor that she started using to be closer to Adeline."

"What?" Rainer's eyes goggled in shock.

"It was from the pain medication. When her surgery was in the paper, her mother's lawyer demanded a test the next day, while you were in Boston. We figured if her lawyer got wind of the surgery, they'd force another test. Jack said not to worry about it, but she freaked, of course."

"I'm so sorry." Rainer shook his head in abject disbelief that a parent could be so awful to their child.

"I would've told you, but she gets so upset."

"No, it's fine," Rainer insisted. "I'd be upset too."

"I'm hoping Paris will get her away from all of this for a while, you know? Other than going to the beach with us, she's never been on a vacation."

"I think you could probably all use a little time off from the press and the election," Governor Haydenshire said. He looked like he could use some time off as well.

"I saw the polls this morning, sir," Rainer complimented his future father-in-law.

"Yeah, me too." Will grinned.

Governor Haydenshire chuckled and nodded. "Yes, but remember, a job can't be called well done until it's complete."

Will grinned. They'd all heard that expression many times before.

"Yeah, well, I'd say unless news breaks that half of us are illegitimate or something, I'm currently standing in the kitchen of the next Crown Governor," Will vowed.

Rainer could tell Governor Haydenshire was pleased, but he would never have admitted that. The polls had him up by seventy-three percentage points with five percent of the Realm still listed as undecided.

While sporting his favorite footie pajamas with the large dump trucks on them, Henry circled around the many sets of legs in his line of sight. He dragged his blanket along the floor until he located Rainer and lifted his arms.

Rainer grinned and scooped him up. Henry tucked his face into Rainer's neck as he began to suck his thumb.

"I really can't tell you how much I appreciate what excellent care you've taken of the boys," Governor Haydenshire complimented Logan and Rainer. Emily gave Rainer an adoring grin as he began patting Henry's back.

"We're glad to help, sir." Rainer couldn't help but think that babysitting wasn't doing much for the campaign, until he recalled the most horrific moments of his entire life when he'd watched Keaton plead for Emily in the hands of Roberto Vasquez.

A little while later, Mrs. Haydenshire lifted Henry from Rainer's grasp and took him to bed as he waved sleepily to the rest of his family. He gave a lethargic, "Happy Birfday, EE," on his way up the stairs. Emily rushed to kiss the twins before they headed off to sleep. Henry wrinkled his nose and promptly wiped off her kiss which made everyone chuckle.

After Emily and Adeline had taken thorough notes of all of the best shopping in Paris, Emily moved to sit in Rainer's lap on the couch.

"I can't believe you're taking me to Paris!" He reveled in her energy swirling in elation all around her. Rainer hugged her tighter. He wanted to feel more of her, and he was thrilled he'd made her so happy.

"I really want to make you Mrs. Lawson, and it was my understanding that a dress would be needed for that to happen," he teased and listened to her giggle sweetly. She paused and studied him. Then she wrapped her arms around his neck.

"Thank you so much. You have no idea what this means to me. I don't deserve you."

Rainer brushed a kiss across her cheek. "That's not true, and I can't wait to see you in Paris. I'm thrilled to get to take you." She laid her head on his shoulder as talk of the election and the new baby spun around them.

Mrs. Haydenshire had an appointment with a medio the next day. They were hoping for some explanation on why the new baby didn't appear to have Gifted energies. Normally, the energy was the first thing to develop, even before organs formed. The energy started it all.

CHAPTER 6
CELEBRATIONS

As everyone else was involved in the many varied conversations floating around the living room, Emily leaned her head up to whisper in Rainer's ear. "So, is Paris it, or do I get another birthday present?" she urged in a heated pant. His trousers strained. Rainer gave her a cocky grin before he leaned back.

"What did you have in mind, baby?"

With a soft, sultry smile, Emily leaned closer and let her hot breath caress over Rainer's neck as she drawled. "If you take me home, I'll show you."

After valiantly stifling a shuddering growl, Rainer locked his eyes on hers and watched as the storm he loved swirled desperately in their emerald depths.

"Are you getting tired, baby?" Rainer called and gave Emily the out she'd asked for. Emily faked a deep yawn and gave a slight nod.

"Yeah, we played really hard today. We worked six Coulomb's webs," she huffed in disdain.

The signature Haydenshire smirk formed on Logan's features as he teased, "Hey, Em, you know Coulomb was French. We could probably find a museum or something so you could pay homage, if you want."

Emily countered with her own signature eye roll. She shook her head. "No thanks," she spat, but Rainer wasn't interested in Coulomb or his law.

He wanted to feel the energy pass between him and Emily. Calculating the distance of the drop-off was woefully unnecessary as he planned to make certain there was no space between them. Emily stood up off of his lap and took Rainer's hand. She pulled him off the couch.

"You aren't leaving already?" Governor Haydenshire lamented. Emily gave him a sweet smile.

"Yeah, Daddy. I'm tired, and I guess I need to start packing."

"And there's another gift Rainer wants to bestow on you. Right, Em?" Garrett chided as he pretended to cough, and the governor pretended he hadn't heard the quip.

Emily shot Garrett a warning glare and then turned back to her father. Her sweet smile returned instantly. With a slight shudder, that the governor probably hoped Emily hadn't caught, he pulled her in for a hug.

"I'm going with your mother to the medio tomorrow, and then I'm hearing trials. So, I don't guess I'll see you until you get back from your trip. Have a good time, and please be careful, and remember whose baby girl you are."

With another slight eye roll, Emily chuckled. "All right, Daddy. Thank you for everything."

After bidding everyone good night, thanking them again for her gifts, and helping Rainer load them into the car, they finally climbed in the Mustang.

"So…good birthday?" he quizzed as he drove home across the fields.

"Best birthday ever!"

As he gave her a wry grin, Rainer rubbed her leg.

"Where are we staying?" Emily sounded completely thrilled.

As he realized that he hadn't really given her much detail on her gift, Rainer smiled. "We're staying at the Ritz until Sunday night, and then we're staying at this place that's Will and Brooke's favorite Sunday and Monday." Emily was buzzing in her excitement.

"The Ritz!" she gasped. "Rainer, how much did all of this cost you?"

Rainer scoffed. "You don't get to ask that."

She appeared momentarily panicked and began biting her lip. "Please, please tell me you didn't spend a fortune. I'll feel terrible."

"You're worth every penny and more."

"Are you just making up for trying to lie on me when I was a baby?"

Rainer laughed at the sheer number of times he'd heard that story. "Yes, I do still feel badly for that," he mocked.

She waggled her eyebrows and a sexy, mischievous grin formed on her lush lips.

"I like it when you lie on me now."

"Do you?"

"I do."

"I'll have to see what I can do about that, but there are several other things I want to do first."

"Like what?" she urged as he led her into the house.

"Oh, don't worry, sweetheart, I'll show you."

Emily followed Rainer inside. He threw his keys on the counter and spun her into him as he kissed her heatedly.

"Happy Birthday, baby."

CHAPTER 7

HEARTBREAKER

The next day, Logan and Rainer brought Henry and Keaton to the guesthouse so that everyone could pack for Paris while they kept up with the little guys.

Emily played with the boys, while Rainer laid out the clothes he would need. Then he and Logan played with the twins, while she put everything into suitcases.

The Haydenshires had given Adeline a ride to the hospital. She still was putting off Logan buying her a car. Mrs. Haydenshire had insisted that Adeline be her primary medio, despite the fact that she was still in training. Brad and Medio Callavander, who had delivered all of the other children and was soon to retire, were assisting her.

Mrs. Haydenshire was having a full battery of tests run, and Adeline was only working a half shift since they were flying out at six the next morning.

Emily was feeding the boys lunch when the Haydenshires and Adeline returned. Rainer lined their suitcases up in the hall.

Mrs. Haydenshire grasped the governor's hand as she studied everyone in the guesthouse.

"What did they say?" Emily begged. She'd been frantic all morning.

"A lot of things." Mrs. Haydenshire seated herself on one of the

51

couches, and Adeline plied her with a large glass of water. Everyone moved closer.

Logan approached cautiously. "What did they say about the poison and everything else?"

"Well," Mrs. Haydenshire's face fell slightly. "They did the tests they were able to do and... what was the test you did that had the concerning result?" Mrs. Haydenshire asked Adeline.

"It's a nuchal translucency, Mrs. Haydenshire."

"What does that test for?" Logan pushed.

Adeline took Logan's hand. "She's going to need to see a specialist, but it could mean there's a chromosomal anomaly."

"Because of the poison?" Logan asked.

Adeline shook her head. "We don't know if there is one yet, and we don't know if the poison caused a complication...or other factors."

Mrs. Haydenshire chuckled at her embarrassment. "Sweetheart, it's fine. You can say 'it might be because of your mother's age.'" Adeline looked like she wanted to melt into the floor as Mrs. Haydenshire continued. "Medio Callavander wants me to take it easy and not do quite so much campaigning over the next few weeks, but I keep telling all of you I will be fine and your little sister will be fine. I know it."

Governor Haydenshire stepped in. "No one is arguing that, but you're still going to stay off your feet and rest and let me finish this campaign. Then I'll be home to take care of both of you."

While giving her husband a wry smile, Mrs. Haydenshire nodded. The twins finished their lunch and crawled up in their mother's lap.

"When you get back from Paris, I want as many of you kids at the house as can be there. I don't want your mother to lift a finger. Do you understand me?" Governor Haydenshire ordered.

"Of course," everyone agreed. The governor gazed at his wife, and Rainer glanced away. The guilt he was trying so hard to hide was pinned on every line of his face and in every muscle of his weary body. His Adminis rhythms tensed with terror.

"I've got to get to the Senate," Governor Haydenshire lamented.

Mrs. Haydenshire gave him a knowing smile. "I'll be fine. You go on. There are a million things I want to do at the house. We haven't been home in so long." Mrs. Haydenshire sounded thrilled to get to work. Every head in the room shook side to side.

"Uh, Mom, you're supposed to rest," Logan insisted, but Emily seemed to have her mother's number.

"How about this? We'll keep Keaton and Henry here, and you go home and rest. Maybe occasionally you can throw a load of laundry in."

Mrs. Haydenshire smiled at her daughter and agreed. Governor Haydenshire brushed a tender kiss across his wife's cheek as he headed back to Arlington to hear trials.

"Do you have everything packed?" Mrs. Haydenshire glanced from Emily to Adeline.

"I haven't even started," Adeline confessed, but she looked thrilled to begin.

"I'm about half done, but I can't decide what to wear to dinner tomorrow night," Emily explained.

"Can I help?" Mrs. Haydenshire stood and headed toward Rainer and Emily's room.

"No," Emily and Adeline drawled sweetly.

"Okay, can I sit on one of your beds and watch you both pack? I haven't been with my girls in so long, and I want to hear all about your plans for your trip," Mrs. Haydenshire begged. The girls agreed.

"Logan, you and Rainer go outside and play," Mrs. Haydenshire ordered. She sounded just the way she had when they were ten and being a little too boisterous in the farmhouse kitchen.

Rainer feigned offense. "I'm pretty sure we're being thrown out."

"No kidding. I mean a guy knows when he's not wanted," Logan drawled.

"Take your brothers with you." Mrs. Haydenshire chuckled at Logan.

With an eye roll, Logan scooped Keaton up. "Come on, Keat. The boys are being excommunicated. Trust me, you'll get used to it."

Rainer followed suit with Henry, who blew Emily and his mother a kiss and made the girls swoon.

"You, my friend, are gonna be a heartbreaker," Rainer teased Henry as they headed out to the back fields to play.

CHAPTER 8

IT'S TIME TO GO

Rainer whimpered as he slammed his hand across his phone the next morning.

"Get up! It's time to go." Emily sounded like she'd been up for a while. Rainer let one eye open and saw her sitting up beside him. An elated smile spread across her beautiful face. Rainer grabbed her hand and pulled her across him so she was straddled over him.

"Hey there, baby. Are you excited or something?"

Emily giggled. "Yes, and it's already ten o'clock in the morning in Paris. Someone could be buying my dress right now."

Rainer laughed at her outright. "We can't have that."

"Exactly! So get up."

"All right, all right." Rainer eased up on his elbows and angled his head up for a kiss. Emily leaned her head down and granted him his unspoken request, before she crawled off of him and pulled him from the bed.

"I'm going to go make sure Logan and Adeline are up." She headed for the door.

"Em, baby." Rainer caught her hand and halted her progress.

"What?"

"I'm thrilled you're so excited, and even though I know you and Logan used to bathe together when you were babies, I'd really appreciate it if you were wearing panties when you go to wake them up." He tried hard not to chuckle.

Emily looked mortified as she realized she was about to go awaken her brother in nothing but one of Rainer's T-shirts that barely covered her backside.

"Okay, I'm losing my mind." She pulled on a pair of underwear and a pair of knit shorts. "Get up. We're going to Paris!" Rainer heard Emily announce. He doubled over laughing as he listened to Logan groan.

"Geez! It's like every freaking Christmas morning only then I got to sleep until six."

Adeline laughed.

"Get up!" Emily demanded again.

"Get the hell out of my room. I'm not wearing anything," Logan ordered.

Emily made a dramatic gagging noise. "Eww, you poor thing, Adeline. That's disgusting." She infuriated her brother.

By five fifteen, they were headed into the Senate. Rainer and Logan were loaded down with luggage. Vindico chuckled as he met them at the jet fleet that belonged to the Senate.

"Okay, remember that evidence is key, not only to the election but to dismantling the Interfeci. Watch your backs. Wretchkinsides has men in Paris and all over Europe. A good friend of mine will meet you at the west entrance of Charles de Gaulle on Sunday, just before you get on the plane, and I'll meet you right here when you land." Vindico concluded his orders to Logan.

Vindico gave them all kind smiles. "Other than that, have fun. Enjoy the press not breathing down your necks for once." Since that sounded wonderful, Rainer thanked Vindico again for giving him the time off and helped Emily to the tarmac to board the jet that would be taking them to Paris.

The Senate jets were a great deal faster than Gifted commercial flights. They required ten pilots and sixteen coolant officers to work the engines, guide the plane, and to keep the engines cool.

After they boarded, a man that Rainer recognized but couldn't name, dressed in a Senate pilot uniform, stopped by their seats and extended his hand. "I'm sure you don't remember me, Rainer. I'm Pete Namphis. I used to fly you and your dad when you were little. I captained his flight crew. It's a pleasure to fly with you again."

"Oh, thank you." He stood and shook Pete's hand. He gestured to Emily who stood as well.

"This is…" but Pete chuckled as he took Emily's hand.

"Emily Haydenshire, your fiancée and Governor Haydenshire's baby girl."

Emily's chin dropped to her chest. "He calls me that everywhere apparently."

"Your dad took you, Will, and Connor with him on a trip to Dallas when you were a baby. You cried the entire flight," Pete informed her with a wry grin.

"I promise not to do that this time." Emily cringed as Pete chuckled.

"Now, I'm not taking the bride and groom on some sort of secret honeymoon am I?" Pete quizzed with a twinkle in his eye. He appeared proud of Rainer, though Rainer couldn't fathom why. It made him uncomfortable. He shook his head.

"Oh, no sir, just a quick trip this time, but I might take you up on that in a few months." Rainer hoped he wasn't giving too much away.

Pete smiled kindly. "I'd be honored, son, and I know the press has been rough on you as of late, but I really believe Joseph would have been so proud of the man you've become."

With the same swell of remorse and fear that always washed over him whenever someone informed him that his father would be proud of him, Rainer thanked Pete and sincerely hoped he was correct.

"Shall we go to Paris?" Pete drawled. Emily and Rainer nodded their excitement. "I know I took you and your dad there when you weren't but seven or eight, Rainer, but have you ever been, Miss Haydenshire?"

"No sir, and please call me Emily."

Pete agreed and told them he hoped they had a wonderful time in the City of Light before he disappeared into the captain's cabin.

"Do you remember coming with your dad?" Emily asked as they reseated themselves and listened to the engines roar to life.

Rainer shook his head as he tried to recall Paris. "Not really. I remember Dad taking me, but I was mad I couldn't stay here and play with you and Logan, so I complained the whole time. We were only there for one night, I think." The now haunting memory riddled him with guilt. Emily reached and squeezed his hand. She supplied him with her heavenly calming rhythms.

"You were just a kid. Give yourself a break. Logan and I are pretty awesome—just don't tell him I said that."

"I heard you," Logan called from a few seats away.

Emily laughed and then gave Rainer another hug. "This is the most amazing birthday present ever. Thank you so much."

CHAPTER 9
PARIS

Three hours later, they were landing at Charles de Gaulle, and Emily was buzzing in her glee.

"Oh my gosh! I'm here. I can't believe I'm actually here." She was all but squealing on the descending airplane. Rainer chuckled.

Adeline seemed almost as excited as Emily, but her nerves appeared to be setting in rapidly. Rainer and Logan watched the girls as their luggage was unloaded from the belly of the plane.

They'd decided to try their best not to let Wretchkinsides, or the evidence that Logan would be bringing back to the states Sunday, intrude on the girls' trip in any way. They would keep them safe without either of them feeling smothered.

"I can't believe I'm here," Adeline stated in awe. "I've never even been out of Virginia or DC." She was simultaneously thrilled and terrified.

Logan wrapped his arm around her protectively. "Well, welcome to Paris, baby. I've never been here either, but I've heard it's supposed to be sort of romantic." He gave her a cocky wink.

Adeline beamed up at him. She looked like she'd never been happier. They made their way down the ramp to the gate, and Rainer held his breath. After releasing it in a relieved hiss, he tried to recall the last time he'd exited an airplane without being met by the press.

Rainer and Logan's tickets had been purchased through Senate representatives, and Rainer had paid for Emily and Adeline's. They'd also been listed as Senate Officials in an effort to keep Wretchkinsides from knowing who was coming to France.

Rainer guided them to the Metro, and they made their way into the city. As they exited, they found it teeming with people, food, flowers, and the most stunning architecture any of them had ever seen.

It was just after two, and shop owners were just reopening after lunch as Parisians bustled in and out of stores, restaurants, cafes, and museums.

Emily gazed lovingly at the surrounding city and the magic it held. Rainer watched her with rapt adoration as they approached The Ritz Paris.

Adeline's mouth fell open as they made their approach to the swanky entrance.

"Logan, I've never..." She trembled and shook her head as she spun to take in the hotel. Logan grimaced. He'd already shared his worries with how Adeline might react to just a few of the things they'd chosen to do to treat the ladies. "I've never even stayed in a hotel. At all."

"Hey, okay." Logan stopped in the middle of the busy sidewalk and wrapped Adeline up in an all-encompassing embrace. Rainer and Emily tried not to listen but overheard Logan's soothing words.

"Listen to me, baby. It's just a room with a bathroom. It'll just be me and you, okay? So, the scariest thing in there will probably be my snoring." That elicited a small grin and a giggle.

"You don't snore." Terror continued to play cruelly in her eyes as she glanced back at the posh hotel. Logan kissed her forehead, and Rainer watched as the motion soothed Adeline.

Her eyes closed as she reveled in his kiss and in the energy he spun around her. In that moment, Rainer knew he was in the midst of the kind of love that was going to last for the next eighty years or more, if they were incredibly lucky. It was the kind of love that knew no depths and no bounds. The kind he shared with Emily.

"Let's just go see the room, and if you don't like it I'll take you somewhere else, okay?" Logan negotiated carefully. With a slight nod, Adeline clung to his arm as he eased her inside the hotel.

"Wow." Emily gasped in awe as she took in baroque décor, dripping with ruffles and overstated moldings that hung around enlarged portraits of French royalty, all over a century old. Her eyes goggled as they passed a restaurant salon in the hotel filled with silver tea sets and snack trays holding delicate noshes all intricately decorated.

"We're having tea there tomorrow," Rainer whispered and was thrilled as her mouth fell open in astonishment. They moved toward the mahogany desk, with inlaid gold and Carrera marble, used for checking in. Rainer smiled at the attendant working and told her he'd made reservations. He gave his and Logan's names for the rooms.

"I don't know how to have tea." Rainer heard Adeline's terror-filled whisper.

"Okay." Logan rubbed her back soothingly. "I've never really had formal tea either, but no one's going to grade us on it, sweetheart. It'll be the four of us, so if you forget to put your napkin in your lap, or you eat with your fingers, no one's going to care." He was trying desperately to allay her fears. "Just relax, baby. I want you to have a good time. No one cares who we are or what we do for once."

The fact that no one in the vast and overstated hotel lobby had turned a head or batted an eyelash when the four of them walked in did seem to put her at ease.

The bellman appeared and relieved Logan and Rainer of the luggage. He asked if they spoke French. Adeline had taken six years of Latin at the Academy as a Valeduto Predilect, and she'd also taken French her last four years. This was substantially more than the two years Rainer, Emily, and Logan had taken to fulfill their foreign language requirements.

"Un peu. Nous parlons anglais," Adeline offered in a hesitant tone. Logan stared at her in awe as the bellman replied.

"Êtes-vous de l'Amerique?"

"Oui," Adeline sounded slightly more confident.

"Well, I do hope you enjoy Paris, Miss…" The bellman smiled kindly at Adeline.

"Oh…uh…Parker. Adeline Parker."

The bellman exited the elevator on the twelfth floor and gestured for everyone to follow him.

"Well, Mademoiselle Parker, here is your suite." He led them down several corridors to a back corner of the hotel where two suites were situated across a small hallway from one another.

He guided Rainer and Emily to theirs next. "Wow!" Emily breathed as she spun to take it all in. Rainer quickly took the key the bellman was offering and handed him several euros after he'd placed their luggage in the room.

He informed them in English that there would be live entertainment in the bar that evening and that the pool was on the third floor. He exited and left Rainer and Emily to goggle over the ornate room.

Rainer watched Emily as she walked around. She gently caressed the silk bedding and the irises and lilies that were in vases set around the tables. Rainer chuckled. She couldn't seem to believe where she was.

"This is just wow!" She smiled sheepishly.

Since Rainer thought the room was really over the top with the large gold bustle that hung over the bed, several candled chandeliers, and with every wall dripping with moldings, inlaid with floral wallpaper, he studied her closely. He took in the columns that stood around the area and against the walls for grandeur alone.

Emily felt out of place. She looked almost afraid to be where they were. He wrapped his arms around her.

"I kind of think it's a little much actually," he soothed and felt her relax. She smiled up at him and nodded.

"I'm so glad you said that." The breath she'd been holding escaped from her lungs. "I still can't believe I'm here. Everything is just amazing. This is the biggest bed I've ever seen." She flitted out from under his arms and went to admire the bathroom.

"Wow!" Her voice echoed off the tiled floor. Rainer chuckled and went to see what had amazed her so thoroughly.

The bathroom was huge, and everything was tiled in marble. The oversized tub was the size of a small swimming pool and twice as large as the tub they'd played in at the Gansevoort Hotel, when they'd visited New York.

It made Rainer think of several interesting things that could be done in the tub. With a heavy smirk, he asked if she might like a bath later. She giggled and nodded. Her eyes danced with light and love as she bit her lip in intrigue. His heart swelled.

She ran her hands over the two marble sinks and then a lowered countertop with a stool for applying makeup. Suddenly, she stopped and threw her arms around him. She kissed his cheek sweetly.

"Thank you! I cannot believe you did all of this for me." Rainer let his hands travel down her back and then used her backside to pull her closer as he stared at her.

"I would do anything for you." He longed for her to understand how much she meant to him and how much he loved her. She beamed up at him and nodded.

"I know. I can't believe how lucky I am."

As he leaned his head down, Rainer lifted her chin tenderly with his hand and breathed a hesitant kiss across her lips. She trembled slightly in his arms.

He kissed her sweetly and then as hunger began to course through his veins he added to the intensity. He reveled in her desire as it began to spin in heated arcs around him.

"We don't have to be at the tower until six." He continued to run his hands over her body. "So, would you like to go wedding gown shopping now or do you want to explore the city with me today and shop with Adeline tomorrow?" Rainer secretly hoped she might want to crawl in the gigantic bed and let him have his way with her delicious body.

He shut that thought down though. He wanted her to do whatever she wanted, and he chastised himself for wanting to keep her holed up in their hotel room when he'd brought her to Paris.

Logan and Adeline were sure to come looking for them soon. He continued to amend his thoughts.

With a lusciously naughty grin, Emily sassed, "Do we have time to try out the humongous bed before dinner?" After giving her a shuddering growl, Rainer tried to think straight, which was a very difficult task when she was furthering her proposition by taking his hand and pulling him toward the bed.

"If you want to hang out with me this afternoon, then Brooke gave me some great ideas of stuff to do, but Logan and Adeline are going to be banging on that door in a few minutes. Let's wait." He forced the words out of his mouth, but she could tell his resolve was weak.

With a hungry glint in her eye, she reached her destination, spun, and pushed him down on the bed.

"We should go out and see the city," he whimpered as she began to unbuckle his belt. With a quick move, she unzipped his trousers and tugged them downward.

"Then I'll be quick," she murmured seductively as she began to lave him with her tongue. He gasped for breath as the room began to spin. He knew he should stop her.

It took him several long minutes to cast around in his mind as he tried to remember why he should make her stop. The feeling of her tongue caressing him, her long soft hair sweeping across him, her mouth around his head was too good. It was just too intoxicating. He couldn't seem to find his resolve.

"Em," he finally choked and pulled away. "Let's just wait, okay? Please," he begged.

"Fine," she mocked. She'd let him guide her mouth off of him, but she'd replaced it with her hands. She traced him gently and then with slightly more force. She drove him out of his mind. He grasped her hands firmly lest he throw her on the bed and have his way with her.

"Let's just get ready for dinner, and then when we get back we can make full use of this room."

"Are you turning me down?" She feigned insult. He whimpered and shook his head.

"You do understand that I am using every ounce of restraint I have in me not to rip your clothes off and throw you on this bed, right?" he asked, only half joking. She giggled.

"All right, I guess, but you have to make it up to me tonight, and

I'm charging interest." His eyes flashed as a groan escaped his chest. It thoroughly delighted her.

"I'll look forward to paying it in ample return. Believe me. In fact, that's all I'll be able to think about at dinner."

Just as he'd suspected, there was a knock on their door a few minutes later. He cocked his jaw to the side, while she touched up her makeup in the bathroom.

"See," he chided. "Wouldn't that have been interesting for your brother to be pounding on the door, while we were making use of the bed?"

Never willing to admit that he'd been right, she smirked. "It would've been just like being at home."

Rainer laughed as he nodded his defeat and went to let Logan and Adeline in to their room.

"Wow, yours is all different." Adeline took in Rainer and Emily's suite.

Emily nodded. "I think they all are. Come on. I want to see yours." With that, she grabbed Adeline's hands and dragged her back to their suite.

"Is she okay?" Rainer whispered as soon as the girls were out of earshot.

"Kind of," Logan hemmed. "I told you this was going to be tough for her. She's never done anything, and this is kind of huge." Rainer tried to think of something to ease Adeline's deep fears of inadequacy.

"We don't have to stay here."

"No." Logan shook his head. "I want her to get used to staying places like this. She deserves this and so much more. I just can't seem to get her to relax and let me take care of her."

Rainer clenched his jaw and refused to say the dozen or so dirty comments that flooded through his brain at that moment. He reminded himself that he and Logan were no longer teenagers, and that Logan had dug deep to confess something like that.

"Why don't we take them out? Let them walk around and get a feel for the city. We could show them how to get to the Champs, use the Metro, all of that. Maybe she'll relax after she knows more about where we are."

Logan gave Rainer a genuine smile. "Thanks. I really appreciate that. You're the best."

"That is just what Emily was saying last night," Rainer goaded. That comment he was unable to keep to himself. Logan laughed and rolled his eyes.

"Yeah, well, what else can she say? She doesn't have anything to compare you to. She's just stuck with your tiny junk and substandard performances," he mocked as he slid the tip of his tongue through his teeth in laughing triumph.

"Can it," Rainer huffed in the customary way they'd always ended sessions of ragging on one another. The girls returned to Rainer and Emily's suite a moment later.

"Shall we go explore?" Rainer urged as Logan gave Adeline a hopeful glance. The girls agreed and after unpacking they all headed out into the teeming streets of Paris.

After indulging in macarons from a patisserie that tasted like heaven, they window-shopped and walked the banks of the Seine. Around five, they headed back to the Ritz and got ready to head out to dinner at the Eiffel Tower.

Emily was ecstatic as she pulled on a black skirt with a low-cut, hunter-green blouse and black high heels. Rainer let a low whistle slide between his teeth as she exited the bathroom.

"Do you think this is okay? It doesn't really look like what all of the French women are wearing."

A slight chuckle escaped Rainer's lips as he took her hand. "I don't know. Let me see." Emily's case of nerves was worse than he'd originally calculated as she moved to him. She hesitantly glanced down at her outfit.

"You look phenomenal, baby. I just wanted to see how to get it off of you." He traced his index finger down the zipper of her skirt and up the center of her backside to illustrate his point.

She shook her head at him, but the naughty glint in her eye had him aching as he released her hand and she walked away to pick up her purse. She checked herself in the mirror on the dresser once more and drew a steadying breath.

"Okay, I think I'm ready." She seemed to steel herself.

"We're just having dinner. Not facing a firing squad." Rainer retied his tie. He didn't want her nerves about where they were eating to intrude on her evening.

"I know, but it's here, and in the Eiffel Tower, and..." She bit her lip again. "I don't know. I'm just a little nervous, I guess." With a wry grin, Rainer pulled her close.

"I happen to have just the cure for nerves."

"Do you?"

"I do."

"And what might that be?"

He held her eyes with his own for a long drawn-out minute. He let the passion and electricity arc heatedly between them just before he devoured her mouth.

He let his hands trace over the deep, V-neckline of the silk blouse and then grasped her breasts. He lamented the fact that they were bound in her bra. His mind spun to her mouth on him earlier, to the way it felt for her to lick and suck him, and for her hair to graze his thighs. The way it felt for her to draw his erotic energy straight from its source. He halted the kiss before he began to pant and beg her to stay in the hotel room with him and for him to eat his dinner off of her.

"I do feel better," she teased in a sweet whisper. Rainer couldn't quite hide his hungry smirk.

"Just wait 'til we get back here, baby. I plan to make you feel deliriously happy." While laughing at him outright, she grabbed her wrap and slung her purse over her arm.

"I look forward to that, Mr. Lawson, and I'm so glad you do actually live up to all of your macho bragging." They laughed together as they exited the room and waited on Logan and Adeline to arrive in the lobby.

"So, we're having tea there tomorrow?" Emily was wide-eyed once again as they passed by the opulent tea parlor in the lobby of the Ritz. Rainer smiled as Logan and Adeline joined them a moment later.

"Yep, that's the deal. You two can shop to your heart's content every day we're here, but at four o'clock you have to hang out with us again."

"Yeah, we have these grand delusions that you like us more than you like each other," Logan quipped.

Everyone laughed as they headed through the lights of Paris by sunset. Rainer had to admit it was beautiful. The architecture and the city itself seemed to hold its secrets over the people dashing about. It was a few miles from the Ritz to the tower so they headed toward the Metro station. Rainer wrapped his arm protectively over Emily's shoulders as they all studied the ancient buildings they were passing by.

CHAPTER 10

HIGH IN THE TOWER

As they neared the tower, there were several crowds of people milling about. Black market salesmen had baby blankets on the grass full of Eiffel Tower memorabilia.

Paris Iodex made a sweep of the area a moment after they arrived, and the illegal sellers gathered their goods and sprinted away.

"That was effective." Rainer laughed as he led them to the entrance for the private elevator that would take them to the restaurant Will had recommended.

He gave his name to the maître d' who, Rainer noted, spoke perfect English. They were led to a table for four in the back corner. It had a spectacular view of the city, obscured only slightly by the steel frames of the tower itself.

"This is amazing." Emily brushed a tender kiss across Rainer's jaw. After pulling out her chair for her, Rainer turned and was taken by the views the table afforded them. As this was a decidedly touristy thing to do, the people seated nearby were speaking many varied languages, several of them English.

They began glancing over the menu with Adeline translating for them as they each had questions. A waiter approached carrying a bottle of wine and asked in French if they'd rather he speak English. They all nodded, and he continued smoothly.

"Would you like to try the wine the chef has selected for this evening's meal?" Rainer raised his eyebrows at Emily to see if she'd like a glass. She nodded.

Rainer ordered a bottle for the table and began studying the people seated around him.

As they sipped the wine, they began listening to Emily and Adeline plan what bridal salons they wanted to go to the next day.

Rainer continued to glance around. He had the distinct impression someone was watching him. He didn't see anyone he recognized and didn't meet any curious stares.

Rainer didn't want anything to ruin this night. A luscious fire was just beginning to spark in Emily's eyes, and he intended to indulge himself in her heat.

With a shrug, he told himself he'd been mistaken and began talking with everyone before the waiter returned to take their orders.

Logan whipped out his phone and Googled sweetbreads, before announcing that they would not be ordering that as an appetizer.

They settled on a seafood platter and foie gras, something none of them had ever eaten. The waiter retuned with their appetizers and everyone dug in. They'd never eaten lunch, and the macarons they'd consumed were long gone.

Logan almost gagged on the foie gras but managed to cover it well as Adeline beamed at him. They consumed the shrimp, lobster, oysters, and clams. Emily tried the escargot at Rainer's urging. He'd eaten it several times with his father and was pleased that she enjoyed it as well.

Rainer tried to eat slowly. He remembered Will and Brooke's warning that the courses in French meals would be served slower to allow them to be enjoyed. He occasionally studied the people seated around him. He thought he'd noticed someone's Gifted energies. He glanced around again, but it was only a slight vibration and it ebbed quickly. Rainer tried to tell himself he was being crazy. Their lives since the election had begun had taken their toll, and now even when they were perfectly safe he worried.

Emily shot Rainer a sly, mischievous grin.

Using the cover of the long tablecloth and the corner booth, she slid her hand up Rainer's leg slightly farther north than she would've done in a restaurant at home. All thoughts of other people in the restaurant quickly left his mind as he raised his eyebrow at her.

His mind whirled. He tuned back to the conversation in time to hear Logan comment, "The best thing about Paris is no one knows us. We can basically do anything we want and not end up in the papers or in Dad's office."

A slight giggle was Adeline's only comment. Rainer found himself unable to respond as Emily's hand slipped further toward his burgeoning erection.

Emily shook her head. "I don't think we'll be doing anything too crazy. Don't forget the entire world is watching this election."

Rainer drew another slow sip of the wine and tried to distract himself from the location of Emily's hand.

Logan nodded. "I know that, but won't it be nice to go in a store without the *Realm Times* reporting that you bought a different brand of cereal and does that mean Rainer Lawson is no longer a fan of Fruit Loops. And what will this mean for the Kellogg's food company? Could this spell disaster?" Logan pretended to hold a microphone in front of his mouth as he commanded his best reporter impersonation. Everyone laughed.

A bowl of corn soup landed in front of Rainer. As he glanced up to thank the waiter, Emily snatched her hand back and offered her appreciation of the salad placed in front of her. They all dove into the second course and were quiet for several long minutes.

As she drew another sip of wine, Emily returned the hand she wasn't using for her fork back to Rainer's leg. She started at his thigh and gained ground quickly. She shifted and crossed her legs differently so he could see more of her thigh under the skirt she'd chosen. Challenge lit in the emerald blaze in her eyes.

Unable to do or say anything with Logan and Adeline sitting right across from them, his brain made a valiant effort to focus on what they were talking about. Other parts of his body willed her hand to slide higher.

Rainer was still trying to focus as he took another bite of his soup and bit down hard on the spoon. He tried not to whimper as she discreetly brushed him for a drawn-out minute and then slid her hand back down his leg.

He shot her a pleading gaze. She smirked and gave him a sexy grin before she let the tines of her fork slowly exit her lips. He shut his eyes and forced himself to continue eating.

Emily's napkin slid off her lap. Rainer reached to get it for her, but she leaned down first and granted him a glimpse all the way down the very low-cut blouse she'd chosen as it pulled away from her chest. She was thoroughly enjoying driving him mad. Rainer cleared his throat and whispered.

"I'm not gonna make it through the next course if you don't stop." The dangerous look in her eye told him she had no intention of stopping and that he was done for.

Emily's sea bass, her favorite fish, was placed in front of her, as was Adeline's chicken. Logan and Rainer had ordered steaks, and Rainer's mouth watered not only from Emily's flirting but also from the delectable plate of meat and potatoes along with a dish of delicate mushrooms that he'd been served.

Logan's brow furrowed. He appeared to be trying to figure out what Rainer and Emily were talking about. He gave up and cut a large bite of his own steak. He turned to make certain that Adeline was enjoying her chicken.

Emily took advantage of Logan's distraction and traced Rainer again. With a wanton, needy gaze, she moved in and grasped him before returning quickly to her meal.

She certainly wasn't going to stop, so Rainer decided if he couldn't stop her he might as well join her. He cocked his jaw to the side and let his eyes smolder over her as he drew a slow sip of wine.

After cutting another piece of meat, he slid his right hand to her leg and let his fingers trail under the hemline of the skirt. He watched her cheeks color as he plied her legs. Not to be outdone, she shook her head at him minutely and a triumphant look rose in her eyes as she discreetly uncrossed her legs and let his hand fall between her thighs. It startled him as he was trying not to look at her lest she win their unspoken lust-filled battle.

With a quick decision to up the ante, Emily pointed out something on the darkened horizon across the tower from where they were seated.

Logan and Adeline turned to look. She grasped him again and whispered how badly she needed to be filled and how hard she wanted to be taken. Her hot breath sizzled on his neck as he swallowed and let the image she'd painted set in his mind. She stopping talking just before Logan and Adeline turned back around.

"Em, there's nothing over there. What the hell?" Logan sounded highly irritated. Still reeling from the things she just asked him to do to her and still feeling her hot breath on his neck, Rainer started to demand the check immediately.

He considered dragging her back to the hotel and throwing her in their bed, but Rainer amended his plans when he reminded himself that he was fully capable of halting an elevator and making certain it didn't open until he was finished.

The savage thoughts took over his brain. After trying desperately to listen to what Logan wanted to do the next day while the girls shopped, Rainer clenched his jaw. Emily continued to shoot Rainer decidedly naughty gazes.

Mercifully the waiter appeared with their desserts. He placed a delicate chocolate and hazelnut ice cream saucer in front of Emily and a strawberry cake in front of Rainer.

While laughing victoriously, Emily scooped up a spoon full of ice cream and locked her eyes on Rainer as she began to lick the spoon seductively. She told him how utterly delicious it was and then asked if he'd like a bite.

Rainer glared at her as he plunged his fork into the cake. He was aching. She'd had him turned on for so long he could hardly bear it. It was the worst case of blue balls he'd had since he was a teenager.

He wasn't certain he'd even be able to walk back to their hotel. As he thought about the hotel, he squeezed her thigh again and pushed the skirt higher. Her eyes flashed as she hesitantly pushed his hand back toward her knee.

"Rainer!" Logan huffed loudly.

"What?"

"I just asked you like seven times if you wanted to go to the Louvre tomorrow. There's supposed to be a Gifted section. Will said it was really cool. It's like you can't even hear me."

"Sorry, uh yeah, sure, whatever you want." Rainer was still not entirely certain what he'd agreed to. His mind was too full of Emily.

As if she'd cast a spell on the waiter, he appeared with the checks and a bowl containing bright red, candied cherries complete with their stems. She laughed outright as the waiter set them down and handed Logan and Rainer the checks.

As he pulled his wallet out of his pocket, Logan glared hatefully at his sister. Adeline excused herself to the restroom and asked Emily if she'd like to accompany her.

"Oh yeah. I'll be right there. You go on," Emily directed, though she never broke Rainer's stare.

"Here, I'll walk you," Logan huffed.

Emily shot Rainer a decidedly wanton grin before drawling the inevitable question that she'd been longing to ask ever since the waiter set down the bowl.

"Go ahead with it then." Rainer chuckled. He was certain he was not going to be able to walk. She raised her eyebrows and lifted the dish.

"Would you care for a cherry, Mr. Lawson? They're delicious." Her voice was low and excited.

With victory most definitely in her sights, she popped the cherry in her mouth, laved it with her tongue, and then slid out of her chair beside him. She made certain he caught glimpses of all of his favorite curves before she joined Adeline in the restroom.

CHAPTER 11
ALL I WANT, ALL I NEED
LOGAN HAYDENSHIRE

Thoroughly impressed with himself for making it all the way back to their suite without shouting at his sister, Logan gave a quick, disdainful wave good night as Rainer dragged Emily into their room.

Not that either Rainer or Emily noticed or returned the gesture. He brushed the small of Adeline's back and guided her through their door.

She was almost in tears, and Logan reconsidered marching across the hall and screeching at Emily to apologize. He shuddered at the thought of what he might see if he did.

Logan decided to leave Emily to Rainer. He was the only person who could ever get through to her anyway. Logan focused on Adeline.

He seated himself on the small settee in their suite and caught Adeline's hand. He guided her to the seat beside him.

"Are you okay?" he soothed. While visibly feigning bravery, Adeline gave Logan a forced smile and nodded.

It was the first time she'd lied to him about how she was feeling in quite a while. He held her eyes with his own and tried not to let it get to him. He'd thought they were through with her lying to cover her emotions. He reminded himself that she only did it because she never thought her feelings were important.

"Come on. It's me, and I know you're not all right." He broached the extremely tenuous line between getting her to talk to him by pricking the surface and easing the pain or accidentally detonating the blasting cap of a woman's emotions.

She shrugged and moved closer to him. She laid her head on his shoulder as he wrapped his long arms around her.

"I should go apologize." She sounded terrified and sorrowful. Logan pulled his head away from hers to study her speculatively.

"What on earth do you have to apologize for?" He tried to modulate his voice but found it extremely difficult.

"Emily can always tell when I'm upset. She knows me so well. I don't want her to worry." She stood, but Logan stopped her.

"Good, it's about time my sister got her head out of Rainer's ass long enough to use her abilities to do something besides give him a hard-on."

"Logan!" Adeline gasped. Her eyes goggled at his fury.

"I'm sorry," he offered, and Adeline attempted to stand again. "Baby…" Logan decided to try a different tactic. "If my little sister still has any clothes on at all, there is something very wrong with Rainer." He spelled out the truth of the matter and willed her to talk to him and forget about Emily.

"I'm really not mad at her."

"You should be." Logan loosened his tie and tossed it aside.

"She didn't do anything wrong. Not really." While unbuttoning the collar of his shirt, Logan shook his head and gave her an incredulous glance.

"She was rude, and she completely ignored us all through dinner. More importantly, she completely ignored you, and quite frankly, I don't want to see the shows she puts on for Rainer."

With a slight smile, Adeline nodded her agreement. "I know, but it's Paris, and she's so excited. It's no big deal, really."

Logan knew she wanted him to forgive Emily. She didn't want him to have a rift with his sister at all and certainly not on her account. He pulled her to him and wrapped her up in his arms again.

"If anyone, including my little sister, is rude to you, sweetheart, it tends to piss me off." He watched a tender smile form on her beautiful face.

"I know, and you'll never know how much that means to me, but I don't want you to be mad at Emily."

Logan forced himself to drop it, for the moment anyway. He kept Adeline tucked in the safety of his protective embrace.

"Do you want to get in the bed that's the size of the barn?" Adeline teased in a hesitant whisper. Logan kissed the side of her head.

"Sure, baby, maybe by the time we leave we'll be used to the time difference." With a sweet smile, Adeline nodded. Suddenly a deep, crimson blush worked up her neck and settled in her cheeks. The sight made Logan's heart race.

"Can we maybe not go to sleep?" She stared at the ground. Her voice snagged on her desire.

A deep, penetrating love washed over him as he watched her ask for him. It was more than he could ever have hoped for. Quickly deciding to pretend he hadn't noticed her embarrassment, Logan reached for her hand. He pulled her beside him.

"Do you feel okay, baby?" He surrounded her body with his own and let them meld together. His shield spilled out around her. He'd only been with her twice since the surgery, and though she'd repeatedly assured him she was fine, she'd hurt after the first time. He'd insisted that she be examined again before they slept together the next time.

The medio had suggested another few days off during her examination.

"I'm fine. I wish you wouldn't worry about me so much. I brought some lube. That will help." With a slight smile, Logan rubbed her back.

"Taking care of you is my job. I'm your Shield. I don't know any other way to be."

"I'm starting to wonder if you even want to," she admitted with tears pricking her onyx eyes.

"Baby, how could you ever, ever think that?" His voice was raw from his astonishment.

She shrugged and drew a deep breath. Logan kissed her. He

concentrated as he tried to read her rhythms. He raised her head, cupped her jaw in his hand, and brushed her lips with his own.

Suddenly, he had it. He caught her energy. He leaned in and added to the fervency and the pressure as he studied what he was feeling from her.

Hesitant hope, desire, worry, apprehension, need, and inadequacy swam deep inside of her in a volatile cocktail.

Logan pulled away. He held her face in both of his hands and stared deeply into the obsidian pools of her eyes. "I love you more than life itself, and being with you is the most important thing in the world to me. How could you ever believe for one single moment that I don't want you like that? I ache for you, baby. I ache to hold you against me and to feel you around me. The sweet sounds you make drive me wild. I want that all of the time. Every second of every day."

"Really?" Her disbelief wounded him. Logan had spent the past several weeks assuring her that he loved her whether they could have sex or not and that he wasn't in need.

He'd vowed that he could and would wait for her forever if she needed him to. Part of his reassurances had been lies. He was desperate to feel her again and to make her feel him.

"Really," he vowed just before devouring her mouth again, but the fear was still there. It was something else. He moved slowly and pulled the pins holding her silky, jet-black hair in the twist she'd fixed it in. He watched it spill down her shoulders. She trembled in his arms as he eased the zipper of her dress down her back slowly.

"Will you just hold me, please?" She clung to him. As he tried to wade through the frantic energy and moods that were spinning through her, Logan halted his progress.

"Can I finish undressing you first? Then I'll take you to bed and hold you for as long as you want, and we can do anything you want to do, but I just want to hold you naked in my arms."

Her eyes flashed heatedly as she turned around for him as he continued to free her from the dress. Unable to stop himself, he stared at her beautiful body as he revealed it. He took in everything from her shoulder blades, to the curvature of her spine, down to her backside that made him ache to knead it and lift it as he entered her.

He watched her walk to the bed and pull off the masses of pillows. She pushed back the silk duvet until she located sheets and blankets. After crawling in, she stared back at him. Need and hunger churned in her dark eyes and in her rhythms. Hesitant expectation played on their rims.

Logan threw off everything he was wearing in a second flat. His heart hammered in his chest. Her breath caught deliciously when the mattress lowered under his weight. He lay back on several of the pillows and encased her in his arms as she laid her head tenderly on his chest.

"So, you do want to?" She refused to meet his gaze.

"More than anything else in the world," Logan vowed again. "But first I want you to tell me what's got you so upset."

"I don't know." She buried her face deeper in his chest, hiding from the world and from the lies she continued to tell him.

Logan's heart swelled as he let her hide. To stand between her and the world was all he'd ever wanted, but he didn't want her to hide from him.

"Baby, come on," he urged. "What's all this about?" He brushed a kiss in her hair and massaged his hands over her body.

"I just don't think I could ever do that," flowed from her mouth in a forced confession.

Before Logan could ask what she couldn't do, she continued. "And you saw Rainer. He loved it. I mean she really knows what to do to… you know…get him going or whatever and I…" She shrugged. "I don't. I'm an obstetrics medio. Shouldn't I know that?"

With a slight shudder, she seemed to strengthen her resolve. She drew a steadying breath, and a slight groan echoed from Logan as she drew from him. It was incredible, but he wanted her to continue talking.

"I just don't think I could ever do that," she vowed again. "Not out in public, in a restaurant, but Rainer was eating it up. He loved what she was doing and…" Her breath hissed from her lungs, and he rescued her.

He was simply unable to watch her equivocate anymore. "And you think I want you to do that?"

She managed a fearful nod. "Baby,"—he shook his head—"I don't want that. I'm not him. We're not them." He took a moment to try not to think of Emily as his sister so he could continue.

He brushed her cheek with his thumb. "Em's always been a spitfire, and if that gets Rainer going, then good for them, I guess. But you drive me wild." He paused to let several of his favorite images of her fill his mind before he continued.

"Look at me," he whispered, and she raised her head tentatively. "When I think about you doing anything at all, it makes me want you. When I watch you at the hospital, the way you take care of everyone, or when we were in school and we would study together, and you would pore over books in the library. I almost failed out because all I wanted to do was sit and stare at you." She gave him a hesitant grin, but she was still skeptical.

"The way you twist your hair up whenever you have a meeting with the higher-ups at the hospital, because you think it makes you look older." He chuckled at the thought.

"It doesn't make me look older?" she squeaked as concern furrowed her brow.

"I don't know, baby. All I can think about when I see you with it like that is how badly I want to unclasp it and let it fall all over me." His vow was low and reverent. She moaned as he braided his hands in her hair and pulled her in for a long, seductive, drawing kiss.

"You know…" he murmured a long moment later. "We're not the only ones who saw my sister's outrageous display this evening. Rainer was too enthralled to notice the waiter and several other guys who were very intrigued, but you see…"—he moved until he was staring down into her eyes as he let his hands glide over her soft fevered flesh —"when I get you like this, I want this all for myself. I'm not sharing. No one else gets to see you like this." He slid his hands to her breasts and groped and massaged. He moaned as he felt her nipples pebble into strained, taut beads under his pliant caress. "I want it all, and I don't want anyone else to even have a little piece of it. You're all mine, and I don't share."

With his proclamation, he pulled off the lace panties he'd left her in and tenderly traced his fingertips over her. He watched as she writhed and rolled, so hungry for his touch. It drove him wild. He listened intently to her breaths pant from her lungs. Her energy gave hungry, needy arcs as it spun, eager to be joined with his.

Unable to stop himself, with her body fevered, swollen, and wet for him, he slipped his fingers between her soft, sweet lips.

Her muscles clenched around his fingers. They pulled him deeper. Her eyes darkened and her face flushed. She was absolute perfection. Her body throbbed under his touch. She whispered his name in the darkness, and he shuddered as fervent need coursed through him.

"Does that feel okay, baby?" He prayed he wouldn't hurt her. "Tell me where the lube you brought is."

"It feels amazing." She panted as her eyes closed in the ecstasy of his touch. Her body gave languid, needy writhes in his hands. He locked her eyes with his. "I don't know if I need it."

"I want it all. I want you to come in my hand and in my mouth, baby," he urged as another moan echoed from her. "I don't ever want to hurt you, sweetheart. I swear I'll be so gentle, but I need you. I need to feel you all around me. Nothing will ever feel as good as you." His voice was strained and rough in his need.

She nodded. Her eyes beseeched him. As he gazed into them, he felt her give way for him as he stretched her as tenderly as he was able.

He delicately prepared her to take all of him. He kept his fingers moving over the places she was most sensitive as her breath stuttered and she swelled. Her muscles cinched even tighter around his hand.

"That's it, baby." He reveled in the knowledge that he knew exactly what to do because she was all his. He kept his fingers gently caressing her just the way she wanted it. "Right there, baby. Right there. I know. That feels so good, doesn't it?" He was desperate to hear her tell him.

"Yes, please don't stop," she begged in heated need as she rode his hand.

"I'm not stopping until I come deep inside of you," he assured her. With that, he had her. She broke hard. Her orgasm seized her body. Her back arched deeply as her energy unraveled for him. It spilled out in heated waves of release.

"I want to drink you, baby." He moved down her body. She'd shut him down the past two times, when he'd tried to take her orally. He was desperate to taste the sweet honey that flowed from her. She wanted it too. He felt her energy spike again as he gave her the warning.

With a deep, guttural growl, he held her thighs with his hands and opened her as he laved his tongue over her slit. The taste of her and the feeling of what he'd just elicited from her, of her energy flowing readily into his mouth, drove him wild.

He wanted more and was beyond the ability to use the head above his waist. He pulled his tongue away. He watched her body roll and buck. She wanted more as well.

"Come here to me," he ordered as he rolled to his back. He pulled her over his face until she was straddling him. He delved deep and kneaded her backside as she moved above him. He sucked her clit and slipped one finger back inside her. He continued to explore her deeply with his tongue. She flooded his mouth. He drank her dry. He licked and sucked the sweet nectar of her. She fell back and looked afraid of what he'd just done.

"I have never tasted anything sweeter, baby. Eating you out is like heaven," he assured her. He flipped again and continued his commands. "Lay down, and spread your legs for me. I'm gonna set the cast, okay?" With a fervent nod, she bucked again, and he summoned. He closed her womb instantly as he was already part of her energy.

"Are you ready for me, baby?"

"Yes, now." Her desperate desire and her permeating need seared through him. It ignited the fire burning deep within his groin.

A groan thundered from his chest as he moved on top of her. He caressed her hips tenderly with his hands and reveled in how good she felt. While he was dragging his tongue over her breasts, sucking and pulling, she began to beg.

Her pleading became fervent, and she reached down to stroke him. His eyes rolled back in his head. She wrapped her fingers around his length, and he pulsed in her hand. She moaned as she pressed him to her clit and bucked. A moment later, she sprang up suddenly and swirled her tongue around his head.

"Oh, hell yeah," fell from his mouth in a shuddering groan. She moaned. The sound reverberated through his length and through his soul. It was incredible, but he wanted inside of her. He wanted to own her.

"Is that what you need, baby? Do you need my energy to fill you full?"

"Now," she begged as she eased her mouth away from him but continued to pull and beg for him with her hands.

"Show me where you want it." He watched as she fell back on the pillows and let her legs fall open for him again. Unable to stop himself, unable to draw it out any longer, he pierced into her. She was so tight he had to steel himself not to lose it immediately.

He thrust gently at first, as not to hurt her. She lifted her hips into his and pulled him deeper as steady, streaming moans sang from her lips.

He took her harder and faster. He added to the friction and force. He felt her swell and let the feeling wash through him. Nothing would ever feel as good as that. Being drowned deep inside of her was otherworldly perfection.

She broke, but he held on. He refused to surrender. He was going to claim her. He was going to make every inch of her belong to him. He was going to prove to her how incredible and indescribably beautiful he thought she was. He was going to show her that she was everything.

"I want another one. Give it to me." He eased his thrusts as the orgasm washed through her then began again. "I want them all. You're all mine," he repeated, and she clenched around him again. His directives seemed to drive her wild.

She gasped and bucked. Her eyes flashed unrestrainedly. Her moans echoed around him as he ground into her.

He let go as the waves crashed through her hard and fast. He held her and refused to allow any space between them. As she stilled, he kissed away the last of her moans and told her how much he loved her.

As the blissful haze of his explosive release began to dissipate, Logan grimaced.

"Uh, Ad, baby, are you okay? I'm sorry. That was too rough." He felt harrowing guilt wash over him, but she giggled softly. The sound soothed his soul.

Her cheeks were a dizzying array of pinks and reds from her climaxes and her embarrassment. "I feel fine. I'm not hurting at all. That was completely amazing."

"You're sure?"

She nodded and moved so he could hold her tighter as she eased her leg over his and wrapped herself around his body.

"Will you promise me something?" Logan blurted out as he swallowed down the guilt that had come over him suddenly.

"Of course."

As he remembered her confessed fears that she didn't do things that would make him want her, he explained. "You drive me wild. Like so wild I can't think sometimes. So, please just promise me if I ever do anything you don't like or don't want to do, that you'll stop me."

She considered for a minute. "Okay, but sometimes you do something that I'm nervous about, but then it ends up being the most incredible thing I've ever felt." She tucked her face into his chest. Heat radiated from her cheeks against him.

He chuckled and kissed the top of her head. It was the only part of her face she was currently allowing him to access.

"I just don't ever want you to do anything you don't want to do."

"Logan…" She eased her head upwards to meet his heartfelt gaze. "I love everything you do, and the things that you say make me feel so beautiful. When I'm wrapped up in your arms, it doesn't matter if we're doing that, or if we're just lying on the couch watching TV. When I'm close enough to you to feel your energy and hear your heartbeat, then it's like, in that moment, nothing bad could ever happen to me because you're there." The devoted plea seemed to spill from her heart with fervor. Logan let her words wash over his soul. They soothed and filled him.

He shoved several more of the pillows off the bed and then lay back on one. He held her tightly on his chest and caressed her face.

"I would never let anything bad happen to you." He whispered for her to go to sleep, that he had her, and that he'd never let her go.

CHAPTER 12

APOLOGIES

RAINER LAWSON

Hazy, orange sunshine warmed Rainer's face as he let his eyes slowly blink open. He pulled Emily tighter into his embrace and let their first night in Paris replay in his mind in slow, vivid motion. She'd driven him wild in the restaurant, and they'd enjoyed each other thoroughly when they'd returned to their suite.

Logan's irritated glare when they'd parted company last night flitted through Rainer's mind as well. He suspected Logan had seen at least some of Emily's show at the tower.

He grimaced. He wasn't certain what to say but supposed he should apologize. He smiled down at Emily. Her hair was splayed wildly across his bare chest, and he let just a few of his favorite fantasies replay in his mind as he watched her sleep.

After glancing at the clock on the bedside table, he leaned and kissed Emily's forehead. Her eyes fluttered open a minute later.

"Hey there, baby. Did you sleep well?"

"Mm-hmm." A deeply satisfied grin spread across her face. "Very well." As he tried to hide his smirk, Rainer kissed the top of her head.

"They're delivering our breakfast this morning, and I thought maybe I should have on clothes when I answer the door," he teased as she yawned deeply.

"I like it better when you don't have clothes on."

He shook his head and edged away from her as she scooted back on her own pillow and allowed him to get up and throw on a pair of jeans. She decided to dress as well, in case the room service attendant should come inside the room. She began reciting all of the places she and Adeline planned on going.

"Hey, what did Logan say about the Louvre last night at dinner? You had me all hot and bothered, and I couldn't pay attention." She laughed with the gleam from the night before still in her eye.

"There's a Gifted section in the Louvre, probably lots of stuff about Coulomb." She rolled her eyes. "But Will told Logan that it's got some cool stuff, and he wanted to see it since you can't go shopping with us today."

Rainer bristled. He didn't want to say what he needed to say. Emily noticed it instantly.

"I kind of think we might've…" he hemmed, but Emily interrupted.

"You mean I might've hurt Adeline's feelings last night, because she's nervous about being here, and I completely ignored her and was a terrible best friend." Rainer wouldn't have put it quite like that, but he didn't argue. "I know. I'm going over there to apologize now," she explained as she pulled on a pair of jeans and an oversized black sweater.

"Do you want me to come with you?"

She leaned up on her tiptoes to brush a kiss across his jaw as she shook her head. "No, I screwed up. I loved flirting with you like that and what it led to…" she teased as she glanced back at the bed and the couch in their room. She was clearly recalling the locales of their amorous lovemaking the evening before. Rainer gave her a sly grin. "But I was rude to them. I shouldn't have done that. I got all caught up in the fact that no one here cares who we are, and I let the freedom of it all and just being in Paris get to me. I need to tell both of them how sorry I am." She marched across the hall.

Several minutes later, Emily reentered the room. She looked like a weight had been lifted off her shoulders. Adeline and Logan followed as the attendant delivered all of their breakfasts. They were supplied with trays of fruit, croissants, and pastries along with rich, dark coffee that none of them particularly loved.

Logan and Adeline gazed at one another the entire time they ate, and Rainer assumed they'd enjoyed their first evening at the Ritz as well. He chuckled and punched Logan on the shoulder.

"So, we still up for the Louvre?"

"Gee, you remembered. I wasn't sure you would seeing how you couldn't keep your mind north of your belt at the restaurant last night."

Rainer glanced at Emily who had turned the color of her hair. Neither of them commented as Logan and Adeline laughed at them.

After the delectable foods were gone, Emily moved to her purse. "Okay," she instructed in what Rainer and Logan instantly identified as her bossy tone. "We have tons of stores to get to today, so we need to head out soon."

Adeline looked thrilled.

Logan's brow furrowed. "I thought you were just going wedding dress shopping?"

"We are," the girls insisted. "But we're shopping for other things as well. I mean it's Paris. Fionna says French lingerie is supposed to be amazing, and she is definitely a lingerie connoisseur. She loves it. So, we definitely want to find lingerie shops."

Logan waggled his eyebrows. "You two take your time then."

A little while later, Logan and Rainer walked the girls to the Metro and reminded them to watch everyone around them constantly.

"Be careful and call me if you feel anything weird," Rainer ordered. Emily and Adeline shared an incredulous glance. He still couldn't shake the feeling that something was off.

Emily kissed his cheek. "We will be fine. We'll call you if we need you. If not, we'll see you back in time for tea. Now go have fun."

CHAPTER 13

RELICS OF THE LOUVRE MUSEUM

Logan and Rainer eased out of the underground station and headed toward the Louvre. As it was Saturday, the Parisian sidewalks were bustling with people. Rainer glanced around. He was suddenly edgy as they neared the museum. He batted away the ever present loom of cigarette smoke.

"So, where's the Gifted area?" Rainer gestured his head toward the opulent museum.

"Will said it's in whatever part is shut down. They move it around so the Non-Gifted people don't get suspicious. They tell them they're setting up new displays or whatever. You have to summon to get in."

Rainer was thankful Logan seemed to have forgiven him and Emily for their behavior in the tower the night before, but he couldn't shake the feeling that he was being watched.

As they made their way into the courtyard of the grand museum, they stared up at its majesty. They paused momentarily to take it in. The building alone was stunning.

They climbed the stairs that led to the imposing marble columns. Logan nudged Rainer's shoulder.

"Hey, does that guy look familiar to you?" He gestured with his head to a man who'd paused and was glancing around the courtyard.

He was studying a map. With a slight headshake, Rainer furrowed his brow. His stomach started to churn as he studied the man.

Logan shrugged. "I could've sworn he was at the tower last night at the restaurant. Not that you remember anyone or anything in that restaurant. My sister's got you eating right out of her hand," he goaded with a disgusted smirk.

Certain he had no defense for his behavior the night before, Rainer decided to raise the white flag, or at least make Logan think he was. He gave a sheepish nod and willed away his reddened cheeks.

"Yeah, she does. I can't help it. I'm head over heels. She drives me crazy, and when we get started she does this thing with her..."

"Ah geez," Logan nearly shouted as he scowled at Rainer. "I do not want to know. Stop talking now!"

Rainer cracked up as Logan had fallen right into the trap he'd set.

Rainer glanced back again as they reached the entrance, but the man Logan had pointed out wasn't in the courtyard anymore. He looked around, but he didn't see him anywhere. He'd disappeared.

After chuckling at Logan, who was still shooting him infuriated glares, Rainer advanced to the entrance stairs and allowed Logan to enter ahead of him.

They followed crowds of tourists and Parisians alike through the entry. Rainer allowed himself a moment to reflect on how long the building had existed and all of the information it stored.

It struck him as amazing as he considered the parts of history that his own father had played a part in, and the fact that the American Realm was centuries younger than the French.

They took a moment to look at a large interactive map near the entrance. Logan pointed to a wing on the ground floor that read *closed for new installation*. "That's it."

Rainer followed him to the closed wing. They waited and allowed several Non-Gifted tourists to pass them by before they turned down the darkened corridor.

"Je suis désolé...." a guard began, but Logan halted him as he and Rainer cupped their hands. Their brilliant green shield casts spun in their hands. The guard smiled and waved them through.

"Surely he could see our energy from around us," Rainer

commented.

"Yeah, but the rules are you have to summon. Gifted kids have energy around them too."

They began their journey with statues of great Gifted scientists that had contributed to the Non-Gifted world. Rainer paused in front of a statue of Coulomb.

The large, marble figure was surrounded by interactive screens. They all displayed how his law was calculated mathematically and gave examples of how he had, in fact, determined that the force of attraction or repulsion between two point charges is directly proportional to the product of magnitude of each charge and indirectly proportional to the square of the distance between them.

Rainer pulled his phone from his pocket and chuckled. "I shouldn't do this."

Logan joined in his laughter and urged him on. Rainer snapped a photo of the entire display and texted it to Emily with the message,

Your favorite Gifted scientist says to tell you hi, baby.

They moved on to a large display on Henry Ford and Rudolf Diesel that they were both drooling over when Emily texted back.

We're having champagne in a fabulous wedding dress boutique, and I'm flipping you off. Rainer laughed heartily.

He'd expected nothing less. He and Logan stood enamored for a long while, just watching the display of different engines running rhythmically.

There was an entire wall devoted to Tesla, and Rainer and Logan both grimaced as they took in the information. Nikola Tesla was probably one of the most Gifted men to ever live. The time that he lived in was his downfall.

He'd wanted to share the Gift of electricity with the Non-Gifted and had figured out the ways to make that happen. It wouldn't have cost the Gifted people anything at all, but the powers that be during those dark days wanted to lord their powers over the Non-Gifted people.

They certainly wouldn't share with them. They had stifled Tesla at every turn. He'd been beaten, starved, and shamed all at the hands of his own people.

Finally a hit man had caught up with him in a hotel room in New York City. They'd caused the accident that had severely injured him, but when it didn't kill him, they'd stopped his heart from beating and walked away.

Rainer hated Tesla's story. It made him sick. He looked away from the large display and saw the man Logan had pointed out in the courtyard earlier. He was whisking away from Rainer quickly.

After reminding himself that they weren't the only Gifted people in Paris, and that tens of thousands of Gifted people from around the world visited the city every year, Rainer tried to push away the feeling of dread that kept washing over him.

As they moved on to the display on Joule and the invention of professional Summation, the man was there again. Logan noted him as well, and with a quick glance at one another, they both turned and followed the stranger.

Rainer almost caught up with him by cutting down a shorter corridor, but the man disappeared. Logan pointed to his left and they sprinted that direction, but he was nowhere to be found.

"I'm not picking up on his energy. How did he get in here?" Logan searched the corridor frantically.

"He's suppressing it." Rainer rushed back to the entrance but found nothing. He phoned Emily to make certain she was all right. She assured him she was fine and they were having a ball. Her delight made his heart beat in rhythm again.

They returned to the Joule display. Rainer snapped pictures of the first Arlington Angels team. They were the first all-women's Summation team in the world and had fought endlessly to allow women to challenge professionally. To make up for his earlier text, he sent that to Emily as well with the message,

The original Angels aren't nearly as pretty as mine.

"Let's go get lunch." Rainer glanced at his watch. It was still early, but he hoped Adeline and Emily weren't wedding gown shopping anymore and maybe they'd let them tag along. They took the twists and turns out of the Gifted section. They were halted by the guard and had to wait several long minutes, until all Non-Gifted people were away from the corridor, before they were allowed to leave.

They finally emerged into the sunlight outside the museum. Logan shielded his eyes and glanced around the courtyard. They began walking and stumbled upon a restaurant that was just opening for business.

After they were seated, they struggled through the menu, but they were able to determine a few sandwiches and salads that looked good. When the waitress returned, Logan attempted to pronounce his choice. He must've butchered it.

"Just tell me in English," the waitress demanded. She'd spoken the command perfectly.

"I'm sorry," Logan hesitated but then placed his order. After ordering his own sandwich and a bowl of soup, Rainer heard the tinkle of the bell on the door.

He wasn't certain why it sounded ominous. He'd heard it half a dozen times since they'd entered. Rainer turned to see the man who had to be following them as he was taken to a table near the back. Rainer's eyes met Logan's concerned glance.

"Do you seriously think he's following us? Do you think he knows about the evidence?" Logan cocked his jaw to the side and narrowed his eyes.

"I don't know, but this is all a little too coincidental." Rainer stood up and pretended to have dropped a napkin so he could scan further. The man was chatting with a different waitress.

Rainer shook his head and tried to remove the frantic feeling settling on him. Their lunches were placed in front of them, and he picked up his sandwich. As he took a bite, his phone chirped.

I found the dress! It's perfect! Now, we're off to find what to wear underneath. Emily's text had his heart lurching momentarily. The reality of their wedding cemented in his soul.

He responded to Emily's text and informed her that he couldn't wait to see her in it. "After we eat, you wanna go check on the girls? Then we can head back to the hotel. Em found her dress."

Logan looked relieved by the very idea of going to make absolutely certain Emily and Adeline were okay.

"Good. Tell her to buy the damn thing because they're not going off by themselves anymore."

CHAPTER 14

IMMINENT THREAT

As he drew a sip of his soda, the hair on the back of Rainer's neck stood. He jerked his head up and swallowed. His eyes flashed dangerously as the man seated himself at their table.

"Who the hell are you?" Logan demanded. He cupped his hand and summoned instantly. Rainer followed suit. He leveled a hate-filled glare at the man.

With an ominous chuckle, the man smirked. "It's not nearly as important who I am as it is who you are, Mr. Haydenshire. Ladies shopping on the Champs today?"

He already knew the answer. Rainer's blood ran cold as he clenched his jaw. The man looked familiar now that he could see his face. He knew he'd seen it somewhere before they'd arrived in Paris.

"Mr. Lawson…" the man drawled. His French accent did nothing to cover his sinister tone. "I saw the little show your fiancée put on for you last night at the tower. She's quite a handful, isn't she?" Bile flooded Rainer's throat as he leaned in.

"Tell me who you are and what the hell you want. Now."

While ignoring Rainer's questions, the man glared.

"Yeah, she's wild. I could tell. Wouldn't mind having a piece of that myself."

Rainer leapt to his feet. His chair shot backwards as he leaned into the man across the table.

"I don't know who the hell you think you are, but if you get anywhere near her, I'll kill you." The man stood and backed away as Logan tried to throw him with a shield. He missed by a millimeter. The guy was fast.

He glared and gave a final quip. "You better hope you find her before I do."

Rainer reeled as he and Logan began to chase the man, but he ducked into an alleyway and disappeared.

Rainer shook from the realization of what the stranger had just threatened.

"Come on! Now!" Logan demanded. As they took off in a furious sprint to the Metro, Rainer cast his phone to display Emily's location. They jumped on the first train headed toward the Champs-Élysées. "They're in Sephora."

Rainer harnessed the engine and Logan cooled, but the engine was too large for the two of them to speed it up. Rainer shook his head and tried Emily's cell.

"Hi, this is Emily. I'm sorry I missed your call…"

"Dammit." Rainer ended the call. They exited and attempted to sprint down the enormous street, but it was just too crowded with tourists.

"Who the hell was that?" Logan demanded.

"I don't know, but I've seen him before." Desperation shook Rainer's voice. "This doesn't make any sense. Who tells a Shield they're planning to kidnap someone?"

"What are we going to do when we find them?"

"We'll go back to the Ritz and call Vindico. We can't arrest him here. We have to contact the French Iodex office." He checked Emily's location again. "Now they're in Zara."

They rushed toward the store, and Rainer realized what he was about to do. He caught Logan's shoulder and gasped for breath.

"We can't just search women's dressing rooms."

While terror and fury pulsed through his shield, Rainer shouted, "Emily!"

No one appeared and he checked the location again. "Fuck, I think there's a delay. Hang on. I'm gonna harness one of the cell towers."

They moved while Rainer tried to force his phone to update more rapidly. They almost knocked down a sales woman in a parfumerie who scowled at them. They took no time to apologize. They scooted by the woman and searched the jewelry store.

"They're not here either!" Frustration perforated Logan's already angry tone.

They moved through several more stores. Rainer shook his head. "Stop. This is stupid. We'll never find them like this. Let me harness and make it work. Then we'll know where we're going."

He tried Emily's cell again. When she didn't answer, he fully harnessed the cell tower and moved the cast to his phone.

CHAPTER 15

LINGERIE STORE HELL

"They're in that lingerie shop." Rainer pointed farther down the road and they took off.

"Mr. Haydenshire, Mr. Lawson..." a well-dressed saleswoman, with her hair done up in a sophisticated twist, gushed. "We were so hoping you both would come in and help Miss Parker and Miss Haydenshire pick out a few things."

Rainer and Logan attempted to catch their breath enough to speak. They clutched at the stitches in their sides.

The sales clerk seemed to have mistaken their lack of verbal acknowledgment for confusion. She smiled broadly.

"You two are rather famous here in Paris as well. Such beautiful girls your fiancées are. I was so pleased they stopped in today. We've been helping them select things you might like, but now that you're here, you can help them decide."

Rainer stammered and gasped. "Where are they?" He started through the store.

The woman was taken aback by his tone. "They're in the back there." She pointed to a large, curtained area of the store. Rainer nodded and tried to console himself with the fact that she was here and she was safe.

He hustled to the room the woman had indicated. Logan was right behind him as Rainer threw back the curtain and ran in. A horrified gasp came from Adeline as her mouth hung open in shock.

Emily and Adeline were standing in what Rainer now realized was a dressing room. They were also wearing the raciest lingerie he'd ever laid eyes on.

He was simultaneously overwhelmed as he stared at Emily in black leather and lace with bows and ties. There were tiny satin ruffles and leather pasties covering her nipples. The see-through G-string completed the confusing ensemble.

He was also thoroughly embarrassed as Adeline was standing in something equally as see-through and ruffled and leather and clearly meant for Logan's eyes only.

Rainer spun quickly and spluttered.

"Adeline, I'm so sorry!" He covered his eyes even though he'd turned around. He didn't know what else to do. Logan spun as well, and as Rainer opened one eye slightly, he took in Logan staring at him with fury emanating from his glare as red energy pulsed through his shield.

With a slight headshake, Logan growled, "Get dressed! We have to get you out of here."

Still stunned by their interruption, Emily gasped, "What are you doing here?" Her embarrassment was evident even though Rainer couldn't see her face.

"Just get dressed, please," Rainer pled. "Then we'll tell you everything, but we have to get you out of here now."

"Why?" Emily ordered. "We aren't finished shopping."

"Em!" Logan screeched. "Just get some fucking clothes on." She jerked the curtain back as she did what he asked. Rainer glanced back at Logan again.

Blood flooded his cheeks as he stammered, "I'm so sorry. You know I didn't mean to. I had no idea. I should've guessed given where we are…but I wasn't thinking. I'm sorry."

As he glared hatefully at Rainer, Logan seemed unable to speak. He tried to think of a way to make Logan understand that he hadn't enjoyed seeing Adeline dressed like that without offending Adeline.

"You've been my best friend since I was born." He paused and dropped his voice to an audible whisper. He tried to sound reassuring. "I didn't want to see her like that. I don't ever want to see her like that. You have to believe me."

Logan seethed. "Just shut up."

Rainer willed the girls to dress quickly. The saleswoman who'd greeted Logan and Rainer whisked back and called through the curtain.

"How did those work, ladies? I bet the boys loved them." As he squeezed his eyes shut, Rainer wanted to melt into the floor.

"Uh," Adeline stammered. "I, uh…I think we'll just get the things we'd already selected, and save these for another time." She sounded mortified which only seemed to further infuriate Logan.

"Of course. I've got everything packaged for you. Will you be paying in cash or shall we start an account for you?" She smiled broadly at Rainer who gave her a half glimpse before returning his gaze to the floor.

"We'll just pay in cash." Emily's voice shook violently as she replied. The saleswoman turned back to Rainer and Logan.

"Mr. Lawson, did you see her in the black waspie? Wasn't she simply exquisite?" Certain he had died and gone to some kind of lingerie store hell, Rainer rubbed his forehead.

"We're in a hurry. Could you just take care of whatever they're buying?" He assumed he was probably purple in his embarrassment. Logan seemed to convulse from his fury.

"Why did you take so long to turn around?" he demanded in an infuriated hiss.

As Rainer had taken less than three seconds to turn, he glared at Logan and declared what he considered to be obvious. "I was looking at Emily!"

With another audible huff, Logan threw his arms in the air.

"Oh come on," Rainer spat. "She's my fiancée. Are you really angry that I saw her like that, or are you mad I saw Adeline? You can't have it both ways."

Logan crossed his arms over his chest and glared like the entire world had pissed him off. He turned his back to Adeline as the girls exited the dressing room loaded down with bags from other stores. They were both the color of overly ripe strawberries.

While trying desperately to focus on the reason they'd entered the store in the first place, Rainer breathed. "Let's just get out of here."

"No!" the girls shrieked and then glanced around to see who might've heard their outburst. Emily continued in a lower tone.

"You tell us why you're here, right now."

Rainer tried not to lose his temper as he explained. "Logan and I thought we were being followed today at the Louvre, and we were. The guy came up to us at lunch and threatened to take you if I didn't get to you first. We need to go back to the Ritz and call Vindico. I need to know who the hell he is, and I need to talk to the Iodex officers here."

The saleswoman returned. She was carrying two large, pink bags, each tied with a black bow, and handed Adeline's purchases to Logan and Emily's to Rainer.

"Enjoy," she offered. They each gave a single nod, took the bags, and exited the store.

Logan seemed to focus solely on getting everyone to safety as he took Adeline's hand. "Are you sure we should go back to the Ritz? They probably know where we're staying."

"I don't know anywhere else to go. I can call Vindico from here, but we're still all out in the open. There's just too many people everywhere to keep them safe here," Rainer concluded.

"We could go to Brooke's mom's house?" Emily offered. Rainer noted the aggrieved notes in her voice.

"I don't know how to get there, and the address is in the room," Rainer lamented. "Plus, I don't want to put her in danger."

"Let's just go," Logan commanded. They took off to the nearest Metro station. Rainer and Logan paced around the girls and studied every person on the Metro car they were in. Neither had a gun.

They reached the stop for the Ritz and each took the girl's hands as they leapt in a furious sprint. They dodged around people, carts, dogs, and strollers as they raced up the steps of the hotel. A sense of impending dread settled harshly in the pit of Rainer's stomach. He ignored glares of the faces flying by.

Rainer summoned instantly and brought an already traveling elevator back to the ground floor. They rushed on, and Logan raised his cupped hand. The elevator rocketed to the twelfth floor.

Steady streaming tears ran down Emily's face, but Rainer wasn't certain if it as the impending threat or Logan seeing her in the racy lingerie that was more than she could bear.

As he tried to swallow down the pain of watching her ache, Rainer knew that him seeing Adeline like that did nothing to soothe her either.

With his heart racing and terror surging through his veins, Rainer forced the doors open.

CHAPTER 16

INCOGNITO

"Very impressive, Mr. Lawson." Rainer instantly recognized the accent and the threatening drawl.

"You want to do this? Let's go! You won't win. I'll kill you," Rainer spat venomously. They moved like the well-oiled machine Vindico had turned them into. Logan threw his cast over the girls while Rainer summoned more of his own power and shot a fluid heat-filled spark of electricity at the man's heart.

"Whoa!" the guy screeched. He leapt to the floor and threw a powerful shield. He deflected Rainer's cast. Whoever he was, he was one hell of a Shield. He was almost as quick as Vindico.

Rainer's heart raced as his cast seared a small hole in the wall and shattered a vase on a table nearby. He turned to cast again, but the man stood and held up his hands.

With fury in her emerald eyes, Emily summoned and ordered Logan to release his shield cast. Everyone in the hallway tried to shield their eyes from the brilliant burning light of her cast with the ring.

"Okay, stop!" the man pled. "Please, just let me tell you who I am. Here…" He lifted his handgun from its holster and held it between his thumb and index finger. "I'm going to give Officer Lawson my gun, and Officer Haydenshire, I'll even let you pat me down. I don't have any other weapons." Rainer took the gun and turned it on the man. He chambered a round and racked the slide in a second flat and then he casted the gun. He wasn't going to miss. The man was a weapon unto himself.

Logan shoved the man up against the wall and patted him down rather forcefully, which he allowed. Logan withdrew a badge from the man's shirt pocket. He flipped it open and studied it momentarily.

"Is this a fake?" he demanded. Rainer caught a glimpse of the Elite French Iodex Captain's badge.

"You're right. I don't want to do this," the man quoted Rainer's threat. "Certainly not with the two of you and her with that ring." He chuckled. "The way Danny bragged about you two, I was worried he might've made a hasty decision when he appointed you two to Elite."

Utter exhaustive confusion rocked through Rainer. The man continued.

"I'm Jean Paul Fitzroy. I'm the Captain of Elite Iodex here in France." He gestured to the badge in Logan's hand. "I went through Special Ops training with Dan in the States. He's one of my best friends. We tracked the largest of Wretchkinsides's installations here in Paris and worked tirelessly to bring it down. Dan would fly back and forth all the time to see Amelia, but in the midst of all of our work, I fell in love with the city and with the woman who is now my wife. So, I took a job with Iodex here, and then Amelia was killed." Fitzroy shuddered slightly. His pain was evident in his tone. "I was a pallbearer in the funeral. I'm sure you've probably already figured out that Dan hasn't handled her death well. I love him like a brother, but he's consumed with his hate and revenge for Wretchkinsides. I was concerned when he hired you on fresh out of the academy. I'm not sure if you've noticed, but his decision-making is questionable at best."

"Why did you do this? Why doubt us?" Rainer demanded. He was still furious.

"I don't know, Mr. Lawson. The last pictures I saw of you, you had your hands up her skirt and your tongue in her navel," Fitzroy fired back. Rainer bristled but couldn't deny the argument. "Dan kept insisting that you were phenomenal officers. The best he has, save your brother." Fitzroy nodded to Logan and Emily. "I just didn't see it. You're too young, not seasoned enough, but you proved me wrong." Fitzroy gestured to the still smoking hole in the wall of the Paris Ritz. "I'll get that taken care of for you." Fitzroy grimaced. He turned back to them and continued.

"I needed to see it before I handed the evidence I've collected over to you. It's taken me years to put some of this together, and I'm not handing it over to some kid who's going to set it down in the chair beside him while he makes out with his girlfriend in an airport lounge." He was smiling as he laid out why he'd done what he'd done. "Please accept my fervent apologies for what I did and what I said." He gestured to Emily.

"What did you say?" she demanded.

Fitzroy gave her a wry smile, winked at her, and shook his head. "But we do have a fairly significant problem." His smile faded quickly.

"Oh yeah. What's that?" Logan challenged.

"Wretchkinsides sent a snatch-and-grab team along with a hit team led by Ferratus into the country just a few hours after you arrived. So, I'm certain you can see where this is going. Officer Haydenshire, let me be the first to congratulate you on your recently extended trip to Paris, and Mr. Lawson, let me be the first to console you on the fact that you'll be leaving a day early."

Conrad Ferratus had recently executed the hit on one of the German Realm Governors. He'd thought a job of that magnitude meant he deserved to be promoted within the Interfeci. He'd apparently mouthed off about wanting to take Cascavel's place as the top hit man. Only he'd been sloppy and had left evidence behind that had led the German Iodex to the Interfeci.

Since then, Iodex officers around the world had been on high alert to discover what was going to happen to Ferratus. Rainer assumed that pulling off the removal of the evidence Fitzroy had collected, and perhaps disposing of him and Logan in the process, might buy him back into Wretchkinsides's good graces. He nodded his defeat.

"Dan gave me each of your cell numbers before you flew out here should anything go awry. You'll be meeting me at the time and airport gate that I text to you in two days' time. I'll send one piece of the information to each of your phones. Do not respond to the texts in any way." Everyone nodded their understanding.

"You won't need to rush on your departure day," Fitzroy stated cryptically to let them know that they would be leaving Monday night probably late. "I'm sorry to ask, but could we, uh…?" He gestured to Rainer and Emily's suite.

"Sure." Rainer unlocked the door and allowed everyone in. The maids had been in to make the bed, and Rainer was thankful that Emily had picked up the nightie she'd worn for him the night before.

"I'm running a sting tomorrow at Charles de Gaulle," Fitzroy explained as soon as Rainer had closed the door. "They know your return tickets were for tomorrow afternoon. I'll have Elite Iodex everywhere. We'll see if we can't take down the team he sent in. You'll actually be flying back separately. I've divided the evidence and heavily encrypted it. You'll have to have both thumb drives to access information on either. So, Logan, you and Miss Parker will fly back about twenty minutes before Rainer and your sister."

"Good." Logan threw another hateful glare at Rainer. His tone visibly confused Fitzroy as Rainer grimaced.

Fitzroy continued with a slight shrug. "Like I said, I am sorry about today, but I had to know you were really the men for this job." With morose nods, after the day they'd had, no one spoke for a moment.

Emily drew a steadying breath and raised her head with a forced smile. "Mr. Fitzroy, sir, we're having tea in the salon downstairs in a little while. Would you care to join us?" She had been raised in a governing family, after all.

Fitzroy smiled. "No, thank you, Miss Haydenshire. I don't want to intrude on any more of your trip, and please call me Fitz. Everyone does. I'll talk with Henri. He runs the tea salon. I'll see that you get the best table in the house. It's the least I can do. Uh, could I ask you one more question?"

Rainer nodded.

"Do you have any idea how Wretchkinsides knew you were coming to Paris? Did you discuss it outside of work? Are you certain your phones aren't cloned?"

"We never discussed it. I didn't say a word about it until her birthday. I was afraid someone would tell her. Maybe someone figured out who I was or what I was doing when I booked the flights. I rarely cast my phone. I know it could be cloned if I do." Rainer shrugged dejectedly.

Fitz nodded. "I'll get a few officers to hang out in the lobby so I make certain you're safe while you have tea. After that, it would really be better if you stayed in your room until I determine how much Ferratus knows about where you are. I've had men all over here today, and it doesn't appear he knows where you're staying. They've called no doubt, but the Ritz is an impeccable hotel. They would never give the names of their guests to anyone."

"We'll be fine," Logan vowed. Rainer nodded his agreement. He didn't want escorts to tea.

"You're a fierce team, to be certain. Just keep them safe." He gestured to the ladies. "And I think I'll keep several guys patrolling around here just in case." A moment later, he was bidding them goodbye, after Rainer returned his pistol and Logan returned his badge.

While trying to let the information he'd just been informed of and the events of the day settle in his brain, Rainer watched as Logan followed Fitzroy out of their suite and stalked quickly into his own. Adeline had followed after him.

The bags Emily had been carrying fell to the floor as she curled up in a ball on their bed. She buried her face in one of the pillows, and to Rainer's horror she began to sob.

"Baby." He rushed to her and wrapped his body around hers. He had no idea what to say to make any of this better. His mind raced. He assumed she was more upset about the potential for kidnapping than the dressing room or about their trip being cut short. Complimenting her on what he'd seen her in seemed like the wrong thing to say, but his brain kept offering that up feebly. He had to acknowledge what had happened.

"Em, baby, shhh," he soothed. "Please don't cry. I'm so sorry. I just...I thought he was really after you. I thought he worked for

Wretchkinsides. I knew I recognized him. I thought it was from Vindico's office wall. I didn't even realize what store we were in."

"I know," she choked. Tears flowed in sheets over her beautiful face. She shook her head convulsively. "You weren't supposed to see that, and I'm so tired of being hunted."

"I know," Rainer soothed. He rubbed her back and caressed her head with his hands. He had no idea what to say, but he wondered who was meant to see the extremely naughty lingerie if not him.

"Ugh," she groaned. "I cannot believe that is when you two busted in!"

"I'm sorry," Rainer offered again. She sat up and shook her head. She allowed him to wipe away a few of her tears.

"It was a joke. We dared each other to try on the raciest things in the store. I can't believe you saw me in that." Her eyes flashed. "I can't believe you saw *her* in that."

With that declaration, she fell back on her pillow and buried her face.

"I really only saw you. I mean I saw her, but I was looking at you." He tried to be truthful. She'd been standing right there. Obviously, she knew what he'd seen.

"Oh my gosh. Logan saw me in that!" she whimpered, as her blush grew more violent. Rainer smiled down at her and brushed her damp hair away from her face.

"Trust me, Logan was only looking at her." She was clearly desperate to believe what he was saying to her. Her chin began to quiver again.

Rainer lay back down beside her and pulled her onto his chest.

"I know it was only a joke"—he kissed her head—"but you looked amazing. If Adeline hadn't been standing there, believe me, I would never have turned around." She clung to him with force and unburied her face.

"I bought a few things. Nothing quite so…" She tried to come up with a word to describe what she'd been wearing. She settled on "… outlandish, though." She returned to her hideaway in his chest. He chuckled and stroked her hair.

"Good, because although you looked stunning in all of that, I had no idea how to get you out of it, and I really wanted to get you out of it."

Finally giving a small laugh, she shook her head at him.

Rainer decided a slight subject change might help.

"Did you buy the gown, sweetheart?" She'd been carrying several bags, but he didn't think any of them were large enough for a wedding gown.

"No," Emily whispered. "I found it, and I love it, but I'm supposed to go back tomorrow to try it on again to make sure it's the one. Then we can take it back with us so Mom can make the alterations." Rainer smiled. He was suddenly overwhelmed as he thought of her dressed all in white and walking toward him on her father's arm.

Talking about the dress seemed to dry her tears. Her eyes lit with excitement as a contented grin spread across her face. Not wanting to ruin the momentary reprieve from her day, Rainer knew he had to go ahead with his warning.

"Em, baby, I don't think you and Adeline can go back tomorrow. Not alone. Not with Wretchkinsides's teams here."

Her face fell and tears welled in her eyes again. "I have to go back. They're holding the dress for me. That's the dress I want."

Rainer held up his hands and reassured. "Okay, okay. I know. I didn't say you couldn't go back at all, but maybe Logan would be willing to go with you, just until we get that evidence home, or I'm sure, seeing what he put us through today, Fitzroy would probably give you an escort to the store. I'd be happy to go. I could stay outside. I swear I won't look at the dress. I would never take that away from you. You know that."

She nodded, but that wasn't at all what she wanted.

"I can take care of myself." She spoke her defiance weakly. He'd heard her utter that phrase so many times growing up it always made him smile. She did point to the ring as he nodded.

"I know that, but I also know that until the evidence is out of the country and in Vindico's hands, we're all in a lot of danger." The thought occurred to him that the reason Emily hadn't picked up on Fitzroy the night before at the tower and the reasons she hadn't felt anything while they were shopping was because Fitz was a good guy. He'd never used his energy to harm another.

With a dejected glance at the door, Rainer knew he had to go talk to Logan. Emily picked up on his nerves.

"You should probably go talk to him." She reached and touched his forearm. Her soothing Receiver's cast worked through his arm and into his heart.

"I will." Rainer was finding it difficult to drag himself from the bed and from the intoxicating feeling of her energy flowing so readily into him. "I just wish I knew what to say."

Emily gave him a reassuring smile as she nodded. "Logan can't believe that everyone doesn't find her as intoxicating as he does. You just have to make him understand that."

CHAPTER 17

MINE

LOGAN HAYDENSHIRE

Fury pulsed through Logan's veins. He couldn't speak. He couldn't even see. His entire body vibrated in his wrath. He glanced at Adeline, and his anger melted slightly.

She was stunned from their afternoon. She shivered all alone on the bed. He knew he should comfort her. He just couldn't seem to figure out how.

He began to pace. He couldn't help it. He was infuriated that Rainer had seen her like that. Using most of his resolve to keep himself from sinking his fists into Rainer's face, he continued to pace. She stared up at him with terror splayed in her eyes.

"Logan, I'm so sorry."

He spun around, completely stunned. He shook his head and forced his voice into what he hoped was a soothing tone.

"Why are you sorry? You didn't do anything."

She stood and moved closer to him, but she remained a few feet away.

"Rainer didn't mean to do that. I don't think he wanted to see me like that at all."

"Then he's a fucking idiot." His rage returned instantly.

"Logan, please," Adeline begged as tears loomed on the horizon.

He wrapped his arms around her. He couldn't stand for her to cry.

Her tears of shame stabbed through his acrimony. "He's your best friend. He didn't intentionally burst in on me in a dressing room. Please don't do this. He loves you almost as much as I do." He'd never heard her beg for something so vehemently. "I honestly can't believe either of you saw me in that."

Logan continued to rub her back and try to calm her as he wondered who was supposed to see her in that. "It was just a stupid thing to do. We'd been picking out what we wanted to wear under our wedding gowns, and we picked out a few things to wear while we were here and at home. Some of the stuff that saleswoman kept showing us was really over the top, so Emily dared me to try one on. I agreed as long as she did, and that's when you busted in." Adeline's cheeks flushed crimson in her embarrassment. She shook her head in disbelief.

Logan was still at a loss as to how to comfort her, and he was still furious with Rainer.

"Please don't be mad at him," she pled again. "I feel terrible. He didn't mean to. He didn't even really look at me. He only saw her. Trust me." Desperately wanting to believe that to be true, Logan drew a deep breath.

"If I agree not to kill Rainer, will you stop crying?" he asked, only half joking.

"Please just forgive him. He's just as embarrassed as I am."

Logan rolled his eyes and shook his head. He couldn't shake the image of Rainer Lawson standing and gaping at her dressed in see-through black lace and leather with nothing covered completely.

Everything he considered to be his and his alone had been revealed to his best friend. Although Logan had certainly seen her naked, and even in lingerie before, even he'd never seen her in anything so racy.

It galled him that Rainer had seen her as well. Even the G-string she'd had on with the rest of the straps and lace had revealed almost as much of her front as it did her backside. He added fuel to the fury swirling inside of him.

He felt like he was being rent in two. He willed himself to try to make her feel better, and not to give in to the ire that was boiling so close to the surface. She clenched her jaw and pulled back.

"Do you remember what Emily was wearing when you came in the room?" Her voice was hopeful.

"Gross, she's my sister. Trust me—I couldn't take my eyes off you, and I don't ever even want to think about my sister in something like that." Revulsion plunged through him, and he convulsed slightly.

"Exactly." Adeline gave him a tentative smile. "I think that's probably exactly how Rainer feels about seeing me. I'm really more of a sister to him in his eyes."

He wanted desperately to believe that. Logan released her to run his hands through his hair. The day had been more than he was capable of handling. He closed his eyes and tried to let what she was saying wash over him. He sank onto the bed.

"I know, okay? I really do. You're just going to have to give me some time. When I think about what he just saw, it makes me physically ill. That's mine. You're mine. All mine. I don't want him to have seen that. I don't want anyone else to have seen that. I do not share."

Adeline gave a hesitant nod. She looked pale and worn as she sank down beside him "I know, and I love that you feel that way, but I really don't think he saw what you saw." There was a knock on the door, and Logan groaned. She squeezed his hand and kissed his cheek.

"Let him apologize," she urged as she made her way to the door. "Because at some point you're going to have to let yourself be scared about Wretchkinsides having men here instead of angry, even though it's easier to feel that."

CHAPTER 18

THE UNDOING OF LOGAN HAYDENSHIRE

RAINER LAWSON

Rainer couldn't recall another time in his entire life he'd been nervous to talk to Logan. The door slowly opened. He forced himself to meet Adeline's eyes and not recoil. Rainer offered her a timid smile.

"Uh." He cleared his throat before forcing himself to go on with it. "I cannot tell you how sorry I am."

"I know. I really wish you hadn't seen me like that, but I'll get over it," she assured him, but her face was glowing crimson. Not having any idea what an appropriate response to that might be, Rainer nodded and gave her a sorrowful look.

"Can I, uh…?" He gestured into their room. Adeline drew a deep breath and glanced back at Logan.

"Sure, I'll just go see what Emily's wearing to tea." She looked pleased with her reason for leaving. With that, they traded places, and Rainer closed the door to Logan's suite with a quick prayer that he could fix the damage he'd done. He glanced around nervously.

"Logan, I, uh…" He directed his eyes to Logan seated on the bed. "I'm sorry. I really didn't even see her. I was only looking at Em and I know"—he held his hands up in utter defeat—"that makes you mad too, but I just…tell me what you want me to do. You've been my best friend for my whole life. You're my partner. I'm marrying your sister.

How can I make this better? I'll do anything." Rainer quickly decided that he wasn't above begging. Logan refused to meet his pleading gaze.

"I'm not mad you were looking at Em," he finally mumbled as he kept his eyes on the bed, glaring at it like it had fangs.

Much to Rainer's chagrin, Logan looked like he'd very much like to take his aggression out with his fists. Rainer already knew that was the case, but he hoped Logan would go on. He stood after a long moment of harrowing silence. His fists were clenched in tight knots as he began to pace.

"I don't know," he erupted but was still keeping his eyes off Rainer. "I don't know what you can do. I can't get it out of my head. It makes me sick." He finally turned his hate-filled eyes on Rainer for a split second but then forced himself to glance away again.

Rainer's heart ached as he felt the fury that pulsed in Logan's shield. He was so angry his energy spiked in waves of red. Rainer tried to think of what to say to convince Logan that seeing Adeline like that hadn't done anything for him.

His mind moved in reverse for a long moment. Rainer knew there had never been anyone Logan had ever wanted except for Adeline.

All through middle and high school and even their first year at the academy, girls would flirt, chase, and play games just trying to get Logan's attention, but he'd never succumbed. He'd made out with Rachel McAdams at a middle school party because he knew she had a crush on him, and he felt sorry for her. His brothers had been harassing him about not having kissed anyone yet.

He'd laid eyes on Adeline Parker at sub-freshman orientation, and that had been it for him. With single-minded focus, he'd worked up the courage to be in the same room with her, then talk to her, and then finally ask her out.

"Em is it for me." Rainer knew in any other situation Logan would most definitely not want to hear what he was about to say. After drawing a steadying breath, Rainer went on anyway. "I know Adeline gets you going, but Emily drives me wild. Taking everything else in our relationship away, Emily has all of the features that to me make up jaw-dropping sex appeal, and please know that I mean no offense, but Adeline just doesn't." He laid everything out on the table, truly willing to do anything to make Logan understand.

Logan studied him for several minutes before huffing dejectedly. "You're Rainer Lawson. You could have whoever you want, and I've always been fine with that. I was good with it all, with the car, and the money, and the looks, head of Ioses Order, and being Joseph Lawson's son, and you're my best friend, but God, man, I swear I will kill you over her."

Rainer tried desperately to think of how to respond to that. The truth of it all bit harder than Logan's fury for the moment.

He shook his head and finally allowed himself to be who he was. He stopped fighting the unearned fame and wealth that his father had bestowed on him. In that moment, he accepted the truth because he couldn't change it.

"Maybe," he admitted. "But you know what? I already have everything I could ever want, and you're Logan Haydenshire, the next Crown Governor's son," he vowed adamantly as Logan's brow furrowed from the sudden realization of what was to come. "You're Will and Garrett's little brother," he reminded him. The Haydenshire men had the reputation of being highly skilled lovers, and it came directly from the top of the line.

"You're one of the finest men I've ever had the privilege of knowing. You're my best friend, my blood brother," he edged, finally getting a slight smile out of Logan. "But friendship, and Emily, and who our fathers are—putting all of that aside for just a minute, you need to understand something, so hear what I'm telling you." His voice rose in accordance with his fervor. "I couldn't have her." He jerked his hand back to the room the girls were in. "Not only because I don't want her, and I would never do that to you, but because she wants you and only you." He continued on, determined to make Logan understand. "You know everyone's always telling me how Em and I were kismet or whatever, and maybe we are, but we're not the only ones.

"Man, I was sitting right beside you when she walked into orientation that night, and I saw your eyes bug out of your head and your mouth hang open. I saw her catch your eye and then glance away. You may not know this, but Adeline's kind of shy," Rainer chided with a wry grin. He was pleased that Logan chuckled. "But I saw that split second when you saw each other. I swear to you. I knew then and there you were sold and so was she. It was done. All the dozens and dozens of girls who'd been chasing you since kindergarten could hang it up because the game was over."

The fury seemed to ease from Logan's face, and his fists unclenched. "Can I ask you something?" He asked with pain perforating his tone.

"I don't know. If I come over there, are you gonna hit me?"

"Maybe," Logan allowed. Rainer decided to chance it knowing that if it would help, he'd let Logan hit him. He moved to sit near his best friend.

Logan seemed to draw courage from the air around him in a long pause. Whatever he wanted to know was obviously important, so Rainer waited patiently.

He drew a deep breath and braced himself. Logan stared into Rainer's eyes.

"Fair warning," Logan drawled. "You better tell me the truth, but if I don't like your answer I will probably pound you."

"Great," Rainer quipped as fear swirled in his stomach. Logan seemed to force himself to go on.

"Do you remember that campout when Garrett and Levi snuck all of those *Playboys* and what were the other ones?" He seemed caught up in the details of his recollection.

Rainer studied him incredulously but supplied, "Uh, as I recall it was *Juggs* and *Spank* and I don't even remember the rest." He grimaced as he recalled that evening.

"Right," Logan agreed. Not certain where this was going, Rainer continued to study his best friend. He and Logan had turned thirteen that summer. Rainer was spending two weeks with the Haydenshires while his father traveled. Rainer had gone on the campout that he'd always been included in. That was the first year that Will and Garrett had talked Governor Haydenshire into staying home and letting them take care of Logan and Rainer. They'd insisted that Logan and Rainer weren't babies anymore and that they would be fine.

As Garrett had just turned twenty-one, making him and Will both in their early twenties, the Haydenshires had agreed. Beer and porn had been passed around in heavy doses and indulged by all of the Haydenshire boys and Rainer. With a slight shudder, Rainer recalled just some of the images he'd seen in *Spank* magazine.

"It's amazing we're not more screwed up," he quipped. Logan chuckled. He seemed momentarily distracted from his interrogation.

"Anyway…I'm sure you remember what happened after they started passing out magazines." He scowled.

With a slight shudder, Rainer recalled Garrett handing out the girly magazines and then spending the rest of the night making fun of Cal, Patrick, Connor, Logan, and Rainer for having the normal male reaction to seeing scantily clad women. After more than a few rounds of harassment, Will had called Garrett on it.

"Leave them alone. We could all sleep under the tent you just popped." Will had effectively shut Garrett up. As the story replayed in Rainer's mind, he suddenly realized where Logan was heading with his question.

"Tell me you are not about to ask me what I think you're about to ask me." He and Logan had talked their way through childhood, through Rainer and Emily's first kiss, and all through adolescence. He'd talked Logan through his first time, but this question was over the top.

Logan stared him down, and Rainer moved off the bed. He was too angry to sit. He began pacing and trying to will calm.

"You really want to know if I got a hard-on after seeing your fiancée in lingerie? That's really what you think of me?" Rainer demanded hotly. His eyes flashed in acrimony. "Are you insane? First of all, I thought someone was trying to kidnap the love of my life, the reason that I exist, so even after seeing her in that getup, I couldn't have if I'd wanted to. Keeping her alive seemed to take precedence over banging her!" he shouted. "Second, I keep telling you I didn't look at Adeline. I was staring at Emily, and you know what, still didn't happen. Man, we're not all fucking wired like you. What did you think? I was gonna see her dressed like that and decide I had to have her? You and Emily be damned?"

All of the pain and fury pent up inside of Logan seemed to exit through his lungs in a battered hiss.

"All right, I know," Logan finally relented. "But that is what happened to me!" he admitted with his face coloring rapidly. "I mean not today, but…I don't know. I spent my whole life watching you and Em, and I kept thinking 'I want to look at a girl the way Rainer drools over my sister. I want someone who'll love me like Em loves him.' I went through school looking for that one girl, and all of the notes in my locker and girls who'd ask their friends to ask me if I'd dance with them—I didn't want any of that. Then, just like you said, she walked into orientation, terrified and all alone, and I couldn't stop staring at her. She took my breath away," Logan confessed in a haggard choke. He refused to meet Rainer's gaze. "But, I also couldn't walk over to her and introduce myself. Trust me, that would've freaked her the hell out." Logan shook his head abashedly as Rainer found himself laughing.

"I get it. Believe me." Rainer returned to his seat on the bed near Logan. "I'm not freaking because you're Em's brother, but if any other guy had seen her dressed like that, I'd be going nuts too." Silence blanketed the room for a moment. "Being Shields is tough sometimes. It overrides our brains."

"Maybe someday we'll laugh and tell our kids about this."

With a hesitant nod, Rainer considered. "I'm gonna go with probably not, but it was a good thought."

Logan's laugh eased the tension that had been churning in Rainer's stomach.

"Yeah, son, let me tell you about the time Aunt Emily dressed up like a dominatrix, and I walked in on her."

"Yeah, so you see how that could be bad."

"I'm sorry I freaked," Logan admitted.

"Totally understandable."

"I just kind of think of all of that as…" Logan hemmed, still trying to apologize feebly.

"Yours," Rainer interjected.

"Yeah, but don't tell her I told you that."

Rainer shook his head. "I won't, but I kind of get the impression she really likes being yours."

"Yeah, I hope."

"Trust me." Rainer offered Logan his hand. With his signature smirk, Logan shook Rainer's hand in the handshake they'd made up when they were kids.

"Shall we take them to have tea and try to figure out what to do about what Fitzroy said and all of the other insane things that have happened today?" Rainer suggested. "Or do you want to talk about how being terrified is actually what pissed you the fuck off?"

"I think I'll just keep pretending that isn't it."

Rainer nodded his adamant agreement.

CHAPTER 19
PROPER TEA

Logan held the door to the tea salon open as they all entered. Henri, a large, round man with soft wrinkles displayed in his smile and a twinkle in his eye, greeted them at the ornate, antique desk situated near the door.

"Officer Lawson, Officer Haydenshire, I presume?" He spoke in English with a heavy French accent. "Captain Fitzroy said you will be coming today, and I save you the very best table with the beautiful views and the romantic fountain. This will be lovely. You see. Follow me."

Adeline and Emily giggled as they followed Henri to the back of the salon, behind an enormous stone fountain with cherubs. The rushing water soothed them, and Rainer immediately understood why the booths in the back would be romantic, as the fountain made them unable to be seen by everyone else in the salon.

Octagonal windows on every side showed off the courtyard gardens that surrounded them which, even in October, were still quite extravagant.

The tables were dressed in the white linen tablecloths and were set with extremely fancy china and crystal. Huge plants and strategically hung curtains made each table feel intimate. He gestured them into the opulent booth, complete with throw pillows. Henri smiled.

"Now, I bring you the very best tea you have ever had, and you will never tell me English tea is the best once you have had my tea. And I bring you all the delights I have created for your tea today." With a bow, Henri made a grand exit as Logan and Rainer shared a chuckle. The mischievous look on Logan's face had Rainer breathing a sigh of relief.

"This is amazing," Adeline gushed, and Emily was bouncing in her seat. They all took a moment to study the priceless antiques placed around the cove where they were seated.

A cozy fire was blazing under a marble mantle opposite the fountain which made the area extremely romantic and soothing. Rainer wrapped his arm around Emily's back as she grinned up at him.

"Do you all want to go swimming tonight? Brooke said the pool here is supposed to be amazing." Emily gave Logan a pleading gaze. "It's heated," she added. Adeline looked nervous as she glanced at Logan.

Rainer, Emily, and Logan had spent most of their summers in the Haydenshire's backyard pool and could all swim well.

Adeline hadn't had the privileged childhood they'd had, and it had taken Logan weeks to even get her in the pool and then even longer to attempt to teach her to swim.

Mrs. Haydenshire had to take Adeline swimsuit shopping as her mother had refused, but Logan hadn't given up on her. By the end of the first summer they'd dated, she was less afraid and even swimming a little. Logan and Rainer had a silent conversation with their eyes.

Rainer shook his head. "Baby, I don't think we can go to the pool. I can't have you somewhere that's so easily accessed until Fitzroy figures out if Ferratus knows where we're staying."

"Oh." Emily tried to hide her fear, but it played on the rims of her emerald eyes. "That's okay," she immediately lied to keep from upsetting him.

Rainer sighed and fought the regret that occasionally pulsed so close to the surface it was palpable to those around him—regret that he couldn't just go out and do things with Emily without either attracting a mob of press or a hoard of people that would like them dead.

Henri returned to their table with a cart that contained a highly polished, ornate, silver tea service and several plate stands. Each contained three platters of finger sandwiches, pastries, and scones.

"Eat, eat," he implored. "Then you will say to me, 'Henri, this is the best food I have ever eaten. Henri, this is the best tea I have ever had. Better than anything in the States.'" He scoffed with a shudder.

They all nodded, laughed, and waited until he'd left before they began pulling things off the trays. Emily poured them all tea from the silver carafe.

After having several of the minute sandwiches, Logan and Rainer shared a disappointed glance.

"Okay, Em,"—Logan smirked and seemed much more himself— "these are great, but we're having a real dinner, right? We can order room service." He held up one of the diminutive sandwiches. "This is not a sandwich."

He finally broke out in laughter with everyone else.

Adeline shook her head at him. "We'll get you something from room service. Think of this as your afternoon snack. Don't be hangry."

"Thank you." He plunged the entire sandwich in his mouth in one bite. He shared a conspiratorial smile with Rainer.

As she took in the atmosphere around them, Emily laid her head on Rainer's shoulder. She seemed content after the insanity of their day. He put his arm around her. The images of her in the racy lingerie still intruded on his brain occasionally.

"I don't think this is as good as Mom's," Emily whispered with a mischievous grin. She held up the teacup.

"Me either," Adeline agreed as Logan and Rainer laughed. "This is so beautiful though." She gestured to the view as the lights of Paris began their magical display as the sun sank toward the river.

Adeline gave a slight shudder but then smiled. "So, before our day went completely insane, did you have fun at the Louvre?"

Rainer's blush returned. He tried to will it away as he nodded.

"Yeah, we should go back. You two should see the displays. It's really incredible."

After shoveling another sandwich in his mouth, Logan agreed. "It was really cool except that we thought we were being followed by a mad man after the two of you, which for me took away from the overall experience a little."

They shook their heads at all that had happened. Rainer settled in and lost himself and his worries, momentarily, in the beautiful scene outside the windows. He let the heat from the fire, the sounds of the steadily rushing water, along with the tea they'd consumed rest and restore him. He cuddled Emily close and tried desperately to reconnect. He pushed away the wounds the day had inflicted and got lost in the healing embrace of a few sweet, simple kisses.

Henri returned after several long restorative minutes and cleared his throat. He chuckled as he'd interrupted their kissing. Rainer noted that he was smiling at them and didn't seem to mind their affection.

"This is why people come to Paris. Did you enjoy your tea then?" He was still beaming at them. They all assured him that they had and thanked him profusely for the table and all of the delicious foods.

Henri glanced at Emily and Adeline's hands. His smile broadened even more.

"You are engaged. No?"

"Yes." Logan and Rainer smiled.

"You must come here to the Ritz for your honeymoon. Our honeymoon suite is crème de la crème. I will arrange it all."

Rainer smiled and shook his head. "We'd love to, Henri, but I've already made arrangements for another destination for our honeymoon. Thank you very much for everything you've done."

Henri seemed genuinely disappointed, but he thanked them for coming and told them to stop back in if they should need anything else.

After taking Logan's offered hand as he helped her out of the booth, Adeline giggled. "So let me go back and feed Logan..." She smirked at him.

"I'm hungry. I'm sorry. I'm a grown-ass man."

"And then are we going to hang out in the rooms or..."

Rainer and Emily held hands as they exited the salon and entered the elevator. Emily's eyes held both love and concern that seemed to overwhelm her as she gazed at Rainer.

He felt her intoxicating cast work through his hand. She was trying to soothe him from their day, from everything they now knew, from everything that the world threatened to rob them of.

The ride began its ascent and no one wanted to talk about what Fitzroy had told them or about the warnings they'd received.

Rainer decided to text Fitzroy in a little while to see if he could get a little backup for escorting the girls back to the bridal salon the next day. It had to be done, and he was no longer pompous enough to forgo every precaution available to him when it came to Emily's safety.

Logan eased Adeline into his arms as the elevator began its ascent. No one casted it. There was no need for it to fly. The four of them wanted to exist inside a cocoon that evening. They'd had enough of the world for one day.

Rainer and Logan shared an unspoken concurrence as the girls tucked into their chests. They didn't have the evidence yet. Wretchkinsides's men didn't seem to know where they were staying.

Perhaps they could take this one night to exist in blissful ignorance, to pretend there weren't dangerous people gunning for them, that for this one night the world could contain only the four of them.

They needed that moment of peace and restoration. They nodded to one another as they entered their separate rooms and agreed to meet the next morning.

"You wanna talk about it?" Emily wrapped her arms around Rainer's waist and tucked her head on his chest after they'd entered their room. She tried to supply him with calming energies, but his shield was frantic and pushed her away.

"Maybe tomorrow." Rainer pulled her closer. He melded their bodies. He didn't want to talk. He didn't want to think. There was just too much at stake.

He couldn't bear the thought of dragging her through an airport and onto a plane carrying the evidence, when Wretchkinsides's men knew they were there. *How had they known?* The infuriating thought pulsed constantly through his mind.

Dozens of Senate representatives flew from DC to Paris on a daily basis with work for the Realm. Only Vindico and the Haydenshires knew where they were going. Rainer had phoned Chloe Sawyer and explained that he'd be taking Emily on a trip to Paris for her birthday and that she'd miss Friday's practice. The Angels had already been given the next week off. The vacation fell in line perfectly with their trip.

He felt stupid and reckless for putting her in the situation that there wasn't any other way out of. Hopeful thoughts reared in his head. Fitzroy and the sting—maybe French Iodex would catch them. Maybe not, he thought morosely.

"Rainer," Emily whispered. He raised his eyebrows and studied her without giving her a verbal response. "We'll be okay. Please, let's not think about it tonight. We're in Paris, and you brought me here. I found the dress I'm going to wear when I marry you. Even with all of the crazy stuff that happened today, I can't tell you how thankful I am to be here with you."

He smiled at her and tried to let it all go. He wanted to do as she'd asked, to just be there with her. With a firm clench of his jaw, he forced himself to shut down the ceaseless worries of his mind and listen to her reassurances to do nothing but feel.

An idea formed from the sporadic jumble of his confusing thoughts. She'd wanted to swim. He couldn't take her to the large pool, but with a wry grin he thought to himself, *I sure as hell could get her wet.*

"Hey Em," he whispered. Her timid, tender smile warmed his heart. "Let me give you a bath, baby. I want to get you nice and hot, and nice and wet." He watched her eyes flash in intrigue as a low fervent moan echoed from her.

She was no longer timid. Hunger swayed in her rhythms as she considered a night all alone in their Parisian suite.

CHAPTER 20

THE SHIELD...

With resolution and determination armored in his drive, Rainer rushed to the bathroom. He turned on the multiple faucets in the grand bath and heated them instantly. He returned to her, and his eyes goggled. A low, shuddered moan thundered from his lungs.

She was standing before him wearing nothing at all. She could buy all the lingerie she wanted, he thought savagely, but there was nothing as gorgeous as that. He let his eyes rake over her beautiful curves on full display for him.

"Come here to me, baby." He guided her into his chest. "You are so damn gorgeous. You make me ache." He gazed into her eyes and then promptly devoured her lips. He lifted her into his arms and cradled her to him.

As he lowered her into the water, she relaxed as she was instantly warmed.

"Get in with me." Her raspy tone was pleading. He stripped in record time and climbed in behind her. She laid back against his chest, seated between his outstretched legs. Her lush backside surrounded his length. It drove him wild.

"Need a bath?" He kissed just beside her ear. A quick, hungry moan escaped her lips as he grabbed one of the sponges provided by the hotel. He poured lavender soap on it and began at her neck. He made small circles all over her and listened to her moans become fervent.

He released the sponge in the water. He wanted to touch her. He wanted his fingers on her soft, silky skin. He poured soap in his hands and started over. He caressed her breasts and washed down her stomach. He moved instantly to her mound, the tender rise of nerve endings he knew were raw with need.

He massaged her thighs and began to let his desires form on his ravenous lips. He kissed and licked her ear lobe as he explained what he wanted to do to her. The energy flowing between them become frantic and intense.

"I want to take you to bed, baby." Her breaths quickened against his own ribs. "I want to lay you out and touch you until you're dripping wet for me. Then I want to drink you." He made her body quiver in greedy anticipation as she began to beg for him to fulfill his promises. "Then I'm gonna fill you up, baby. I want to drown in you. I want to hear you scream and make you take it until I explode deep inside of you. Then I want to see my cum drip out of you."

She groaned out a desperate, "Yes." Her heart raced. Her breaths were quick and needy.

With a wanton look in her eye, she spun and positioned herself on her knees. Emily locked her eyes with his.

She grabbed the sponge and poured the soap on it once more. She dipped her hand under the water and dragged it gently over his cock. She began moving it up and down the straining, throbbing length of him.

Rainer gripped the sides of the tub. A shuddered growl erupted from his chest as his body tensed from the sensation. Unable to stop himself, he stood and let the water pour down his body. He was desperate for her, desperate for release, desperate to feel her wrapped tightly around him.

"Come on," he ordered. He held out his hand for her and watched her eyes flash with desire. He grabbed and heated a huge towel. He began drying her off as he kissed each patch of perfect skin that he dried. Once he'd run the towel all over her, he wrapped her in it and grabbed another one off the shelf. He dried off quickly before dropping it and pulling her to the bed.

He laid her down and forced himself to slow. He wanted to take his time as he reveled in her lying in their bed, her body thrumming and her eyes needy from wanting him.

A gasped breath caught in his throat as she reached and grabbed his steel-hard length. She ran her fingertips over him so softly the feeling was exquisite.

She sat up and pulled him into her mouth. She caressed and spun her tongue over his head. His knees began to give way as his body tensed and trembled from the heavenly sensation.

He brushed her face through a stuttered groan and guided her back down. He climbed over and covered all of her with his body. He was her Shield. He would let nothing harm her. She was his.

He let his hands slide over her fevered flesh. While shifting to her side slightly, he let his fingertips trace over the tender red curls between her legs. The silken paradise made only for him. He would occupy her fully. He would stand between her and the world. *She's mine, all mine* pulsed constantly in his mind.

Emily's body gave a desperate buck. She spread her legs for him and showed him what she wanted. He let his index finger circle between her swollen lips. They were throbbing in desperate desire.

"Are you wet for me, baby." She gasped and writhed. With that, he slipped two fingers inside of her and opened her for him. With a groan of supreme satisfaction he moved deeper. "Oh, yeah. So wet and needy all for me." Her muscles clenched around his hand as he amped up the friction of his touch. Her orgasm was moments away. Her breaths seemed elusive as her head shook back and forth on the pillow. He moved his fingers over the spot where she was most sensitive and summoned from inside of her. He closed her womb.

"Yes..." gasped from her as she took in the heavy dose of his energy. Hot, wet, sex dripped around his fingers.

He forced himself to concentrate as he felt her energy climb high. She let him continue to build her. He moved quickly and dragged his tongue over her clit. She spiraled wildly and screamed out his name as her climax consumed her. Her rhythms arced to their highest tilt.

He replaced his fingers with his tongue and drank everything he'd elicited from her. Her energy flowed into this mouth and filled his soul.

She convulsed as the powerful orgasm shattered through her. He watched her pulse. Her body's pressure built. It was intoxicating. He needed to feel it with her. He couldn't wait.

Rainer moved his mouth to her lips and kissed her heatedly as he spread her legs. He dropped low and urged her open.

Then, with a shuddered groan, he plunged her depths as she cried out for him. His mind whirled from the exquisite sensation. She was perfect. She felt like heaven. She met his every thrust and called out for him. Her eyes closed in pleasure as she gasped for breath.

She trembled around him as he pushed deeper. She was his. He watched her. Her moans seared like a siren's song, imprinting his soul with her heat. He felt her give way. She swelled, and he picked up speed.

"That feels so good." She gasped and bucked again.

Rainer kept his thrusts deep and unrelenting. He reveled in their energy joining as one. His body trembled as his eyes rolled back. It was astounding. He buried himself deeper.

Nothing else made sense but to take more of her. She writhed. Her temperature spiked. Her body flushed for him. She wrapped her hands around his back and he felt her nails dig into him.

"Oh… I'm gonna…" She couldn't tell him. She couldn't catch her breath, but he needed no warning. He could feel her release licking and trembling around his throbbing cock. He could see her energy rising in frantic arcs. The floodgates were unable to hold back her climax. He pushed harder.

"That's it, baby. Give it to me. You feel so damn good. I'm gonna explode when you let it go. It's all mine. Just give it to me."

Her eyes flew open. His words drove her over. Her body seized and contorted as the waves flooded through her, and with one final, ragged push he spread her legs wide and lost it all.

He held her as she convulsed. He watched what he'd done to her. Rainer was unable to believe he was lucky enough to get to be the guy that watched something so exquisitely beautiful. When she stilled, he withdrew as tenderly as he was able and fell onto the bed beside her. He kept her wrapped in his arms.

She tucked her head under his chin. He brushed a tender kiss on her forehead as they reveled in their rhythms as they spun and danced around them and glowed from their passion.

CHAPTER 21

MISSING PIECE

"You are incredible. I love you so much." He felt her smile against his chest. She clung to him. She refused to ease her arms from around him, and he didn't want her to. "Are you okay, baby?" She leaned her head up with a replete smile on her face.

"I'm perfect. That was amazing, and I know you're worrying. I just wish you knew what that means to me, what being here means to me, what you mean to me...." Her explanation drowned in concern over him.

"Baby, no." Rainer immediately squeezed her tighter. "That means everything to me too. Please don't think my worry over everything going on means that being with you doesn't mean as much to me, or that I was distracted, or anything like that." He willed her to understand. "I know you felt it, but I just..." He tried to think of the words to explain what she'd felt from him while they were together.

A sudden understanding of why Vindico had scoffed over being with a Receiver had Rainer reeling. He loved that Emily could read him so thoroughly even when it meant he had to explain some things. That only meant that they needed to talk, he reminded himself.

Still rubbing her back, he drew a steadying breath. He inhaled the scent of her and let it soothe him.

"I'm worried and a little irritated."

She sat up, crossed her legs, and gazed at him. "Why are you irritated?"

Rainer chuckled as he stared up at her. "You expect me to talk while you sit there completely naked showing off everything that makes me ache?" He gestured to her crotch on full display. She'd folded her legs like a pretzel.

She rolled her eyes. "Would you like me to get dressed?"

Rainer rubbed his hand down her thigh to her backside. He shook his head. "That is not ever something I want."

"So talk," she urged.

"Okay, but if at some point during this conversation, I lay you down and crawl all over you then you should consider yourself warned."

"I think I'll take my chances."

Rainer let his fingers continue to glide along her thigh as he considered what he wanted to say first. "I don't know. I wanted to bring you here, get away from it all, let you shop to your heart's content, see all the sights, and then take you to all of the sexy places Paris has to offer, but I just brought everything with us."

Emily studied him and then gave him a sweet smile. "I know today didn't go exactly as planned…." They both laughed outright at the truthfulness of that statement. "But Adeline and I did have an amazing morning, and I found a fabulous dress. Tea was out of this world." She blushed slightly and shrugged. "I thought all of this…"—she gestured to the bed—"was pretty hot. Tomorrow we can go back and get my dress, and shop, and eat, and do all of those things you said you wanted to do. As long as Fitzroy catches the guys, we can do all of it. He seemed up to the task."

Rainer grinned at her optimism. "I know, baby. I just…" He shook his head in frustrated disbelief. "How did he know we'd be here? No one knew where I was bringing you except Vindico and your family."

"And Fitzroy," Emily stated thoughtfully. Rainer considered that.

"Yeah, and I don't even know who the hell he is, but he sure seems to know a lot about me."

"You could call Vindico. If you're worried about it."

"That's a good idea." Rainer eased from the bed to locate his cell.

He found it in the pocket of the slacks he'd worn to tea. He fished it out and sank onto the bed beside Emily.

She leaned forward, up on her knees, and pressed her breasts into his back as she let her arms hang loosely around his shoulders. She kissed his cheek. The motion eased Rainer's harried thoughts and soothed his soul.

Before he could hit Vindico's name, there was a knock on the door.

"Please do not be doing what I know you're doing!" Logan's voice pled.

Rainer debated moving to the door and moaning or calling out Emily's name in heated passion, but he just chuckled.

"Little busy, Logan. D'you need something?" Rainer reveled in the flirtatious kisses Emily was whispering down his neck and back as she groped his pecs.

"Vindico's on the phone, man. I'm sorry. I told him you were busy, but he said to interrupt you because he has to talk to you now."

"Okay, hang on a sec." Rainer was too curious to pretend to be agitated. Emily had pulled away as soon as she'd heard Logan's request. She threw on a pair of panties and some black knit leggings and one of Rainer's T-shirts.

Rainer hoisted on a clean pair of boxers and the pair of jeans he'd worn earlier in the day. He opened the door. Logan gave him a sorrowful expression as he handed Rainer Adeline's cell phone.

Rainer furrowed his brow and held up the phone in a silent question.

Logan shook his head and shrugged. "That's what he called on."

"This is Rainer," he answered.

"Lawson," Vindico barked. "Listen, I'm sorry, but this couldn't wait."

"No, it's fine. We were, uh…" He blushed as he realized that he'd been about to inform his boss and his best friend that he and Emily had finished their session. "It's fine," he concluded as Vindico gave a slight chuckle.

"Listen to me, not to rain on your vacation, but I'll be on the next flight out to Paris. I think your cell has been cloned."

"What? How?" Rainer panicked as just some of the conversations and texts that he and Emily had traded back and forth over the past few weeks began to replay in his mind.

"Not what or how but who?" Vindico spat. "I called Miss Parker's cell because I'm certain it hasn't been compromised, but that's the only phone you should use until I get there. I got all three of you new phones. You can pay me back later."

"Okay, thanks." Rainer swallowed and his heart raced. The information he'd just been given pounded against the recesses of his mind. "All right, fine. Who then?" he demanded.

"Yeah, I have news on that as well. Just meet me in the bar of the hotel you're staying in," he stated cryptically. "In about three hours. Like I said, I'm about to board. Oh and Lawson," Vindico eased, "Chloe Sawyer has been hospitalized. She was attacked outside of her home. She was on the phone with Garrett when it happened. He was on his way over. He got there in time to save her and arrest two of Wretchkinsides's thugs. They're trying to force Medio Sawyer to sell the Angels. He's the majority holder. It seems Marlisa is tired of trying to cheat to win and the Sirens are 0-4. So, she asked Daddy to buy her the Angels. I didn't know if you wanted to tell Emily or if you wanted me to." Utter shock rocked through Rainer.

"Is she okay?" Rainer choked as he glanced at Emily. She'd immediately felt his panic. How was he going to tell her this?

"She held them off until Garrett got there. She's got a few bumps and bruises. They've healed her, but Sawyer insisted she be kept overnight. I can tell you more once I'm there. I'll meet you in a little while."

Rainer rolled his left wrist and noted the time.

"Okay." Panic coursed through his body. Vindico ended the call, and Rainer handed Adeline's cell back to Logan.

"What'd he say?" Logan studied Rainer.

Rainer shook his head and tried to sort through everything he'd just learned. He drew a steadying breath and reached for Emily. Terror took up residence in her eyes.

"Uh," Rainer tried to think systematically. "Where's Adeline?" he asked Logan. His face colored.

"She's in our room." Logan insinuated that perhaps Adeline wasn't fully clothed.

"Right, sorry, but go get her. I think she needs to hear this."

"Sure, yeah, just hang on a sec."

"Just come in whenever she's ready." Rainer slunk back to their bed.

A few minutes later, Logan and Adeline returned.

Rainer paced and tried to decide where to begin. Logan seemed to sense Rainer's confusion.

"Okay, why did he call on Ad's cell?" He was clearly trying to guide Rainer through his explanation.

Rainer nodded. He appreciated the gesture. "He thinks my cell was cloned and maybe yours and Em's too."

"What?" Emily gasped. She immediately panicked. Rainer was certain she was recalling the same things he had. He moved to her as she curled up into a ball and laid her head in his lap. Devastation etched her eyes. If his phone was cloned, then every picture she'd sent, every flirtatious and dirty thing they'd said, had been seen by others.

"That would explain how Wretchkinsides knew we were here." Adeline gave Emily a sympathetic gaze.

"But how?" Emily sprang up off of Rainer's lap.

"I don't know. It would've taken someone who caught me amplifying the signal and knew the number of the phone. I don't ever talk to anyone but you and Logan." He shook his head and tried to think of anywhere he'd been that he'd amplified the phone signal enough that another Gifted person could have caught and locked onto the particle displacement that is slightly different in every cellular phone. The sinusoidal wave reading could be captured and copied onto a duplicate phone.

"And who knows our phone numbers?" Logan huffed in disbelief. "Besides my family."

Rainer couldn't come up with anyone.

"Vindico thinks he knows who did it, and he's on his way here now. He wants us to meet him in the bar in a few hours."

"Okay." Emily continued to study Rainer. Her eyes penetrated his. "What else is wrong?" She knew him far too well. Even if he'd been able to stall on telling her about Chloe, the fact that they'd just made love made her more perceptive and more aware of Rainer's energy than any other time.

She could pick up on every single arc or flow of his energy for several hours after they'd finished, as long as he'd released inside of her.

Rainer pulled her back close to him. He caressed her thigh. He could feel her nervous energy pulse even through her leggings. "Baby," he soothed, "Chloe was attacked outside of her home. She's okay," he immediately assured her as tears welled in Emily's eyes.

"What happened?" Logan looked shocked as well. Emily's chin trembled, and her body gave a convulsive shudder. It was too much. She adored Chloe even if they really didn't have that much in common.

Rainer pulled her close. He wrapped his arms around her as tears began to pour down her sweet face.

"She was on the phone with Garrett. He was on his way there. She was attacked, but he got there in time. He arrested the men. She's fine, only a few bumps and bruises. Her dad's keeping her in the hospital overnight just to make sure she's okay."

"Did they attack her because of Garrett?" Logan choked. His question was laced with raw terror.

"No." Rainer shook his head, still holding Emily tightly. She pulled away from his embrace and tried to wipe away the tears.

"Why did they attack Chloe?"

He didn't know how to tell her that Wretchkinsides was trying to buy the Angels. She loved being an Angel. She'd worked so hard to make this her career. It was all she'd ever wanted. She'd been planning to challenge for the Angels since she was a little girl.

"Rainer," she begged in a hushed plea. "Tell me. You're scaring me." Her voice quivered in her fear.

"It's okay, Em," Logan soothed almost without thought. He'd always looked after her, and her tears pricked his heart as well.

"Tell me," she urged again.

"Wretchkinsides is going to try and buy the Angels. He had Chloe attacked to try and scare Medio Sawyer into selling his shares." Rainer modulated his voice to what he hoped was a soothing tone.

Emily shook her head combatively. "He can't buy us. We're not for sale!"

Logan and Rainer shared a sickened glance as Rainer forced himself to tell her everything.

"Em, the Angels are a business just like anything else. If Wretchkinsides can become the majority stockholder, then he would be the team owner." He choked as Emily began to sob in earnest.

Logan and Adeline stood. Grief filled both of their faces.

"We're just gonna…" Logan pointed out the door. "We'll meet you downstairs in a little while."

Rainer held Emily and let her soak down his bare chest.

NOTHING GOOD

A little while later, Emily was pulling off Rainer's T-shirt and the leggings she'd put on.

"What are you doing, baby?" Rainer was still watching over her obsessively. She offered him a weary smile.

"I can't go to the bar of the Paris Ritz in leggings and a T-shirt," she reminded him. Rainer knew she was correct, and he began changing back into his slacks and white dress shirt. People may walk around in America like that, but it didn't happen in Paris.

Logan waved them over to a table in the corner of the posh bar. The heavy wood tones and lush hunter-green carpet gave an intimate, quiet feel to the space. Liquor bottles were on display behind the vast marble bar. Most of them would cost more than one of his paychecks.

Rainer pulled the black, leather chair out for Emily and took the seat beside her as they waited on Vindico to arrive from the airport.

"Are you okay?" Logan quizzed his little sister.

"I don't have any other choice, do I?"

A waitress approached, and Logan and Rainer ordered beer. Emily and Adeline each ordered a glass of wine. A few minutes later, Vindico appeared.

He looked harried as he rushed toward them. He sank down in the only empty chair and sighed. He looked thoroughly exhausted. The waitress returned.

"Oh, uh, Glenmorangie at least a ten…s'il vous plait," Vindico ordered, though it was more a command than a request. Rainer was rather impressed with how his boss had slipped into a relatively convincing French accent at the end. The waitress continued on in English, however.

"We have ten, twelve and eighteen?" The waitress turned on a flirtatious grin as she moved closer to Vindico. She blinked slowly and her back arched to add to her cleavage. With a slight eye roll, Vindico sighed.

"The eighteen." The waitress, who was brushing her hair behind her shoulder, let her bottom lip protrude and shoved her cleavage in Vindico's face.

"We have everything you need, sir," she cooed in a light French accent. "On zee rocks, oui?"

"No, and I'm kind of in the middle of something here." He shut her down firmly. With a huff, the waitress returned to the bar. They made small talk until she returned with a tray of their drinks and sauntered back to the bar.

After drawing a slow, smooth sip of the Scotch, Vindico swallowed and then drew a deep breath. He laid three brand-new iPhones on the table, then summoned and set the cast to keep anyone else in the relatively empty bar from being able to hear their conversation.

"I take it you told her." Vindico gestured to Emily's swollen, red eyes. Rainer nodded and drew another long sip of his beer. Vindico turned to Emily consolingly. He started but then paused.

"I never know what to call you," he admitted with a slight chuckle. Emily grinned. It was the first Rainer had seen in the last several hours.

"You used to call me Will and Garrett's annoying baby sister."

Vindico nodded and laughed his defeat.

"Yeah, that's probably true. Sorry about that."

Logan and Rainer laughed as well.

"Emily?" Vindico tried and Emily nodded her agreement. "I will do everything in my power to make certain that Wretchkinsides never gets his mitts on the Angels. He's without his top man since I nailed Pendergrath. I don't think he can make the purchase unless Pendergrath gets his money and his teams back in the country." He turned back to Logan and Rainer. "I've given O'Ryan a little time off from Felsink, as he's the one who alerted me to the attempted buyout. I informed him that the more information he coughs up, the longer his reprieve will be."

Mitchell O'Ryan's father had been arrested several months before. Insurance fraud, fraudulent banking, bribery, and several other white-collar crimes had landed him in Felsink with a four-year sentence. As his wife was the sister of Wretchkinsides's wife, Lucinda, Vindico had turned him as an informant. He'd only serve months of his sentence in exchange for information on Wretchkinsides and the Interfeci.

"I didn't know you'd been back to Felsink," Logan commented. Rainer assumed Vindico must've gone when he and Logan were looking after the twins.

"Yeah, I went last weekend," Vindico explained as he drew another slow sip of his Scotch.

"So do you ever, like, not work?" Logan quizzed as he finished his beer.

"No." Vindico looked like the very idea was preposterous.

Already growing weary of the small talk, Rainer cleared his throat. "What's up with my phone?"

Vindico drew a deep breath. "I know yours has been cloned. I don't know about theirs." He gestured from Logan to Emily. "Replacing theirs is precautionary. Fitz called me this morning to make certain your cells were safe, and it got me to thinking. I couldn't figure out how Wretchkinsides learned that you all were in Paris so quickly." He shook his head and appeared highly annoyed. "But, Fitz has a guy imbedded deep in the Interfeci." He dropped his low, gravelly voice to a hissed whisper even though he was holding the sound barrier cast firmly. "A few hours ago, he sent Fitz these photos." He laid out several small black-and-white photos on the table.

Rainer gasped. He lifted one of the pictures. He was unable to believe what he was seeing. He shook his head and turned to Vindico for an explanation. "Are you freaking kidding me?"

Emily and Logan's mouths fell open simultaneously as Adeline shook her head in stunned disbelief.

Rainer picked up another of the photos of his Uncle Stan, seated at a table in what appeared to be The Tantra. He was with none other than Dominic Wretchkinsides and Cascavel, the man Rainer and Emily had seen on the beach at the beginning of the summer with the snake sleeve tattoos. There were two other higher-ups in the Interfeci seated at the table as well.

"Bridgette didn't know he was your uncle, but when I showed her the picture, she confirmed that he'd been in several times with Nic and the boys," Vindico spat furiously. "Listen to me, Lawson. You do not hold court with Wretchkinsides unless you're doing something big. There are members of the Interfeci who have never even seen his face."

Rainer let the implications of what Vindico was saying wash through him. His body rejected the information. Violent revulsion threatened to overwhelm him. "I assumed your uncle might have Logan and Emily's cell numbers from when you were younger," Vindico explained why he'd suspected all of their phones might have been cloned.

"Only Logan's," Rainer managed to choke out.

"Good," Vindico drawled. "We're going to have some fun then."

Rainer's shield was weighted with terror. The air he breathed seemed suddenly laced with lead. What was Stan going to do? Stan's threat at the trial lodged itself in his gut. He shook himself slightly and waited to hear Vindico's plan.

"I'm staying with Fitz and Maddie tonight. I haven't seen my godsons in a while, so this works out well. In a little while, Fitz will text both of your old phones with where he'll be in order to supply Logan and Miss Parker here with the thumb drive of evidence he's collected. Then Fitz and I will see who shows up tomorrow, but I have a feeling we'll be taking out Ferratus and his little snatch-and-grab team."

"Do you want some help?" Logan offered, but Vindico shook his head.

"No, I don't want you to take your eyes off of the two of them, but thanks for the offer. I'll be taking the information home with me tomorrow afternoon. That way you won't have to try and get them on a plane with that level of evidence." That was the first thing all evening that brought Rainer any form of relief.

"After I put all of this together and booked one of the jets to get out here, I traced your uncle's bank account. There's been a recent deposit of $10,000 and there's another four hundred thousand pending. I don't know what Wretchkinsides is planning, but be careful. This is how he works. That deposit won't post until Stan has done whatever Wretchkinsides has commanded in order for him to get that money. Fitz's guy is trying desperately to find out what it is, but so far no luck."

Rainer's heart raced. He wasn't surprised that his uncle was trying to do him in. It terrified him that he'd teamed up with a snake like Wretchkinsides. His uncle's stupidity had always been a comfort to Rainer, but now he wasn't the one doing the thinking.

"I've had a few guys stationed near your uncle's apartment, but he hasn't been by in a few days. Either Wretchkinsides is already done with him and has disposed of him, or he's put him up somewhere a little nicer while he gets his work done." Vindico drew the last sip of his Scotch. "I'm sorry. I know this isn't exactly the kind of trip you wanted to give her for her birthday." Vindico did look devastated to be the bearer of bad news.

"Emily, I'd really like you to take the new phone as well. I feel certain your number could've been accessed as Rainer was probably talking to you at the point he amplified his phone and whoever was following him caught the waves."

"Oh, okay. Thank you." Emily picked up one of the new phone boxes. She still looked stunned over all they'd just learned, and she was busy trying to send soothing pulses through Rainer's hand.

"Can I…talk to you alone for a second, before you leave? I need some help tomorrow, and I need to ask you something," Rainer begged.

Vindico studied him and then nodded. "Yeah, of course." He moved to a table for two on the other side of the bar. He gestured for Rainer to sit down. Rainer tried to sort through the dozens of thoughts all swirling violently in his mind.

"Are you okay?" Concern tensed in Vindico's double-banded rhythm strains.

"I don't know," Rainer admitted. "I already know the answer to this, but..." He wasn't certain he wanted the verbal confirmation, but he went ahead with it anyway.

"What?" Vindico quizzed.

"When my phone was cloned, does that mean they've only been able to hear the conversations or they can access everything on there —texts, data, whatever?" Rainer suddenly felt feverish and faint as just a few of the images and the banter he'd engaged Emily in coiled in his mind.

Vindico's brow furrowed for a moment and then realization formed on his chiseled features. He gave Rainer a sorrowful expression and shook his head.

"I'm sorry, Lawson. I really am. I can only imagine how violated you feel or she'll feel when you tell her." He gestured his head back to Emily who was studying the two of them from across the bar. "I'm sure your texts were seen as well. With the election in just a few weeks and with Peterson's connection with Wretchkinsides, I also wouldn't be surprised if they ended up in some campaign propaganda." Rainer let his head fall into his hands.

"That bad?" Vindico eased. Rainer nodded. He tried not to whimper in front of his boss. "Okay, I give you permission for approximately the next sixty seconds to tell me to go to hell, but I'm gonna try to help you."

Rainer raised his head.

"Pictures?" Vindico quizzed quietly. "I assume her, since you don't seem like the selfie in the gym mirror of your biceps type, and please tell me you did not send her a picture of your junk."

"No, it was her," Rainer answered audibly for the first time. His voice sounded distant and distraught even to him.

"Is her face in them?"

Rainer shook his head. "No," he answered without volume. His cheeks colored rapidly. He'd looked at those snapshots a dozen times in the last week. He'd memorized every detail. He'd jacked off to one.

"Hey." Vindico shook his head and lowered his voice even further. "This isn't like the belly shot. You're a grown man. You weren't putting her on display. Those were messages meant for your eyes only from the girl you've been with since birth and that you're engaged to marry. It's not your fault your cell got cloned, and neither of you did anything wrong."

Rainer tried desperately to believe what he was telling him. With another hesitant glance, Vindico considered for a long drawn moment before his face lit with a wry smile.

"Okay, let's say Governor Haydenshire had to see either the messages or the photos. Which would you rather him see?"

This actually make Rainer chuckle at the way Vindico had gone about his inquisition.

"The photos." He thought of just a few of the things he'd informed Emily he wanted to do to her via their texts. Him telling her he was going to tear her up ricocheted violently in his mind. Vindico chuckled.

"That's good."

"How exactly?"

"There's no way to prove that messages published in some of Peterson's 'vote for me' bullshit actually came from either of your phones unless he comes out and admits to working with Dominic Wretchkinsides and that he had your phone cloned. That doesn't seem very likely. They could've copied any iPhone messages. Hell, they could've written them themselves and captured the screens. If there are no..."—he hemmed momentarily before going on—"compromising photos that would be easily recognizable as Emily then they don't have a lot of proof that they're from either of you."

Rainer tried to feel the relief Vindico was attempting to supply him, but the thought of his uncle and Wretchkinsides's men having any part of his and Emily's relationship made him violently ill.

"Now that I really think about it, I doubt he uses them. Unless the polls change dramatically, your future father-in-law has already discounted so much of the propaganda Peterson's already used, he seems to be reining it in, at least a little," Vindico stated thoughtfully. "I really am sorry about all of this. Try to enjoy your day tomorrow. Let me take care of Ferratus. You go take care of her. Watch your back. I don't know what your uncle is supposed to do for that money, but it's nothing good." He gestured his head back to Emily who was biting her lip so hard Rainer was concerned she was going to draw blood.

"Yeah, I actually need a little more help," he managed.

"What's that?" Vindico seemed willing to do most anything.

"She found a wedding gown here that she really wants. She has an appointment tomorrow morning at nine to try it on again and then buy it. She doesn't want me to see it, but I can't let her go back to the store with just Adeline. Logan and I were going to take them and stand outside. I wouldn't mind a few extra sets of eyes though."

"Good thinking. That's how excellent Iodex officers think and act. I tell you what. Fitz and I will both be there. We're running the sting a little later in the day. It shouldn't be a problem." Rainer extended his hand to Vindico. He looked very pleased with the gesture.

Vindico shook Rainer's hand and then with a wave to Logan, Adeline, and Emily, he scooted from the bar and disappeared out into the chilly Parisian night.

"What did you ask him?" Emily eased as Rainer returned to the table.

"We'll talk about it later, okay?"

She stood as Rainer threw down enough euros for their drinks, and Logan and Adeline followed them on to the elevators.

CHAPTER 23

ABSOLUTION

The morning light seemed to carry absolution on its hesitant rays. Rainer allowed himself to forget all of the harrowing details of the night before, as he held Emily on his chest.

She was safe. She was tucked up beside him, and he allowed himself a few minutes to revel in her energy. It was flowing in even, steady thrums as she slept. He glanced down and lamented her swollen eyes. He shuddered as thoughts of his confession from the night before ricocheted through his mind. He'd had to tell her that the pictures of her cleavage, her thigh, and the flirtatious banter they kept up most days had most definitely been viewed by his uncle and half of the Interfeci.

Her eyes blinked open. She'd picked up on his trepidation even in her sleep.

"What's wrong?" she whimpered in an adorable squeak. He smiled and shook his head.

"Hey there, sweetheart."

"Tell me what's wrong."

"Just worried about you, and about the fact that until this moment I completely forgot that we're supposed to stay somewhere different tonight. Somewhere I don't want to stay with Logan and Adeline."

"Why?" She nuzzled her face on his chest, making him smile as he massaged his hands over her back and tried to work out the stress from the day before. He worked his hands upwards and tenderly caressed her face.

"Remember me telling you it's where Will and Brooke stayed on their honeymoon, and we also have to call Brooke's mother because we won't be here tomorrow night."

"Okay, but why don't you want to stay there with Logan and Adeline?"

"Well…" Rainer hemmed. He wasn't certain why he was blushing.

"What?"

"It's supposed to be a couples-only hotel. There are only seven rooms, and they're supposed to be pretty provocative, I guess." He hoped she wouldn't be offended that he'd booked them a suite there.

Emily smirked. "You're telling me that my big brother told you we should stay at a hotel designed for sex?" she managed before her giggles overtook her. Rainer joined in her laughter.

"Yeah, he's a lot more accepting of your sex life than the rest of the men in your family." He was thrilled to hear her laugh after he'd soothed her tears for so long.

"I think Keaton and Henry are okay with it," she teased.

"Anyway," he chuckled, "I'm kind of worried Logan would be pissed if he found out where I'd been planning on taking you. I'm gonna call and cancel it, and I'll just add a night on here. Hopefully, we can just keep this suite one more evening. I doubt they could even get a room there now. I've had ours booked for months."

"Whatever you want to do."

Rainer kissed the top of her head.

She studied him. "Are you sure you don't want to talk about Stan?" she tried again. She'd tried a dozen times the night before.

"I really don't. I don't want to talk about him or think about him. If Wretchkinsides killed him, I don't even know how to feel about that. How am I supposed to feel? He was a horrible person that never did anything but abuse me. He was awful to my parents. I don't have any idea what I'm supposed to feel. Honestly, I'm tired of letting him ruin my life. He doesn't deserve to live rent free in my head, and he sure as hell doesn't have the right to ruin the time I want to spend with you." Rainer laid it all on the line. He wasn't trying to keep anything from her. He truthfully didn't know what to feel.

Emily kissed his cheek. "I think what you feel is angry, and I also think that's absolutely okay."

"Please. I do not want to talk about him."

"Okay, but if you ever do…"

"You're the only person I ever talk to about stuff like that," he reminded her.

"I know, but I just always want you to know that I'm here in all of this with you."

"I know, baby. You're how I survive it."

She grinned. "Okay, no Stan. So, do you know what we should do now?" She suddenly sounded thrilled. Rainer was ecstatic. She seemed to have let the horrific intrusions with their phones go at least for a little while.

"What's that, Miss Haydenshire?" He turned on his side so she was lying beside him, tucked under his chin and in the protection of his entire body.

She wriggled delightedly as she folded herself into him. "We should get ready and then go get my dress that you are not allowed under any circumstances to see."

Rainer had tried to get used to the overwhelming love that welled in his soul from just being with her. The spark that always lit in his heart, usually traveled to the tips of his fingers, and then settled in his groin. It was his very life force. He'd decided recently that he hoped he never became accustomed to it. He loved the feeling. It righted his world each and every time he felt it.

"I swear, baby, I'll stay outside the boutique the entire time unless something happens. I want our wedding day to be perfect for you. I don't want to see the dress until you're walking down the aisle."

"I can't wait."

Rainer kissed her cheek. "Me either."

Before they left for breakfast, Rainer phoned the other hotel. His mind tumbled over the suite he'd booked. There was a large bed that was mounted from one of the walls in the bedroom. Cloud murals and mirrors made up most of the walls. It was to make one feel as if they were making love in the sky.

The entire suite, and every suite at the hotel, was designed to indulge the five senses. It was complete with a view of the river, red lacquered walls, and furniture made for two, and everything about the design was steeped in eroticism.

As Rainer explained that he needed someone who spoke English and then proceeded to cancel the room, he decided that perhaps he didn't want Emily staying there. He wasn't certain the suite was them especially after everything that had happened. It seemed they couldn't ever do anything without someone finding out. A night or two at a hotel specifically designed for carnal pleasures would make quite a front page.

With a determined nod, Rainer ended the call and waited on Emily to finish getting ready.

CHAPTER 24

INSIDE AND OUT

After another delectable breakfast at a café near the dress shop, Logan and Rainer escorted the girls back to La Belle. It was a century-old home that had billowing wedding gowns on bright display in the windows. Fitzroy and Vindico joined them a moment later.

Both Vindico and Logan looked uncomfortable with the mere thought of entering a bridal salon. Fitzroy laughed and offered Emily his arm.

"I will gladly escort you in and keep you safe, Mademoiselle Haydenshire. As I have been married for many years, I am not frightened of the fabled white gown that terrifies lesser men," he chastised Logan and Vindico. Emily and Adeline laughed.

Vindico rolled his eyes. "Just take her to get the dress, Fitz."

"How long is she going to take?" Logan whined as soon as Fitzroy checked the shop thoroughly and then escorted the girls inside. Rainer could see him as he took post in the entryway to wait.

Vindico rolled his eyes. "I would assume the approximate time it takes women to buy what they definitely consider the most important dress of their lives."

Rainer nodded his agreement. "It's her wedding gown. Blow off, man. She can take as long as she damn well pleases."

"Geez," Logan spat. "I know you got laid last night so what's your problem?"

Rainer shook his head. He hadn't meant to take out his bad mood on Logan, but he was shocked Logan made that kind of quip in front of Vindico. Their boss was laughing heartily and didn't seem to mind.

"I don't know," he sighed. "My uncle and whatever the hell he's up to, and everything else that's gone disastrously wrong on this trip."

Vindico's brow furrowed. "Hey, even with all of the crap that's happened, she seems completely thrilled." He gestured his head into the shop.

Logan changed his tune as well. "You wanted her to pick out the dress, and she did. We don't have to go on any more shopping excursions up and down the Eastern Seaboard. So, all in all, not too bad, right?"

Rainer tried to focus on the good instead of everything that had gone so horribly wrong.

Two men approached in French Iodex uniforms. Vindico bristled.

"Chief Vindico, sir. How are you?" one of the men spoke kindly. The other said nothing and appeared annoyed to be there.

"I'm good, Oliver. How are you?" Vindico offered politely.

"Very good, sir. Have you met Officer Malden? He's a new hire. I was just showing him this beat. Captain Fitzroy said you'd be here this morning."

"We've met," Vindico sneered. "These are two of my top officers, Lawson and Haydenshire."

Rainer and Logan offered polite smiles. Rainer couldn't figure out why Malden looked so uncomfortable. Something about him seemed almost familiar. With another kind wave from Oliver, he and Malden continued on their way.

Logan waited until they were out of earshot. "Why don't you like that guy, Malden, or whatever?"

"He bugs me. He has since Fitz hired him. He's a pompous prick and that's sort of my gig, so maybe that's it." Vindico chuckled.

Rainer laughed, but he would never have agreed out loud anyway.

Suddenly Adeline stuck her head out of the front door of the shop. "Rainer, Emily needs you." Rainer wasn't certain what to do.

"Why? What's wrong? I'm not supposed to go in there." He had been given very specific instructions. With a slight giggle, Adeline beamed at him. "She's not still in the gown. But it's completely magical. She looks resplendent, just like a princess." Logan chuckled at her exuberance. "They just need you to sign something, I think."

"Okay." Rainer drew a deep breath as he edged up the stairs to the shop. Upon entering, Rainer thought he'd stepped into some kind of alternate universe. He was assaulted by pink carpeting and walls with massive, gilded mirrors hung every few feet.

Bright lighting illuminated the space and made sweat dew on the back of his neck. Every available surface was covered in silk, satin, and lace. The fragrance of roses and baby's breath permeated the air. Rainer froze. He wasn't certain which direction he was supposed to turn.

An older woman with her jet-black hair tucked into a tight bun approached.

"Monsieur Lawson, je presume?" she drawled.

"Uh...oui," Rainer offered. After placing her hand on Rainer's shoulder, she led him to the center of the white lace, womblike area. Emily was standing at an antique desk. She looked concerned.

"What's wrong, baby?" Rainer prayed nothing had happened with her gown. He wasn't sure how much more bad news she could endure.

"Nothing. At least I hope it's nothing. There was some kind of security breach at the Senate Bank, and I don't have the other checkbooks. So, they need both of our signatures on all purchases over a hundred dollars. It's...definitely...over a hundred dollars."

Rainer chuckled. "I kind of assumed it would be." As Rainer added his signature under Emily's for the money to be withdrawn from their account, he assumed that either Mr. Buffett or Will had probably tried to alert him as to the breach.

He'd turned his old phone off for good after he'd received the fake text from Fitzroy the night before. No one but Emily had his new number.

Rainer had secured their suite at the Ritz for an additional night so

Emily had the dress sent there. Utter elation filled her eyes as she glided along the streets of Paris beside him.

The delight he felt from her as he held her hand made everything that had gone wrong seem to fall away as he reveled in her exhilaration.

Vindico and Fitzroy waved their goodbyes as soon as the dress had been purchased. They had an hour to get to the airport to try to take down Ferratus. Rainer had never seen Vindico more focused.

"Stay out in public. Shop, eat, whatever. Stay away from the hotel and stay together until I let you know what happened," Vindico commanded.

Rainer and Logan agreed. Fitzroy fell in line beside Vindico, and something about their armored drive had Rainer certain that the Interfeci was going to lose a few key members that afternoon.

The Parisian air lightened around them. Possibility and hopefulness sprung in Rainer's soul. Maybe they could have a day to themselves to just enjoy one another. Maybe their vacation wasn't completely ruined.

He would worry about Stan when they returned home. He turned to gaze at Emily. She wore a content smile. Excitement and curiosity lit in her emerald eyes as she took in the enchantment and allure of the city before them.

CHAPTER 25

CONFESSIONS OF ADELINE PARKER

With a quick conversation, both Logan and Rainer vowed to take the girls anywhere they wanted to go. The girls had a ball in the perfumeries and in pharmacies that contained more beauty products and potions than either Logan or Rainer had ever seen before.

Adeline fussed over the price of a perfume she'd admired and Logan had purchased.

"I only said it smelled really good, not 'please buy it for me immediately,'" she lamented as they walked to a boulangerie for lunch.

Logan kissed the side of her head. "Yeah, but you would never say 'please buy this for me' about anything, so I took 'wow, that smells amazing' as your way of saying, 'Hey Logan, get off your ass and buy your fiancée some perfume.'"

"Thank you." Adeline wrapped her arms around Logan's neck and squeezed him. "I still can't even believe I'm here and that you got me French perfume."

Rainer and Emily shared a grin. Logan looked thoroughly delighted that he'd been able to spoil Adeline a little.

"And we got loads of French lingerie, and you got that amazing skirt yesterday," Emily added as Rainer held the door open for everyone.

"I know, and you got the most gorgeous wedding dress I've ever seen," Adeline added. Both girls were on the brink of jumping up and down. It hadn't been lost on either Rainer or Logan that their hotel suites were full to bursting with shopping bags. They'd joked at the amount the girls had accomplished in one day's time.

"Are you going to go back to get those boots?" Adeline asked Emily. Rainer and Logan led them to a table and tried to pry the ladies from their fashion conquests just long enough for them to tell them what they'd like to eat.

They both felt terrible that their jobs and Wretchkinsides had put such a pall on their trip. They were eager for the girls to do anything they wanted before they all had to head home the next day.

"If you want boots, let's go get them," Rainer urged, after ordering his and Emily's food.

"I don't know. They were kind of expensive. I still can't believe I walked into one Parisian bridal boutique and found the dress that has been in my head since I was eight."

"Yeah, but we looked at so many at home you really knew what you wanted," Adeline reminded her after thanking the waiter for her water.

"That's true. I'm sorry about that." Emily felt bad that she'd dragged Adeline to so many stores before they'd come to Paris.

Adeline smiled at her. "I loved going to all of the wedding dress shops. You always knew you'd get married since you were little. I never thought anyone would want to marry me, so I never thought about what kind of dress I would want or anything."

Logan looked crestfallen. "How could you say something like that? How could you think something like that?"

"I don't know. I didn't mean it like that. I just never really thought about it, I guess. You really are my knight in shining armor. It just seemed like too much to ever really hope that someone would want to rescue me. I guess I always assumed I'd have to rescue myself." She tried to form her deep childhood fears into words. The effect had the entire table choked up.

As he shook his head in stunned disbelief, Logan wrapped his arms around her and began whispering reassurances in her ear that had Adeline beaming.

Emily and Rainer politely looked away and pretended to talk about the Parisian architecture.

Several minutes later, their lunches arrived and everyone ate in silence. Adeline continued to glance Logan's way coyly and with a hint of flirtation. She couldn't seem to keep her eyes off of him. Whatever Logan had whispered in her ear had made her entire day.

Logan and Rainer's new cell phones chirped. Logan sighed and fished his from his pocket as Rainer did the same.

"Now I've got to go in and reset all of my ringtones," Logan lamented. His last text tone had been the Venton fight chant. Delighted smiles broadcast from their faces.

"What?" Emily asked.

The texts from Vindico said,

> Thought I'd send you some pics you wouldn't mind showing around. I plan on making Monahan my wallpaper.

The pictures were of Ferratus, three other scowling men that Rainer assumed were the rest of the snatch-and-grab team, and Dedric Monahan, another of Wretchkinsides's underbosses. He was the one who ran most of the Interfeci operations in Romania. They were all behind bars in what Rainer assumed must be the French Parliament building.

"Damn, they're badass," Logan admired Vindico and Fitzroy's work. Rainer nodded his agreement.

"Yeah, when they worked together, they must've been unstoppable." Rainer tried to imagine Vindico and Fitzroy being a partnered team. Another text came through a moment later.

Try to enjoy the rest of your day. Sorry for all the trouble, and Fitz wants me to offer you four tickets to the Moulin Rouge show tonight. Maddie was a dancer when she and Fitz met so she can get tickets whenever she wants. He feels bad about all he put you through yesterday. He felt worse after I yelled at him for an hour last night, but anyway I'd take her up on it. It's a very Parisian show to see. Headed back to DC now. Just text Fitz and let him know,

was the parting line along with Fitzroy's cell number.

"Wow, a show?" Emily's eyes lit. Rainer chuckled as he studied Logan and Adeline. He'd done a great deal of research for this trip. He knew what kind of show took place at the Moulin Rouge, but it didn't appear that any of his travel companions did.

"It *is* a very Parisian thing to do, but I'm not sure you're going to be comfortable at the Moulin Rouge." Truthfully, he wasn't certain where Emily would stand on topless dance shows.

"Why?" she quizzed.

"Well," Rainer considered. His eyes landed on a brochure display just outside of the boulangerie. "Hang on a sec." He scooted from the booth and out the front door. It took him less than a second to find a brochure for the Moulin Rouge, as it was an extremely popular tourist attraction. He carried the brochure back to the table. "Because…" He handed the paper to Emily.

Still giving him a quizzical smile, she flipped open the tri-folded paper. Her eyes goggled as her mouth fell open.

"Oh," she choked. Rainer was unable to contain his laughter. "Wow!" She handed the brochure to Logan who took one glance at it and closed it immediately.

"But there were kids in the audience of those pictures." Emily's brow furrowed. Rainer took a quick bite of the soup that had been placed at his seat during his absence.

"That's just not a big deal here like it is at home. Europeans are much more accepting of life and sex," Rainer explained.

Adeline had perused the brochure as well and giggled slightly at Logan's reaction. "I wouldn't mind seeing it," she admitted.

Emily nodded. "Is that how we want to spend our last night here?"

"It is a very touristy event," Rainer offered though he really didn't care one way or the other.

"If Fitzroy's wife used to be a dancer and we decide not to go, how do we turn them down politely?" Emily asked.

Rainer thought for a few minutes then shrugged. "I'll just tell them we had other plans since it's our last night in Paris, but thank them for the invite."

"She must be beautiful," Adeline vowed.

"All the women here are beautiful. I'm starting to get a complex," Emily huffed.

Logan and Rainer rolled their eyes. "Have you seen every single French male we've walked by check you two out?" Rainer quickly pointed out. This observation seemed to delight Emily, but it embarrassed Adeline.

After lunch, everyone decided that since Vindico and Fitzroy had taken care of the imminent threats, the couples would part ways until dinner.

Adeline wanted to see the displays on Gifted medicine in the Louvre. Rainer and Emily were planning on visiting a few of the smaller museums and sights and doing some more shopping.

Emily informed her brother that she and Rainer were going to make out in important locations throughout Paris and perhaps purchase the boots she'd seen the day before.

"Hey, what they're doing sounds like way more fun," Logan had teased Adeline. She'd rolled her eyes and giggled.

"We can do that too, after we go to the Louvre."

CHAPTER 26

THOROUGHLY PARIS

They returned several hours later after exploring all of Paris's grandeur. They showered, and Rainer pulled on another dress shirt and tie along with his slacks. They'd decided against the Moulin Rouge when Rainer stumbled upon reservations at a restaurant that was supposed to be phenomenal. He'd called to check on cancellations and had lucked out.

He reclined on the bed and watched a French soccer game, though he understood none of what the announcers were screaming, while he waited on Emily to emerge from the bathroom.

She appeared a few minutes later and spun for Rainer as his mouth dropped.

"Wow!" he exclaimed.

"Too much?" She was wearing a purple button-down shirt with several of the top buttons unclasped and a miniskirt. To top it all off she had on the long, brown, high-heeled boots that zipped past her knee that they'd purchased a few hours before. A large portion of her thigh was visible, and Rainer had to remind himself not to drool.

"Uh, wow," he stammered again. He began thinking about unbuttoning the rest of the buttons on her shirt and reaching his hands under the skirt. She blushed.

"So you like it?" She somehow seemed unsure.

"Uh, yeah. You look gorgeous, but I'm absolutely certain that we should just stay in."

Emily rolled her eyes as she pulled him toward the door. "We just did that this afternoon."

"You say that like it means I shouldn't want to do it again now?" He feigned confusion.

"No, I'm just saying I'll take good care of you when we get back. It is our last night in the most romantic city in the world." She guided him out into the hallway to wait on Logan and Adeline.

Rainer began telling her how luscious she looked and earned himself several kisses. They were rather involved in each other when Rainer heard Adeline giggle. Emily spun as heat began a slow creep up her neck and settled in her cheeks.

"Oh…uh, sorry. We were just waiting on you."

"Uh-huh." Logan rolled his eyes. Adeline and Emily both squealed as they examined each other's new outfits. The effect made Rainer and Logan shudder.

The restaurant they'd selected was only a few blocks away, so they walked and enjoyed the lights of Paris as the sun gave off its last vestiges of daylight.

"I'm so glad we got to stay another night." Adeline stared contentedly at the beautiful sights and sounds of the city.

"Yeah, today was amazing," Logan agreed. The faraway look in his eye let Rainer and Emily know they weren't the only ones who'd spent a little time in a hotel room that afternoon.

They entered the tiny, rustic restaurant filled with candlelight. The tables were constructed of huge wine casks that were turned on their ends. Bench seating ran all along the walls and made a pattern in the center of the restaurant with the wine barrels placed around indeterminately. It allowed for a table of two or a large group to sit along the benches together.

After choosing the barrel in the back corner, they slid along the benches until everyone was seated. The food smelled amazing, and a waiter supplied them with glasses of wine.

While drawing a sip of her wine, Emily scooted closer to Rainer as he wrapped one arm over her and used the other to flip through the menu.

After translating some of the menu as best as she could for everyone, Adeline tucked under Logan's arm.

The waiter smiled as he set down a platter of artichoke tartlets. He asked what they'd like. As it turned out, he didn't speak any English so Adeline attempted to order for all of them, which took a good deal of time. Everyone tried the artichokes and agreed that they were good.

As more and more patrons crowded the restaurant, Rainer was surprised that it remained relatively quiet. He supposed the candlelit atmosphere had something to do with the laid-back ease inside the eatery.

When a large party crowded around the two tables nearest them, Emily scooted over to allow room for everyone to fit. Somehow, being crowded together with her very nearly seated in his lap felt more romantic than if it had been just the two of them in a restaurant seated across from one another.

After the soups, the main courses were served. The food and the wine were outstanding, and everyone was having a wonderful time talking and laughing.

They let the wine mellow them as they discussed their day and what would be going on once they returned home.

The dessert course included decadent hot chocolate, fruits, and cheeses that could be dunked in the warmed sauce. Emily pulled off a hunk of croissant and dunked it in her large mug. As some of it dribbled down her thumb, she licked it off.

Rainer watched intently. She wasn't even trying, and she was driving him wild. He stole a quick kiss on her cheek.

Two older Frenchmen entered the restaurant and were greeted by the large party seated next to them. The men scooted onto the benches and didn't seem to notice that there really wasn't any room. Emily slid into Rainer's lap, and Adeline followed suit into Logan's.

No one seemed to mind the new seating arrangements. Since she was sitting in his lap, Emily noticed the effect her licking the chocolate off of her fingers had caused and smirked at Rainer.

He raised his eyebrows at her, hoping the candlelight disguised his slight blush. He let his arm fall across her lap between the top of the boots and the bottom of her skirt. She giggled soundlessly as the effect she was having became more pronounced.

Thankfully, Logan and Adeline didn't seem to notice her laughter as he was whispering in her ear, and she was smiling and blushing in the candlelight.

While bringing a small tray of candies and their check, the waiter smiled at Emily and Adeline in the boys' laps. He offered an apology in badly broken English about the regulars always taking up all the table space. Smiling at him, Logan assured him they didn't mind which Adeline repeated in French, and the waiter nodded his agreement. He complimented Adeline and gave her a wink.

Logan narrowed his eyes in a scowl, but Adeline shook her head and kissed him, which seemed to reassure him quickly. It took quite a bit of maneuvering to exit the table, but after a few moments, several members of the party seated nearest them got up and allowed everyone to scoot out of the benches.

They walked back the long way to take in the Paris skyline, lit by the Eiffel Tower in its center. They came upon a street performer, obviously a Gifted individual who was feigning magician, as he used his hands to set paper on fire and then quickly put it out.

Logan rolled his eyes, but the performer made Rainer think of his Uncle Stan's performances at Non-Gifted children's birthday parties, where he charged ridiculous amounts of money to perform mediocre magic tricks using his lacking gifts.

That was the last person he wanted to think of while he tried to make their last night in Paris romantic and all that Emily wanted it to be. He shut those thoughts down.

Emily began to shiver as the temperature fell, so Rainer shrugged out of his jacket and draped it over her shoulders. He reveled in her adoring smile.

CHAPTER 27

IT RAINS AND IT POURS

Rainer awoke the next morning to rain pouring from the sky and Emily pouting. He was alone in the bed. Emily was frowning at the window as she attempted to stuff all of her purchases from their trip into her suitcase. Rainer stretched and yawned.

"Hey there." He watched her shudder at the thunder. Storms in Paris apparently frightened her just as much as the ones at home.

"Hey," she sighed. "Fitzroy texted over our flight information and said we weren't carrying any evidence about a dozen times."

Rainer picked up his new phone to read the texts. Fitzroy was following protocol in case Rainer's new phone had, in some bizarre twist, been compromised as well.

They spent the morning eating a fantastic breakfast from a bakery and walking around and seeing the sights of Paris in the drizzling rain, once more, before returning to check out of the Ritz. They gathered their things to take the train back to Charles de Gaulle.

"Be careful," Emily fussed for the tenth time as Rainer shifted slightly. He was carrying the large, cumbersome white zip-up garment bag that contained her dress.

"I am, baby."

"Em," Logan spat. "What the hell do you think he's gonna do, set it on fire?"

"Logan," Rainer and Adeline scolded simultaneously as Emily stuck her tongue out at her big brother.

Rainer tried not to think that the dress must have a train as the bottom of the bag was twice as heavy as the top. Emily didn't want him to know anything about it until the moment he saw her walking down the aisle. He could envision it though. He could see her walking down an aisle in her parents' back fields, on her father's arm, dressed all in white. He let his mind travel as the train did.

Their wedding night, their honeymoon, buying a house of their own, her pregnant with his child, taking care of her, raising a family with her. Rainer was overwhelmed with the emotion of it all coming on him so suddenly.

"Hey Em," he called over the roar of the Metro. She turned to him and smiled. "When do you want to get our wedding bands, baby?" She gazed up at him and looked like the simple question had made her entire day.

"Soon, I guess. I want to get yours engraved so…" Rainer thought of the engravings on his parents' wedding bands now tucked in the safety deposit box in their bedroom. Before Rainer could respond, they'd reached the stop for the airport, and Rainer gingerly carried the dress and one of their suitcases through the crowded station. He felt badly that Emily and Logan were carrying the rest of their luggage, but there wasn't much he could do.

A few hours later, they exited the plane to flash bulbs and reporters screaming questions at them. Rainer sighed and wrapped his arm around Emily.

"Welcome home, baby," he lamented. Emily turned her face into Rainer's neck as they moved quickly toward the Hummer.

"Logan, Logan, Logan," chanted from the reporters.

"What do they want me for?" Logan grumped.

"Do you think your parents will keep the baby even if it isn't Gifted?" called a reporter right beside Rainer.

"What?" Logan turned to Adeline who shook her head and urged Logan onward to the car.

Rainer released the cast and carefully scanned and rescanned the Hummer for anything that wasn't supposed to be there before he allowed anyone to enter. They slammed the doors closed, and Rainer backed out quickly.

"What the hell was that all about?" Logan demanded.

"One of the possibilities of what might be wrong with the new baby is that she might not be Gifted, but how did they find that out?" Adeline gestured her thumb back to the throngs of press scattering behind the Hummer. Rainer turned on the car radio and then summoned until he tuned in a local Gifted talk station.

"Governor Haydenshire's numbers continue to plummet as news that the newest little Haydenshire might be disabled come to light," the reporter drawled. "I think we're just concerned that Governor and Mrs. Haydenshire might have overextended themselves this time," sneered the woman being asked for comment. With an audible huff, Emily turned off the radio.

"We need to go check on your mom," Adeline insisted.

CHAPTER 28
HOPE

When they entered the farmhouse kitchen, Mrs. Haydenshire was sitting at the kitchen table sipping tea with Governor Carrington and Serena. Her eyes were red and swollen. Governor Haydenshire was pacing and sporting a furious scowl. Judy Young, the governor's campaign manager, was standing off to the side with a devastated expression.

Governor Haydenshire smiled as soon as Emily entered the room.

"Daddy." Emily moved to him as he hugged her and kissed her forehead.

"Well, baby girl, do we have a dress?" He seemed to be forcing himself to think of something besides what had to be on his mind. Mrs. Haydenshire hugged everyone and welcomed them home. Emily nodded as she studied her parents.

"Where is it?" Mrs. Haydenshire did sound genuinely thrilled.

"It's in the Hummer, but tell me what happened while we were gone."

Mrs. Haydenshire glanced around to all of the inquisitive stares she was receiving. "Well," she started as Governor Haydenshire quickly escorted her back to her seat at the table. "I, uh, had a few problems Saturday," she explained hesitantly. "So, your father insisted I see that specialist Adeline recommended."

Adeline sank down in another chair at the table and nodded. "What did she say?"

"They did several other tests that I've never even heard of before, and mind you I've had ten children." She drew a steadying breath. "Anyway, there is something different about the baby." She placed her hand on her slightly protruding stomach. "Strong heart rate, strong brain function, everything..." Mrs. Haydenshire seemed to draw peace from her statement as everyone nodded. "But she appears to have an extra chromosome, and her cells, right now, don't appear to carry the Gifted energies, but they were quick to tell me that they might develop later.

"But, as you know, in recent history there hasn't been a child born having either parent be Gifted that didn't have the energy. I think it surprised everyone. What I'm so thoroughly shocked over is the reaction in the Realm." Her tears returned. It visibly wounded the governor. He grasped her hand. She drew from him in heavy doses.

"Peterson paid off a receptionist working with the medio specialist and rushed the story to the press. The prejudices we've worked so hard to eradicate from Gifted people seem to have been there all along, just lurking under the surface," Governor Haydenshire concluded in an infuriated huff.

"So, people are voting for Peterson because there's something wrong with the baby?" Logan sounded shocked.

"There is nothing wrong with the baby," Mrs. Haydenshire declared. "She's just different. I don't understand what's wrong with that. All ten of you are different. Every child in the Realm is different. Why is this such a huge deal?"

"I'm making a speech tonight. I'm going to tell the Realm everything we know and how disappointed I am in the reaction. So, we'll see where that lands us, but I'm not going to play Peterson's game of picking and choosing pieces of my life to put out for the Realm to see. If they want me as their Crown, then they take the love of my life." He stared deeply into Mrs. Haydenshire's tear-filled eyes. "And they take all eleven of my children, whether they're Gifted or not, or here with us or not."

Everyone stared at the ground as memories of Cal replayed vividly in their minds.

"Wait, an extra chromosome?" Adeline's brow furrowed. "You mean the baby has Down Syndrome?" She looked extremely concerned.

"Well, sweetheart, we're really not certain. We don't know how it will manifest itself given the fact that we are Gifted." Mrs. Haydenshire smiled sweetly at Adeline.

"But we can't heal that," fell from her mouth without her seeming to have meant to say it out loud.

"No." Mrs. Haydenshire shook her head. Her smile made a timid return as she continued to draw on the love of her adoring husband. "No more than we could cure Emily of being my sassy redhead, or her daddy's baby girl, or Rainer of loving cars, or Logan of making people laugh, and we wouldn't want to." The strength and dignity in her voice rang with every syllable. "So,"—Mrs. Haydenshire stood—"your father has a speech to get ready to give, and I want to see this wedding gown. Then I think Hope and I would like a nap." She smiled kindly at Emily.

"Hope?" Emily's voice shook as she reached and Rainer grasped her hand. Her mother smiled and rubbed her hand over her stomach again.

"I think that seems appropriate," she informed them. "But your father likes Abigail."

"It means strength." He gazed at his wife.

Emily nodded and smiled at her parents through her tears. "I think Abigail Hope is a beautiful name, and it's perfect."

"Me too." Mrs. Haydenshire winked at her. "Now send that strapping stud you're marrying out to the car to get your dress." Everyone laughed, and Rainer immediately followed his orders.

A little while later, Emily tried on her gown for her parents. Her mother pinned the waist where it needed to be taken in and marked the hem, all while Logan and Rainer played outside with the twins. Governor Haydenshire appeared outside, but this time he was the one who had been overcome with emotion.

"Is it too late to tell you that you can't give her the ring?" He choked slightly as he shook his head. Rainer laughed along with Logan.

"I'm gonna go with yes sir," Rainer eased.

Governor Haydenshire chuckled, but the day appeared to have been more than he could take. "I had a feeling you would." He gave Rainer a wry smile. "All right, well, as if your mother hasn't been through enough, I'm heading out yet again to try and beg for a job I'm not certain I even want anymore." He shook his head in indignation.

Logan sighed. "Is there anything we can do to help, Dad?"

"Just look after her for me. You know how you feel about Adeline, son?"

"Yeah, of course." Logan's brow furrowed as he pushed Keaton on the swings.

"That's precisely how much your mother means to me times eleven," Governor Haydenshire vowed. As his gaze fell on Rainer, he shook his head again. "Make that times twelve."

Rainer was deeply touched. "Sir, my dad used to tell me that being Crown was an honor he wouldn't wish on his best friend."

Governor Haydenshire laughed. "That's precisely what Regis said." He fished in his pocket for his keys and sighed. "I'm off. I hope to be home to kiss them good night and try to actually be somewhat helpful to your mother."

"She knows you love her, Dad," Logan assured him.

"Knowing it and feeling it are two very different things, son, and thinking like that will land you in a divorce lawyer's office faster than you can say I do." Governor Haydenshire looked concerned as he studied Logan. "Don't ever forget that."

"I was only trying to help."

"I understand that, but you making incredibly unintelligent comments doesn't help."

"Okay, sorry, geez," Logan spat.

"We're going to talk more about this when my life has begun to resemble something sane," Governor Haydenshire informed Logan as he walked briskly toward his car.

~

Rainer, Emily, Adeline, and Logan all stayed at the farmhouse to look after the twins so that Mrs. Haydenshire could try to rest.

Levi came over and made dinner for everyone. He stayed to watch the governor's speech. Tension crackled through the living room as Governor Haydenshire took the podium in the Senate. There was no audience, and Rainer noted how terribly alone the governor looked.

Emily laced her fingers in Rainer's. Her energy was anxious and troubled. Rainer wrapped his arms around her instead and tried to soothe her. They all watched as the man they respected more than any other stated his case.

The governor cleared his throat, narrowed his eyes in on the cameras, and vowed that he loved his wife and his family, and that they would love their eleventh child whether the Realm wanted them to or not. He stated that he didn't believe that Gifted energies made a person's worth or relevance, and that if the baby didn't have the energies that his other children had that it wouldn't make her less of a person or mean that her family wouldn't love her just as much as they loved all of their children.

He lambasted the Realm for thinking that a Non-Gifted child would mean that he couldn't do the job he'd been asked to do, and he stated that the decline in his poll numbers after his opponent willfully and wrongfully committed an egregious invasion of privacy proved that his work was far from done.

His tone shifted to a snarl as he pointed out that the simpleminded opinion that Gifted people were somehow better than Non-Gifted meant that the prejudices that had led to so many invasions, wars, and the loss of life, in every capacity, in every nation around the world were obviously still there.

He vowed that he wouldn't stop until he felt he'd done his duty to make the Gifted Realm understand that they were no better than the Non-Gifted world. He laid it on the line, and everyone waited with bated breath to see the results.

CHAPTER 29
THE PRICE AND THE VALUE

By Wednesday evening, Governor Haydenshire's numbers were strong once again, and it appeared that the Realm took their reprimand fairly well. Rainer climbed into the Mustang a little after five. He was looking forward to the plans for the evening.

Before they'd gone to Paris, Emily had reminded Rainer that the oil in the Hummer needed to be changed, and he'd called Sam to see if he could do that and help Rainer replace the clutch on the Mustang after they took him out to dinner.

Sam had been only too happy to help. Emily had suggested that they take Keaton and Henry with them. Rainer was certain they would love all of the cars that were typically at Sam's shop, and it would give Mrs. Haydenshire a break.

With only two weeks left until the election, Rainer had just escorted Governor Haydenshire to a plane headed to Portland to campaign on the West Coast for a few days.

Serving as her security, Rainer had followed Emily to practice that morning and was going to follow her to Sam's.

Garrett and Vindico had been at the farmhouse all day to look after the twins and make certain everyone was safe.

Garrett had agreed to meet Rainer and Emily at the arena to give them the twins and to take Chloe out to dinner.

Rainer smiled at Emily as he pulled in the parking deck. She was already loading the boys into the Hummer. He flashed his badge at all of the additional security and then parked beside her. As he exited his car, he realized she'd been crying.

"What's wrong?" He panicked.

"Nothing," she lied.

"Hey." He caught her hands and spun her toward him. "What's wrong?"

Her eyes closed. She shook her head as she swallowed down her emotion.

"Can we talk about it later, please?" At that moment, Fionna appeared. She'd changed out of her practice uniform and into a black micro miniskirt and a sequined blouse. Garrett let a loud wolf whistle slide through his teeth.

"Who's the lucky guy?" he teased.

Fionna shook her head. "His name is Chad. It's just dinner. He's kinda boring, but I don't mind letting him take me to expensive Italian in the city. He's definitely not hard on the eyes," she admitted with a giggle.

"Neither are you, baby." Garrett tousled her hair. Fionna rolled her eyes.

She turned to Emily. "I know you're kind of bummed, but I swear it'll be fun. You can room with me, and you'll fall in love with the kids. I promise." Fionna gave Emily a tender hug. Emily nodded and forced a smile.

"Okay," she agreed in strained enthusiasm. Fionna gave her a sweet smile before she climbed in her canary-yellow MR2 and flew out of the parking deck.

"What was that all about?" Rainer quizzed. Emily relented and leaned against Rainer's chest.

"Uh...well..." she began as Rainer rubbed her back and waited on her to talk. "The Angels are going to Brazil to work in the orphanage Garrett volunteers at all the time." She choked back more tears.

"Oh." Guilt for wanting to demand that she stay home with him tensed in Rainer's shield. "When?"

"We leave November first." She pulled away to look him in the eye as he nodded. "And we'll be gone for most of the month." She managed the words just before her tears began to fall in earnest.

"Wow." Rainer held her and tried to imagine her being gone for the entire month of November. The longest they'd ever been apart was barely two weeks, and she'd flown across an ocean to bring him back. They couldn't exist apart. It just didn't work.

"We leave the morning after the inaugural ball." She shuddered. Rainer nodded his understanding.

"Hey, okay." He forced himself to smile. "I'll miss you like crazy, but this is why you wanted to be an Angel to do the service work. Remember?"

Emily nodded and began trying to wipe away her tears.

"I know. I'm being ridiculous. It's just that's a really long time, and I'm so worried about Mom and the baby, and you, and..." her explanation was drowned in renewed tears. "I just have a terrible feeling."

"I know." He assured her that she didn't have to explain her resistance. The twins began fussing, and Rainer drew a steadying breath. "Let's take them to see Sam, and then we'll talk when we get back home." Emily seemed relieved both to know that Rainer understood and to be leaving the arena. He brushed a kiss across her cheek and wiped away a few more tears.

"We'll be fine, baby. I promise. You're going to have an amazing experience," he vowed as she climbed in the Hummer. She summoned and turned on her phone. The Wi-Fi picked up the signal and began playing nursery rhymes for the boys.

Rainer returned to the Mustang. His heart ached as guilt took up residence in his stomach. He knew Emily would love being with the orphans and that it was selfish to lament her going, but he couldn't help it. He didn't want her to be away from him for a day, much less weeks. His stomach churned as he cranked the Mustang and followed Emily out of the parking deck.

Garrett and Chloe followed behind Rainer. They were heading the same general direction. Garrett phoned while Rainer drove.

"Is she okay?" Garrett asked.

"I don't know. I didn't really get to talk to her much." Rainer watched Emily's eyes in the rearview mirror of her SUV.

"I know you two are like symbiotic or whatever, but this'll be good for her."

"I know." Rainer wasn't really in the mood to talk to Garrett. They pulled onto the interstate as Rainer listened to Garrett drone on about Emily and the orphanage.

"Shit," he spat as a Dodge Charger cut him off. The driver edged sharply between the Mustang and Emily's Hummer. Rainer slammed on his brakes.

"Moron," Garrett huffed. "I wish people would freaking learn how to drive," he spat as Rainer vehemently agreed. He willed his heart to beat in rhythm again. The Charger cut over and almost took out a Hyundai in the left lane.

"What is wrong with that guy?" Rainer eased closer to Emily and glared at the offending driver. The hair on the back of his neck rose. He thought he recognized the driver of the Charger.

Certain he'd been mistaken, he drew a deep breath and stayed close to Emily's bumper. She waved to him in the rear view, and he blew her a kiss. Garrett asked him if Sam might be willing to help him find a replacement for his Highlander.

"I'm sure he'd be glad to." Suddenly, a silver Jaguar flew past Rainer and pulled over directly in front of Emily. She slammed on the brakes. Rainer saw the twins lurch forward in their car seats.

"What the hell?" Garrett spat. After checking all of his mirrors frantically, Rainer's shield flared.

"Garrett," he panted. "Who's in that Olds Alero on your rear left?" Panic surged through his veins. Hysteria set in quickly.

"Shit," Garrett cursed. "That's him. Chloe! Call Em's cell. Tell her to get off at the next exit. Tell her we're being chased," he demanded. "Stay on the phone with me, Rainer. We're gonna have to tag team them to get them away from Em."

Rainer glanced in his rearview mirror and watched Chloe call Emily. He looked forward and watched Emily answer her cell.

With every harrowing heartbeat, the details fell into place. The discussions and planning for the trip to Paris hadn't been the only plans Wretchkinsides and the Interfeci had heard.

This was what his Uncle Stan had to do to earn the rest of the money. He had to run Emily's car off the interstate while she was carrying the twins. Vile revulsion washed through Rainer as he moved to Emily's driver side and blocked her from being hit from the side. He clenched his jaw as the Charger clipped his front bumper.

The Jag swerved in and out of several lanes in front of Emily. Tears leaked from her eyes as her chin trembled. She slammed on her brakes again.

In a quick move, Garrett zipped around Rainer and instructed Chloe to tell Emily to slam on her brakes. He sideswiped the Jag with his SUV. The Jag fishtailed into the emergency lane. The driver emerged screaming loudly and brandishing a pistol, which he pointed at Garrett's Highlander.

Rainer rolled down his window and shot his fierce shield at the driver. He threw him in the air and behind his own car. The gun flew off the overpass.

"Garrett, tell Chloe to tell Em to cast the Hummer," Rainer demanded. Garrett followed his instructions. The Hummer began to glow a brilliant green.

The Charger moved in front of Rainer and slammed on his brakes. It forced Rainer to swerve around him.

"Dammit," he spat. He jerked the Mustang over now in front of Emily as Garrett caught up to her from behind. The Charger was now directly beside her.

Rainer could see Henry sobbing through his rear window. Garrett moved behind the Charger and bumped him from the rear.

Suddenly his uncle's Alero pulled to Emily's passenger side, and Rainer watched in horror as his uncle, his only living relative, pulled a pistol and took aim.

"Oh shit!" Garrett shouted. "Rainer, you've got to stop him. She's freaking. Her shield is weakening. She can't hold that much power for this long."

Like watching a horror movie he already knew the ending of, Rainer's pulse rang in his ears as he watched his uncle rack the slide of the pistol.

He was never going to stop. It was never going to end. The money would always be more important, and Emily would always be his preferred target. *I'll always take care of her, sir.* Rainer's fervent vow to Governor Haydenshire pounded in his skull.

Tears stung his eyes as he shook his head. He gasped for breath and swerved hard to his right. His blood ran cold. He threw the most powerful heat shield he'd ever thrown out of his window and into his uncle's car.

He watched in horror as the car fishtailed out of control. It spun and screeched in harrowing, terror-filled chaos. It hit the guardrail, and Rainer shot another stream of heated electricity into the car just before the engine ignited and the car burst into flames.

Rainer was trying and failing to choke back sobs by the time he pulled the Mustang into the emergency lane behind Emily. He fled his car as she raced from the Hummer and into his arms.

Garrett pulled in behind them. "Dan's on his way. The state police have the other two drivers." Garrett physically held Rainer upright as Rainer sobbed into Emily's neck. He heard Vindico's Agusta roar to the scene as Henry was lifted from the Hummer and handed to Rainer. Keaton was handed to Garrett by one of the DC police officers.

Henry allowed Rainer a moment of clarity and realization of what he'd just done.

"Are you okay?" Vindico soothed.

"No." Rainer didn't see any point in lying as Henry buried his head in Rainer's neck and patted his face with his tiny wet hand.

"Hey. You look at me." Vindico moved directly in front of Rainer's face. "That was a hell of a thing you just did. One of the bravest things I've ever seen." He gestured to the smoldering remains of his uncle's car. "And you did it for her and for them." He tousled Henry's hair. "You're a hell of a shield. I'm proud of you, Lawson."

The squeal of the tires and the roar of the explosion that continued to detonate in his mind was all that Rainer could hear. Vindico's words of reassurance and praise sounded distant and distorted by the harrowing shrill of murder.

CHAPTER 30
AN ICY SEA OF TEARS

Rainer sat on the sofa in their house with the entire Haydenshire family moving around him and staring at him like he'd been placed on suicide watch. Governor Haydenshire had flown back home as soon as he'd landed in Portland and had been told what had happened.

Emily stayed steadfastly beside Rainer. She kept her soothing Receiver's cast around him. She cried intermittently as she tried to soothe him, but he was unable to lower his shield enough to allow her to access him fully. He just couldn't seem to let anyone through.

Logan was anguished. He'd tried desperately to soothe Rainer or at least make him smile, but all Rainer could see was his father's face before him everywhere he looked.

Trying to look his father in the eye and tell him that he'd just killed his only brother was unspeakably horrible, and yet Rainer couldn't remove the harrowing image from his mind.

Vindico and Garrett had urged him to go out with them for a beer, but Rainer had adamantly refused. He was terrified to leave Emily's sight. He was choking in some kind of abyss. He could only breathe if she was there.

He tried to determine what time it was or what was happening in the house around him. It felt like some sort of horrible dream where he could see everyone, but no one could see him.

He heard a bell and turned the direction of the sound, but was unable to determine that it had been the doorbell, that he himself had installed, until Governor Carrington and Governor Vindico issued through the door. Dan and Governor Willow followed them. Governor Haydenshire thanked them for coming, but Rainer wasn't certain why they were there. The chasm between him and the rest of the world was just too wide.

He forced his gaze to Governor Haydenshire. He still wasn't really able to see him. He saw the governor's head gesture to the empty seat on the couch beside Emily.

Suddenly Logan seated himself next to Emily. He tousled her hair and made a slight smile appear on her beautiful face.

Memories of the day his father had been killed seared through Rainer's mind in alarming detail. Adults all trying desperately to get him to talk about his feelings or to tell him what a hero his father had been, and just like now, he didn't want to hear any of it.

All he'd wanted when he was fourteen years old, and all he wanted now, was for everyone but Emily to leave him alone. He wanted to hold her. He desperately needed to feel the healing warmth of her. He wanted the rest of the world to fade away into the hell that it was. He wanted it all to just leave him be. All he wanted was her.

The sudden realization shook Rainer, and he wrapped both of his arms around Emily. He was able to let his shield down just enough to allow her in. A genuine and instantaneous smile lit her face as she closed her eyes and immediately supplied him with her energy in drowning doses.

He reveled in it. He didn't care at all who was watching or if anyone else realized what had just happened between them.

Mrs. Haydenshire grinned at him. She wiped away her tears, and he knew that she was aware that he'd finally shattered through his body's stubborn will, and he'd let her in.

Breath returned to his lungs like she'd pulled him from the icy sea that had swallowed him whole. His lungs ached. His heart beat disjointedly. It seemed unable to find rhythm. His nostrils burned, and his face felt wet, but he didn't understand why.

Emily reached and ran her thumb over his cheek. It took Rainer another moment to understand that he was crying again. He shook himself as awareness seeped slowly back into his being. He refused to cry in front of Vindico and the board of governors and the former Crown. He chastised himself.

Governor Haydenshire shook his head and seated himself on the ottoman in front of Rainer. He was joined by the ensemble of men he'd called in to help.

"I shed more tears than I care to remember over your father, Rainer, and over you, son," he vowed consolingly. "And we've all lived through enough hell to understand that tears don't make you weak. They're the result of courageous acts and of conquering fear."

"Yeah, and sometimes they're just because life is just too damn much to deal with," Vindico vowed as his father slapped his shoulder and gave him a sorrowful gaze.

Rainer offered no response. So, after sharing uncomfortable glances with his gathered team, Governor Haydenshire began again.

Emily very discreetly slid her hand up the back of Rainer's shirt so she could fill him with more of her.

The motion was like a soothing balm she poured in his soul. It healed and bound him, and Rainer fought the urge to plead with her to take him to bed and hold him against her with nothing between them.

"It's all right," Governor Haydenshire soothed. "You sit there and let her heal you, son, because she is absolutely your other half. And she is the only person strong enough to help you through this. And for all of my teasing and irritation, the two of you were made to be and no one would deny you her, but I just want you to listen to us for a few minutes." While offering a slight nod, Rainer tried to force himself to concentrate. Governor Carrington slid beside Governor Haydenshire.

"Rainer," he began in his low, smooth intonation. His dark eyes were kind and soothing. "You've got us all here, with a few additions that the years have provided." He nodded to Vindico and Will and Logan.

At that moment, Henry toddled over and wiggled into Rainer's lap. Rainer held him with the arm that wasn't around Emily. He felt Henry as well. He was trying, in all of his limited capabilities, not even really aware of why he was doing it, to soothe Rainer as well. He laid his head against Rainer's shoulder and sucked his thumb. He patted Rainer's back with his other hand. Everyone chuckled at the motion as Rainer hugged Henry to him.

"Like I said, the years have provided a few of us with more welcomed additions than others." Governor Carrington beamed at Henry as he slapped Governor Haydenshire on the back. Henry continued to suck his thumb and pat Rainer. "So, here we are, the men who knew your father better than anyone else, save you, but I need you to understand something, son." He held Rainer's gaze with his own. "Your father would've done the very same thing that you did today, and I would swear on his life, and on my own, that he's very proud of your actions," Governor Carrington stated firmly. He never broke from Rainer's gaze.

"My father would've found some other way to save them." Rainer spoke the first words he'd uttered since he'd returned home.

"Man, I was right there," Garrett vowed. "There wasn't anything else you could've done. She couldn't hold the shield that long, not and drive and be scared out of her mind. Her energy is emotional, and her emotions were under assault. He was going to shoot her and wreck the car. He wasn't going to be dissuaded. You saved her life. You saved all of them." His voice rose in accordance with his fervor.

"He's right." Governor Vindico offered him a patient smile. "Sometimes we want so badly for there to be another choice, but the one that presents itself is the choice. Not every action is an option."

"He's right, Lawson." Vindico nodded to his father. "Assuming there was some other miraculous way you could've stopped him today, he wasn't going to quit. Wretchkinsides would've just kept upping the ante. That's how he plays. He pushes until he gets results, and she was always going to be his chosen target. It would've always been when she was in her car so she couldn't feel them coming. Everyone knows what happened to her several years ago when she was in the accident. He was using the most terrifying moments of her life against her. That's the kind of evil we're dealing with. What would've happened if you hadn't been there tonight?"

Rainer's heart seized. He couldn't go there. He couldn't think that way. It was more than he was capable of handling. With sudden, certain assuredness, Rainer knew exactly what he wanted.

He cradled Henry in his arms and turned to give Emily a pleading gaze. Emily blinked back tears of her own and nodded. She understood Rainer needed an escape. He needed an out, if only for tonight. He needed to be nowhere and everywhere with her. She leaned and whispered in his ear. She asked if what she thought he wanted was correct. He nodded adamantly, and she turned not to her father but to Vindico.

"I assume he can have a couple of days off," she commanded.

"Yeah, that's protocol. He needs to stay out of the office until Monday at least."

Everyone stared at him. Rainer thought no one had understood but her, but he was mistaken.

"Hey, you go on, and if we can get Friday off we'll meet you down there tomorrow night," Logan urged.

"Can we use a jet?" Emily pled to her father. "Please."

"Sure," Governor Haydenshire agreed though he was still giving them curious stares.

"Emily, why don't you go get yourselves packed, sweetheart. I'll get you some food together," Mrs. Haydenshire directed. She looked relieved that there was something Rainer wanted that she could help supply.

"I'm exhausted and completely fried. Normally I know what my kids want, but where are you going?" Governor Haydenshire asked.

"The beach house," Emily called as she headed to their room. She began throwing their clothes into suitcases.

"That's a really good idea." Vindico seemed pleased as well.

Governor Haydenshire pulled his cell phone from his pocket.

"I doubt one of the jets would get you out of here without the press being alerted." He arranged a small commuter flight and a car to meet them at the tiny Virginia Beach airport.

"Now," he addressed the room at large. "No one but the people in this room know where they're going. Let's try and keep it that way." Everyone promised to keep Rainer's hideaway quiet. For a brief moment, Rainer felt something he hadn't felt since the horrific evening had begun. He felt hope.

It was no longer vacation season. There would be very few people at the beach. There wouldn't even be a car in the driveway, and all he wanted was to lie in bed with Emily and stare out at the endless ocean. He needed to let it wash away his devastation. He needed to cling to the only person who ever truly brought him peace.

Mrs. Haydenshire began handing out instructions. She sent Brooke and Will back to the farmhouse to get pints of frozen crab soup and the cornbread she'd fixed earlier to pack in the cooler she was preparing.

Garrett's Highlander and Rainer's Mustang had been towed to Sam's to fix the damage they'd done sideswiping the Jag and rear-ending the Charger. Levi volunteered to take Rainer and Emily to the airport.

Rainer felt bad that everyone was preparing to help him escape reality, while he sat on the couch and watched them work. He slid forward to offer to help, but Henry had fallen asleep against his chest. He raised his eyebrows to Governor Haydenshire and offered him Henry.

"He looks pretty comfortable. You just sit back and let him sleep," Governor Haydenshire soothed.

In all of the years he'd been madly in love with Emily Haydenshire, Rainer had never known her to pack as quickly as she packed for their impromptu beach trip. All of the men in their home were visibly impressed when Emily emerged from their bedroom with a suitcase, two duffle bags, and a toiletry bag.

"Trust me, she only moves that fast for Rainer," Patrick quipped, and everyone chuckled.

"Here, I've got it, Em." Levi loaded their luggage in his car.

"Okay," Mrs. Haydenshire casted and loaded two very large

Styrofoam coolers full to bursting with food which Will and Patrick added to the luggage in Levi's car.

"Here." Logan and Adeline issued through the kitchen door. They were carrying a bag from the gas station they always stopped at on their way to the beach. The bag contained several chilled Dr Peppers. "I even got her cinnamon candy for you," Logan chided.

"Thanks, man," Rainer choked. He still wasn't certain why he couldn't seem to get a handle on his emotions.

"We'll see you tomorrow night, okay?"

"Yeah, that'd be good." Rainer truthfully wasn't certain he wanted Logan and Adeline to come. All he knew in that endless moment of terror was that he wanted just one night alone with Emily where no one knew where to find them.

"Hey, Em, come here a minute," Garrett ordered.

"What?" She sounded irritated at the delay.

"Would you just come here? You need to hear this." Garrett pointed back into her and Rainer's bedroom. He closed the door behind them as soon as she'd entered.

Just a little over an hour later, Rainer took the bags from the driver and tipped him as Emily unlocked the door to the Haydenshire's beach house.

Rainer inhaled deeply. He allowed the memories to sweep through him. The scent of suntan lotion, frying bacon, the salty ocean air, and plank wood decking relaxed Rainer's tightly clenched muscles for the first time in hours.

His jaw unhinged slightly as Emily took his hand and led him into the house. She turned and locked the door to keep the rest of the world at bay.

"Thank you for coming with me." He pulled Emily close and wrapped his arms over her body. He clung to her. Emily shook her head and brushed a kiss across his jaw.

"You always take such good care of me. You take care of everyone. I'm thrilled to get to take care of you," she whispered sweetly. "We don't even have to leave the house for the next few days if you don't want. We have plenty of food, and we can just lie around and just be us. We can let it all go for a while, okay?" Rainer felt his face form a smile. It was an odd sensation.

"That sounds perfect." His voice was rough and gravelly from his horrific day.

"I'm going to unpack the food. Do you want to come with me, or do you want to go on to bed?"

"I want to stay with you." He was well aware that he sounded like he was six years old. Emily smiled and took his hand again. She led him to the kitchen and turned on just one light over the stove. She kept the house swathed in soothing darkness.

Rainer sank down on one of the stools at the counter bar, and Emily pulled a beer from one of the coolers, popped it open, and set it in front of him. She began loading food into the refrigerator and pantry. When she finished, she turned and smiled at him. She came to stand between his bent knees, wrapped her arms around his chest, and laid her head on his shoulder.

"You know, when I was driving and the boys were crying, I was so scared," she admitted hesitantly. Rainer squeezed her tighter into his arms. "But I knew I just had to listen to Chloe tell me what you wanted me to do. I knew that you would never let anything happen to me. I knew I was safe because you were there." She pulled her head away and gazed deeply into his tear-filled eyes.

He couldn't seem to find his voice, and he didn't know what to say as he held her close. He never wanted to let her go.

"Let's go to bed, okay?" Emily soothed as Rainer nodded. He wasn't certain he could sleep, but he wanted desperately to be wrapped up in her soothing embrace.

He followed her to the bedroom they'd used the last time they'd been in the house all alone, and she leaned up on her tiptoes, kissed his cheek, and moved to the closet. She pulled out fresh sheets and blankets and several quilts.

"I love you," he murmured. The emotion of everything he felt at that moment was overwhelming. His voice was ragged and low.

"I love you too, and I know how much you love me. I can feel it. I know it's not something I'll ever deserve, but it's also something I could never live without." She touched his face tenderly as he let his eyes close from the caress. He focused on nothing but her.

She summoned as she moved away from him. She sealed heat into the fibers of the sheets. She spread them on the bed and then did the same for the blankets and quilt as she added them. Rainer watched the warm pink glow in her hand darken to a soft blue as she fluffed several pillows and added the cooled cases and then placed them on the bed. As she moved back to him, she summoned once again and pulled the light from all but the smallest lamp in the room.

CHAPTER 31

...AND HIS RECEIVER

"Come to bed with me," she whispered.

As he watched her, with all of the love he felt for her filling him, restoring him, and fortifying him, she began removing her clothes. Rainer swallowed down the tenuous emotion that had overwhelmed him all night.

"Can I please kiss you?" His voice shook violently as he blinked back more tears. She drew a steadying breath and gave him a heartbroken gaze.

"Of course. Why wouldn't you be able to kiss me?" She didn't understand. He shook his head, unable to say the word murderer. "Rainer..." She blinked back tears of her own.

His body sought hers without his awareness. She angled her head and gazed up at him. Her eyes were heavy with anguish as he leaned down and kissed her sweetly, tenderly without expectation that there would be anything more than the kiss.

He held her face in his hands and caressed her as she wrapped her arms around his back and melded their bodies together. He began to braid his fingers through her long, auburn tresses, still guiding her mouth with his other hand.

He wanted to get lost in her. If she didn't want to do anything but kiss him for hours, he was fine with that. As long as she was beside him, as long as the world would stay safely outside their bedroom door, and they could exist alone in this time and space, he might survive.

She let her tongue sweep in his mouth and fill him with the very essence of her. He crushed her to him. He was desperate to feel more of her, but she pulled away. He shuddered as she broke from the kiss. He couldn't fight it. The emotion threatened to drown him in a tidal wave once again.

"Look at me." Emily's voice was calm and soothing. "You didn't do anything wrong, and don't you dare stand there calling yourself a murderer. Don't you dare!" Rainer convulsed at the word as she began sobbing. "Because you are not that," Emily vowed. "You saved my life. You saved Keaton and Henry. I couldn't hold the shield anymore. The ring doesn't work like that. It's a huge amount of energy at first, but I have to be emotionally able to keep it up." He shook his head and stared at the ground.

"Look at me!" she demanded again. He let his head rise to study her. "What do you say to me when it storms and you hold me in our bed and the thunder scares me?" Rainer didn't reply. "You say, 'I've got you, and I'll never let anything happen to you. I'll never let you go.' And when Henry is afraid, and he wants you and you pick him up, you always say, 'It's okay, little man, I've got you.' That's exactly what you did. You had us, and you didn't let us go. That's not a murderer, Rainer. That's the most amazing man I've ever met or that I'll ever know." She wiped away her own tears and clenched her jaw before she continued.

"The choice you had was me or him. That was the only choice. So tell me, do you still think you should've chosen differently, because there wasn't another option?" With that, he wrapped his arms around her and sobbed convulsively.

"I was so fucking scared. I was terrified." He shuddered.

"I know." Emily held him tightly. She let him cry for a long while until she finally brushed away the last of his tears.

"See, I'm the lucky one because I didn't have to be brave or be the hero this time because you were there. I didn't have to make a decision like that, but I am so proud of you. You were amazing. Hey," she soothed. "Do you remember when we were little and I almost ran into that copperhead by the swing set?"

"Yeah." He rubbed his eyes with the heels of his hands and then massaged his temples. He allowed himself to remember how long Wretchkinsides had been after her, and hoped maybe there really hadn't been another choice.

"Do you remember what your dad said to you when you threw your shield and got between me and the snake?" Rainer tried desperately to believe what she was telling him. Emily smiled at him. She kept him tucked tightly to her. "He said, 'Take Emily back up to the porch, son. Keep her safe,'" she reminded him.

"And then after he killed the snake he said, 'I'm really proud of the way you kept her safe.'" She completed his father's vow verbatim. "And you know what? That's exactly what he would say to you if he were standing in this room with us right now."

"I hope," he choked. He just couldn't reconcile what everyone had been telling him all evening.

"I know," she vowed. Then she continued to remove her clothes. She fumbled with the buttons on her blouse. He pulled her to him. He helped her remove her shirt and threw it on the floor. He was desperate to feel her again. He brushed his hands over her face and stroked her cheeks with his thumbs tenderly. She leaned in and angled her head upward toward his.

He let the tip of his tongue trace gently over her kiss-swollen lips, and she opened them slightly. She moved her bottom lip between his, allowing him to trace and suck it as he inhaled deeply and filled all of his senses with her.

She pulled away slightly, and he brushed soft kisses from her lips, down her neck, and across her collarbone. He listened as a soft moan escaped her. Her scent was stronger here and it soothed some of the terror that pulsed in his shield.

After pulling everything else she was wearing off, she began to strip him. She fumbled with his belt buckle. Her hands were shaking. He stopped her.

"I've got it, baby."

"Rainer." She climbed into the warm bed and waited on him to
join her.

"Hmm?" he managed.

"Come here," she beckoned as he stripped. He sank into the soft
bed and wrapped her up in his arms. "Everything will be okay," she
soothed as he pulled her closer.

He finally decided to just believe her, to shut down the impending
doom that swirled violently in his head. He held her as she moved so
that every part of him was touching a part of her. She let her energy
swirl around him. It swathed him and cosseted him in the serenity
of her.

"Do you remember the night after my dad and everyone found out
about the belly shot?" she whispered in the moonlit room.

"Yeah." Rainer wondered what had her thinking about that.

"Do you remember we were in bed, and I told you that I wanted
you to take it all away, to make everything else disappear even for just
a little while?"

"Yeah." Rainer remembered it was the first time he'd kept her
casted in his shield while they'd made love.

Emily kissed his chest and rubbed her hands over his naked body
as she pushed her delicious, soothing energy into him. "You have
always been my Shield. You've always protected me. But I can make it
all go away for a little while too, if you want, because I'm your
Receiver. Let me have everything you try so hard to keep in your
shield. That's why I'm here on this earth to be that for you. That's how
my whole world works," she offered, and he stopped short of turning
her down instantly.

As he felt her energy surrounding him, he was suddenly desperate
to permeate her so that she could fill him completely. He needed relief
from the harrowing grief and the crushing guilt.

With urgent need like he'd never known before, he didn't want to
think. He couldn't. It was too much to work through. It was too much
to carry. He wanted to get lost in her and to fill her with him. He
needed to hear the sweet sounds she made when they were together.
He wanted to wrap himself up in her, to breathe in her scent, to taste

her, to feel her, and make her feel him. He wanted desperately to drown in her energy.

She seemed to understand what he needed so emphatically at that moment as she rolled to her side and traced her hands down his chest and then up his length. He shuddered. He knew he'd never deserve her or the amazing way she understood him, but overwhelming thankfulness filled his soul as he moaned and captured her lips with his again.

He devoured her mouth like her lips held his redemption. He moved his kisses down her neck and then brushed them across her breasts. He laved her with his tongue and drank in the sweet, salty dew on her skin as she gave him a hushed moan. They swelled for him.

He trembled as he traced his hands down her body, working from instinct alone. She swayed beside him. She was still moving her hand over him and making him leave all thought for another time. She was able to make him do nothing but feel. He let his fingers play softly just outside of her swollen lips as she shivered deliciously under his touch.

To know her, to know where she liked to be touched, to know how she sounded when she lost control, the way she looked, the way she tensed, the knowledge overwhelmed him. He wanted to make love to her all night. He needed to push the world away from them. He needed to exist only in the ecstasy of the two of them together.

He kissed her again. He was still tracing her with slight, tender touches that elicited sweet sighs of love and need. He panted as her breath caught as she blinked heavily and held his eyes with her own.

She spread her legs for him, and he groaned. The feeling was once again overwhelming. He would never deserve everything she offered him. He let the tip of his finger trace over her opening, and she gave a soft shuddered moan.

It was a sound of expectation that he would allow her to make the world slip away if only for a little while. That together they could get lost in each other. They could cling to the only thing that really mattered and let everything else go. That she would baptize him anew, cleanse him of obligatory sin that had consumed him.

His mind was at war with his body. He didn't deserve her. He didn't deserve this. He'd just killed his uncle. This was wrong. He couldn't drown the horrible day in her. He didn't deserve the reprieve, but she moved her luscious curves against him, arched her back so her breasts fell against his chest, and her energy flowed in heavy soothing waves of warmth and healing love all around him.

Craving need permeated his entire being. It filled his heart and his soul. She was everything, and when he held her, when he touched her, when he was with her, as no one else had ever been or would ever be, it seemed everything might really be all right. There was hope in the way they moved together as one.

He traced over her once more and then slipped his fingers inside of her. He let her moan pull him toward ecstasy. He surrendered to his own desire, his desperate need. He drowned in the futility of the war. He was fraught with terror. His heart ached, and she was the only cure. He gave himself over to her. He let her energy surround him, let her bind him and heal his aching desperation.

The wet heat that contained the sweet ecstasy of her slipped around his fingers as a groan overtook him. The physical form of her energy overwhelmed him and made him whole once again. Her responses to him were all consuming. She was perfect. She was his other half, like a puzzle that needed no other pieces to be complete.

She bucked as he stroked her. He moved his fingers to where she was most sensitive and reveled again in his knowledge of her.

The slick, wet heat poured from her now as she shuddered. It began to wash away the burdens the world had strained upon them. She was his own personal baptismal fount. She tensed and swelled in his hands, ripe from his tender touches in just the right places. A moan hung on her lips as her breath caught.

The deeper he pushed the more of her filled him as he concentrated. He wanted to give her everything. He wanted to revel in the ecstasy of the two of them together and let the world fade away.

Just before she lost it completely, she moaned again and he let everything else go. She relaxed around him and let him drive her. She let him take her where he wanted her to be.

He swirled his fingers inside of her once more, and she broke. She panted and writhed. She called out for him as her muscles seized around his hand.

He watched her. Her face contorted in ecstasy. Her body tensed and rolled from his touch. Unable to draw it out any longer, desperation permeated his soul.

She opened her eyes and gazed into his as he moved over her. He kissed her. He sucked her luscious lips and her tongue. He explored her, tasted her intoxicating energy, and felt selfish for drinking down all she was offering and coming back for more of the healing waters she offered.

She broke away and gasped for breath. She raised her hips.

"I want you." She breathed in heady need. "I want you to make me yours. I want you to take all of me. I want to make it better. I want every single piece of you. I love each and every part of you." It wasn't a plea she'd planned or uttered to add to his enjoyment.

It was the way their world worked. She needed him just like he required her. Nothing else mattered, and letting all of the horrors of the world go, he spread her swollen lips, wet from need and from his caresses, and he pushed into her slowly.

He allowed himself to feel her and nothing else as she surrounded him. She enveloped him inch by inch. She gasped as he stretched her and formed her around his length. He groaned from the utter bliss and the way she felt as she wrapped tightly around him like she was made for him alone.

It was complete perfection. She surrounded him not only in her body but in her energy. She healed him thoroughly.

He began to thrust as she took him deeper. Her body moved in time with his. She kept her cast pulsing through his skin. They moved in perfect accord without pretense or lust. It was with deep, penetrating love that their energy spun together and soothed them both.

She writhed around him and met his every thrust. She pulled him deeper and tighter as she swelled around him. She encased him in the sweetest silk. Her body moved until they were one.

A shuddered moan escaped her mouth. She called out for him. His name caught on her lips as he brought her nearer. He groaned as his body began to feel stronger as the horrors the day had brought began to slip away. She drained him of the dismay and the terror. She pulled the fear and the terrifying hopelessness. She took it all from his shield and filled it with her devoted, adoring love.

Her heady groan satisfied him. He needed to hear her, needed her to call his name, to moan and pant and let him know that he was meeting all of her needs. He needed to know that he was everything she needed him to be in that moment and forever.

He met her with reassurances all his own. He pushed and rocked her. He nurtured her and tended to her every desire because fulfilling her was all that mattered. It drove him as his heart pounded and he panted and sweated from the effort. The feeling of her enveloping him and calling for him to fill her drove him wild.

He was consumed with nothing but her. She filled his senses and completed him thoroughly. Her body climaxed around his, and he let himself go with her. He filled her with all of him as they drowned the tedium of the world in the mix of their release.

As she writhed, he clung to her. He allowed no space between their bodies as he withdrew from her begrudgingly. She refused to release him. She held him tight and kept her arms wrapped around his chest and back. Their legs remained entangled together. His release brought on drowning exhaustion. He clung to her as she somehow continued to soothe him.

"Rainer," she whispered.

"What, baby?" He finally seemed to recognize the sound of his own voice.

"Go to sleep. I've got you, and I'll never let you go."

CHAPTER 32
TWO WAYS

Rainer awoke the next morning after having been up several times in the night. He would awaken with his heart racing and his body covered in sweat from the horrific nightmares.

Emily had been right there each and every time to soothe him back to sleep, but this time he was all alone. Panic seared through his veins as he frantically searched the room.

"Em?" he pled, and suddenly she was there.

"I'm so sorry." She appeared from the bathroom.

"It's okay," Rainer lied. He had to get it together. He couldn't go on like this. She deserved a man, not a child.

"How are you feeling?" She traced her hand up and down his chest. Her energy was weaker. He could tell instantly. She'd soothed him all night, and she was still exhausted. Guilt settled harshly in the pit of his stomach. He was supposed to take care of her, not the other way around. He shook his head, disgusted with himself.

"I'm sorry I lost it last night."

Emily shook her head. "Sweetheart, you know this is supposed to work two ways, right? I'm going to be your wife, and you certainly took care of me yesterday. Let me take care of you now. You don't have to be okay for me, and if you need to talk then I'll listen, and if you need to sleep then I'll be right here, and if you just want to stay holed up here in the house then all I want is to be right beside you. And sometimes life isn't going to go exactly the way we planned or the way we want, and sometimes it's going to be awful, but as long as we always turn to each other to deal with the bad times then I know it's gonna be a really great life."

Rainer cradled her closely and kissed her cheek. "I could never ever tell you how much I love you or what you mean to me, but I know I don't deserve you." He refused to give in to any more emotion other than his love for her.

"That isn't true, and I love you too," she admonished with a sweet grin.

"Let's go back to sleep. I'm sorry I kept you up all night."

"Oh, you mean like when you barely slept for two weeks straight because you refused to leave my hospital room," she reminded him. "See, both ways."

"All right, I got it." Rainer brushed another kiss across her cheek. He was still reveling in her energy. His voice was gravelly from sobbing the night before.

"Now would you like to sleep some more or do you want some breakfast?" she quizzed with a slight yawn.

"I really want to hold you beside me and try my damnedest to let us both sleep some more." He tried to mentally compose himself enough to let everything that had happened the day before go, at least for a little while.

It was after one in the afternoon the next time Rainer awoke. His eyes blinked open, and he drew a deep breath. He took a moment to revel in Emily still lying on his chest, completely naked. He never wanted to leave the bed. He just wanted to lie there holding her and ignore the rest of the world. It was too much. He couldn't deal with it anymore.

A memory erupted in his mind suddenly. He and Logan were walking around the lake, freezing, and barely fourteen years old. Mrs. Haydenshire had urged Logan to talk to Rainer.

The custody trial had been the night before, and Rainer's formerly

206

black eye still ached, but Garrett had healed it as soon as he'd coaxed Rainer to be able to lower his shield. At fourteen years of age, Logan had no idea what to say to Rainer.

"It's really cool you get to live with us now," he'd commented hopefully.

"Yeah." Rainer kicked a stone with the toe of his sneaker. As excited as he was to not have to live with his uncle anymore, he didn't want to live at the farm. He wanted to live with his dad.

He wanted to go home, and for his father to come home from the Senate and make dinner. He wanted him to ask about his day, and about Emily, and to help him with his homework. Logan had nodded uncomfortably but had nothing else to offer as fourteen-year-old boys are neither verbose nor extremely empathetic.

As they walked, exhaustion had overtaken Rainer. He'd spent the two previous nights on the stoop of his uncle's apartment. Stan had locked him out with no dinner as he'd left to pick up a prostitute and some liquor.

Rainer recalled how heavy he'd felt at that moment. It was like trying to walk through quicksand. He was unable to hold his eyes open. He shook himself to stay awake and to keep the world from swallowing him whole. It had all been too much for him to bear that evening as well.

Emily had appeared suddenly. She'd brought Logan and Rainer a plate of Mrs. Haydenshire's chocolate chip cookies straight from the oven, warm and gooey, and she'd handed Rainer a glass full of cold milk.

"Let's go eat them in the loft."

Rainer remembered every detail. They'd followed her back to the barn.

When they'd arrived at the ladder, Emily had handed Logan several cookies and then instructed, "You can leave now."

Logan rolled his eyes. "Whatever, Em. He's my best friend. I'm supposed to make him feel better."

Rainer recalled feeling extremely uncomfortable as he was being discussed.

"And you've done all that you can, and you're basically terrible at it so now it's my turn. Bye, Logan," she'd sassed and began her climb up the ladder.

"What if he doesn't want to hang out with you?"

"I do," Rainer had choked instantly. He was never certain why he'd said it, but he knew that it was the complete truth. He didn't want to walk around the lake with Logan trying feebly to make him feel better when nothing would—nothing but Emily.

Rainer let his eyes close as he came back to the present. He breathed in the scent of her hair as he realized that the world was only too heavy if he wasn't with her. She wriggled beside him and then her eyes blinked open.

"Hey there," he whispered. Her broad beaming grin warmed his heart.

"Feeling a little better, I take it?" Rainer nodded. "Good, because I'm starving. I'm going to make us food."

Rainer chuckled and then immediately found the sensation odd. He crawled out of bed and headed to the bathroom.

When he emerged, he pulled on a pair of basketball shorts and a sweatshirt and then headed to the kitchen. Emily grinned at him as she fried up bacon and eggs. She was spoiling him thoroughly.

Thankful that he could do something, Rainer perked a pot of coffee and poured Emily a cup. He added cream and sugar and then made one for himself. He slowed and forced himself to really taste the coffee as he glanced out the front windows of the house.

He saw a news truck circle the block, but it didn't stop near the beach house. They didn't seem to if know anyone was there, but they were definitely on the prowl. Rainer returned to the kitchen with a sigh.

"I saw them already." Emily took in the dejected look on his face. "But like I said, Mom packed us tons of food, and we can stay in the house until Sunday night if you want to just hang out."

"I don't want to keep you holed up here. If you want to go somewhere, I'm going to have to face them sometime." Before she could reply, Rainer's cell rang. Logan's name was on the screen.

"Hey," he cleared his throat. His voice was still rough from his emotion.

"Hey man, listen," Logan began. "Adeline and I will come down if you want. We're happy to, but if we come, the press will be all over you. They're getting vicious. Everyone wants a comment, and no one can find you or Em so it just keeps getting worse." He sounded thoroughly disgusted. Rainer appreciated the sacrifice and the offer.

"What was in the papers today?" He cleared his throat again and tried desperately to sound normal.

Logan ignored his voice and supplied, "Mostly that your uncle was killed in a car accident, and a few reports that Iodex took him out along with two other members of Interfeci. No one knows what really happened. They just want to know your reaction to it for now."

His reaction to it was certainly not something Rainer wanted in the papers. He was still trying to get over his mortification that he'd cried in front of Vindico and then completely broken down in front of Emily.

"If you don't mind not coming and covering for me at work, I'd really appreciate it." Not only would he never deserve Emily, he'd never deserve a friend like Logan.

"No, it's cool. Garrett and I are taking care of the twins. Dad threw everyone out last night. He informed his security detail, his press agents, campaign manager, and the whole load of them that he was spending the night alone with Mom, and that they weren't to be disturbed." Logan shuddered audibly as Rainer felt his cheeks pull into a smile for the first time since the afternoon before.

"Good for him."

Logan begrudgingly agreed. "Anyway, Dan says to take all the time you need, but to be back in the office Monday." He chuckled. "You and Em just chill, but I'm serious—if you go out and you're spotted, it'll be like Grand Central Station there. If I were you, I'd shut the blinds and get comfortable."

"Yeah, I think that's exactly what we're gonna do." Rainer ended the call and moved to Emily. He kissed her cheek as she scooped bacon and eggs onto two plates and beamed at him.

They sank onto the sofa in the living room as another news van circled the block.

"The term shark attack comes to mind." Emily rolled her eyes as they both made certain to stay away from the front windows.

"I feel terrible. We're at the beach. It's your favorite place in the world, and you can't even go out to the water." Rainer knew that his guilt should just go ahead and declare permanent residence in his gut.

Emily shook her head and studied him speculatively. "First of all, it's the middle of October, and it's freezing out there." She gestured to the gray sky and the swirling Atlantic waters, which Rainer was certain were quite cold by now. "And my favorite place in the world to be is wherever you are."

The statement that it was the middle of October and then her assurances that she wanted to be wherever he was forced the information he'd received just before their fateful car ride to the forefront of his mind. Emily leaned up off of him. Her back had been to his chest as they'd attempted to eat tangled up in one another.

"What? What's wrong? I had you all calm."

Rainer drew a deep breath and finished off his eggs. They were delicious, and he was starving.

"Brazil." He tried to gauge her.

With an irritated huff, she shook her head. "I'm not going, so stop thinking about it."

"Em…" Rainer furrowed his brow. He wasn't letting her stay home because of him.

"Rainer," she quoted right back. He set his now empty plate down on the coffee table and moved so he could look into her eyes.

"Baby, you can't stay home because of me. I'll be fine. I mean, I guess you and Garrett and everyone else are right. I didn't have a choice, and I'll get over it eventually." He wondered if he was being heartless and crass.

The appalling image of his uncle leaning out the window of his Alero and chambering a pistol aimed directly at Emily's head had his stomach churning instantly.

Concerned his breakfast might make a rapid reappearance, Rainer decided maybe he really hadn't had a choice.

"I know you will," Emily vowed. "But I can't leave you until you are, and Mom and the new baby, and the twins, and the election, and my first niece." She began enumerating all of the excuses she'd come up with not to leave.

Rainer let her get all of them listed without interruption. When she finally exhausted all of the reasons she had to stay, he kissed her cheek.

"You know as well as I do that part of being an Angel is participating in the service projects, and I know that the projects are usually a little closer to home. But this is going to be amazing. I don't want you to miss out on an opportunity like this because you're worried about me." Rainer didn't point out that per her contract, if she didn't participate in the service projects she would not be playing the next season. Emily knew that. She didn't need to be reminded.

"We're going to be gone a really long time, and Brazil is really far away," she choked. "What if you need me?"

Rainer cuddled her closer on the couch. He was immensely thankful to feel like he was comforting her now. "I could come see you in the middle or something. I know you'll be working, but I'd love to help." She shook her head with a defeated sigh.

"No guys. That was one of the rules. Only Garrett can come to make sure we get there safely and everything."

"But Garrett goes down there all the time and works," Rainer argued.

"It's not the orphanage's rule. It's the team owners' rules." Rainer's heart sank. He hadn't realized how much he'd been counting on flying down to see Emily on the weekends.

"I just don't want to think about it right now, okay?"

Rainer continued to cradle her tenderly in his arms. "Yeah, me either." He brushed her hair off of her shoulders and kissed her cheek. "But how about this? After we go to your dad's inaugural ball that night, I'll take you somewhere and we'll have a night, just the two of us. Whatever you want to do, okay?" His mind was still trying feebly to figure out some way to see her in Brazil. She nodded with an audible huff as she turned and buried her face in his chest. The motion in that moment righted Rainer's world as he hugged her.

"You're assuming Dad is going to win."

"He's gonna win. He has to. There isn't another choice." Rainer couldn't fathom watching all of his father's work falling by the wayside if Peterson took office and Wretchkinsides ruled supreme.

"And when I get back, you'll kick Logan and Adeline out so we don't have to get dressed all weekend?" She bit her lip and gave him a mischievous grin.

As he noted how good it felt to laugh with her, Rainer nodded. He never wanted to let something like her sweet laugh or that sexy grin be taken for granted. He couldn't survive without them.

"Oh yeah, baby. That will not be a problem." His vow made her giggle. They lay on the couch and cuddled for a while. They dozed in and out and watched a cooking competition marathon on the Food Network.

CHAPTER 33
ALONE WITH YOU

"Wanna watch a movie?" Emily quizzed as the sun began to set behind the heavy clouds.

"Sure." Rainer headed to the kitchen to heat up some of Mrs. Haydenshire's crab soup for the two of them. Emily began flipping through the movies. She stopped on *The Fast and the Furious*.

"No." Rainer shuddered. His reaction was defensive, but he wasn't certain why.

Emily studied him. She looked concerned. "I take it you also don't want to watch *Gone in 60 Seconds?*"

Rainer shook his head. He didn't want to meet her worried gaze.

All of his and Logan's macho talk that had been taking place since before they could even drive about car chases being awesome, and what they would do if they were ever involved in one, washed over Rainer with a tidal wave of nausea.

He might not always feel that way, but at that moment, as he summoned and waved his hand over the soup bowls, if he never saw another car chase in a movie it would be too soon.

Rainer shuddered as he placed the soup bowls on plates and added cornbread. He carried them into the living room.

"I'll probably regret this, but I kind of want to see what's on the news," he admitted hesitantly.

"Are you sure?"

Rainer tried to brace himself as he nodded.

"Okay." Emily summoned and projected on the TV until she located the Gifted news channels. She halted on a picture of Logan scowling outside of the Senate building.

"Realm news has been anxiously awaiting the arrival of Lawson's best friend, Logan Haydenshire. Logan, Logan..." The pert woman, who appeared to have had several cups of coffee too many, raced to Logan as he tried to escape into the Pentagon.

With an obvious sigh, Logan glared at the reporter.

"Logan!" The woman plastered on a fake smile. "Cat Harris." She batted her eyelashes. "Any idea where Rainer Lawson has disappeared to in the light of his uncle's fatal car wreck yesterday afternoon?" Logan seemed to consider the question for several seconds. He made the woman hopeful.

"Yeah, I have an idea."

Emily and Rainer both laughed as they continued to watch what was obviously a clip from that morning. Cat's eyes flashed as she gave an ostentatious laugh at Logan's quip.

"You heard it here first, folks. Realm News has the source right here in person," she drawled to the camera. Logan cocked his jaw to the side and tried hard not to laugh.

"So, where is Rainer mourning the loss of his only living relative, his uncle, Stan Lawson?" She feigned deep concern over Rainer's loss as she gave Logan a pensive stare.

"I'm not really certain, but I'm sure wherever Rainer is he appreciates the press giving him time to grieve the loss of his uncle without their intrusion into his personal affairs."

Emily bit her lip, clearly not certain if she should laugh, but the frustrated look on Cat Harris's face was hilarious. She gave an uncomfortable laugh for the camera and then urged.

"This has to be a devastating loss for Rainer. I'm certain that you must know where he is. We'd heard you are to be Rainer's best man in his and your younger sister's wedding this spring?" she tried hopefully. This was the press's latest tactic to try and wheedle information out of any of Emily's brothers about the wedding.

"Really?" Logan mocked. "That's the first I've heard of it." Rainer laughed outright. He could tell Logan was enjoying driving Cat Harris to distraction.

"So, Logan, as Rainer's best friend since childhood, what do you think must be going through Rainer's mind, as he is now the last living relative of Joseph Lawson, and where have he and your sister disappeared to?" She tried yet again with a different sound bite.

With a sigh, Logan checked his watch. "Like I said, I'm certain Rainer appreciates being left alone. I'm certain he's deeply saddened over his uncle's passing, and we would all appreciate him being given some space to deal with the loss."

With that, Logan shook his head as Cat tried to follow him past the security boxes into Iodex. She was halted by the guards as she continued to call questions out to Logan who was disappearing behind the massive steel doors.

The next video was of Governor Haydenshire landing in Portland, having delayed his trip a day.

"Governor, how is Mrs. Haydenshire handling this pregnancy knowing that the child will have developmental disorders that could prevent it from being Gifted?" Another overly animated reporter raced to keep up with the governor.

"You don't know anything about my child, and my wife handles every situation with a tremendous amount of grace and dignity," the governor quipped angrily.

"And what can you tell us about Rainer Lawson's uncle's accident and about his and your daughter's disappearance after the story of Stan Lawson's untimely death broke yesterday?"

"I can tell you that I'm deeply saddened for Rainer's loss, and I will make a plea to the press to leave both him and Emily alone as they deal with this devastating news." The governor stopped near the baggage claim of PDX airport.

"So, you're confirming that Rainer and Emily are currently somewhere together?" the reporter pressed.

"I'm not confirming anything," Governor Haydenshire stated

smoothly. "I'm asking that you give Rainer a little space." He reached to pick up his suitcase off the luggage turnstile and made a quick exit into the car awaiting on him outside of the airport.

The next shot was of the street that the Haydenshires' farm was on, but the press wasn't allowed to get close enough to actually get any shots of either house.

"We've been here all day, folks, anxious to hear from either Rainer or Emily about the fatal car crash that killed Rainer's uncle, Joseph Lawson's only brother, yesterday during rush hour. Thus far, we've not seen either Officer Lawson or Miss Haydenshire, so we have to assume they are staying close to home here on the farm. When they emerge, we'll be here to get the first quote from Rainer since hearing of his uncle's demise," an unseen reporter vowed. Emily rolled her eyes and changed the channel.

"Reports are swirling that Rainer Lawson's uncle, Stan Lawson, was taken out by an Iodex officer. He was allegedly working with known felon, Dominic Wretchkinsides, and with the Interfeci Criminal Organization. We have no confirmation of this, but it is appearing that this is true. Here, here..." A young, overly anxious man in a cheap suit and red tie rushed toward Vindico as he was leaving the Iodex office carrying a stack of files and his laptop.

Rainer knew he wasn't going home. He was going to have dinner, probably at Frye's, and was planning on working while he ate.

"Chief Vindico, can we get any information on the accident that took Stan Lawson's life yesterday? Was it an Iodex officer that caused the accident? Was Officer Lawson being chased?" The man ran alongside Vindico.

"That's an ongoing investigation. I can't comment." Vindico gave the typical canned answer for the press regarding anything any Iodex officer didn't want to discuss.

"If he was being pursued by Iodex, will there be an investigation or any reprimand for causing Stan Lawson to crash?" the reporter pushed harder.

"Certainly not. There is no evidence to suggest that he was being pursued. He wrecked his car. Unfortunately, it happens every day. I give my regards to Officer Lawson in the loss of his uncle." With a goading smirk, he pulled his badge.

"When will Officer Lawson be reporting back in to work?"

"I'm finished. How about yourself?"

The reporter's eyes goggled over the badge flashed in his face.

"Uh…yes, sir," the reporter sighed as Vindico issued quickly inside of Frye's. He slammed the glass-paned door in the reporter's face. Emily shook her head and turned to Rainer.

"Are we finished or shall I find more?" With a slight grin, she pulled up on her tiptoes and pointed out the front windows as there were two news vans still parked across the street. They appeared to be watching and waiting on cars to appear. "This is kinda fun though."

Rainer had to agree. Despite everything that had happened, being holed up with her in their sanctuary while the Realm searched for them was oddly enjoyable, as long as Rainer refused to allow the haunting memories of the day before back into his mind. They stopped talking and turned back to the television as Garrett came on to the screen. He'd been stopped outside of Iodex as well.

"Officer Haydenshire, Officer Haydenshire, there are conflicting reports about whether or not you, and perhaps Rainer Lawson, were present at the time of Stan Lawson's fatal accident yesterday? Can you confirm this?" Cat Harris pounced as soon as Garrett parked his Harley.

"That's an ongoing investigation. I can't comment." Garrett hoisted his helmet under his arm as he flashed his badge at the security booth.

"And where are Rainer and Emily now?" Cat demanded quickly.

"No idea," Garrett lied with ease.

"Can you tell us if they're on your family's farm in McLean? Your brother Logan led us to believe they were." Cat didn't seem to have any trouble lying either.

"Then why are you asking me?"

"So, they are on Haydenshire Farm."

Garrett rolled his eyes. "Wherever they are, I'm certain Rainer would appreciate some time to grieve his uncle in peace," was Garrett's final quip as he scooted quickly past the same steel doors Logan had disappeared behind.

Cat assured her viewers that she wouldn't rest until Rainer was located and they had a comment on the loss of his uncle.

Suddenly, a reporter emerged from one of the vans outside. They halted right at the Haydenshires' property line. Rainer's stomach churned as Emily turned off the TV, though no light should have been visible from the screens on the windows.

The reporter was on her cell phone, and Rainer opened a sound wave cast. Emily projected it for him so they could make out the conversation. They made certain to stay out of sight. The woman trespassed overtly, coming very close to the house.

"But they aren't here. We've been watching the house all day. No cars, no lights, nothing," she insisted. "Yeah, okay, I'll send the piece over as soon as we shoot."

They didn't have to use a cast as the cameraman began filming. They could hear her without it.

"We're here outside of Governor and Mrs. Haydenshire's summer home in Virginia Beach. Channel 719 thought perhaps Rainer Lawson and his fiancée, Emily Haydenshire, might take respite here, but thus far we've not seen either of the highly sought after couple.

"In the wake of the fatal accident that took the life of Stan Lawson, Rainer's only living relative, it appears Rainer and Emily have decided to grieve in quiet. No one has seen them all day. The Haydenshire family has been very tight-lipped about their whereabouts. If they show up here at the Haydenshire beach house, we'll be certain to let you know and to get their reaction to the accident." The woman hurried off of the property, climbed back into the van, and ordered the cameraman to send the copy to Ted.

"Seriously, that's news?" Emily huffed as she and Rainer eased back into the living room.

"The good part is that once it airs, your dad can scream and yell about her being on the property."

Emily picked up the plate with her soup bowl and bread, sank onto the couch, and shook her head. "What is it they want you to say?"

"If I told them what happened, I'm fairly certain it would be a huge story." Guilt washed through him once more.

"In which you would still be cast as the hero," Emily vowed.

Rainer shook his head. He still couldn't understand it. He'd saved Emily from certain death and the twins as well. As terrified as he'd been, he knew deep down he hadn't had another choice.

He allowed himself to dig deep to try and navigate his way through his ever-shifting emotions. He finally allowed himself to understand that if it had been any of Wretchkinsides's men in the car, aiming a gun at Emily, he would never have even hesitated to do what he'd done. It was that he'd allowed himself hope. That hope was what was so horrible to bear.

A very small part of Rainer had hoped for his uncle. He'd hoped that Stan would eventually change and become an entirely different man. Rainer knew it was a childish dream, not the reality they'd lived. He'd had no evidence to suggest that his uncle would ever change, but still the hope had remained.

Wretchkinsides knew that. The thought had Rainer convulsing. For the first time since he'd heard Vindico's harrowing tale of Amelia's death did he really understand the depraved, dark, evil that was Dominic Wretchkinsides.

His uncle certainly hadn't meant much to Wretchkinsides. He was far too uneducated, too impatient, and too lazy to have ever climbed the ranks in the Interfeci. Rainer shook his head as he finally allowed himself to consider all that had taken place.

"Wretchkinsides didn't think I'd be able to kill him," he stated out loud. The statement shocked Emily. She set her plate back on the table and slid beside him on the couch.

She nodded. "Keep going."

"That's why he chose him, and with a huge payoff like that, I'm sure Stan agreed to do just about anything. When he didn't get anything from the trial, Wretchkinsides came in and offered him what Stan most wanted."

"Right." Emily reached for Rainer's hand. "And he wasn't really in the Interfeci. He'd never murdered anyone before or done any of the other things that blacken your energy," she explained but was unable to say the word rape. "So, I wouldn't have been able to feel him coming. He was the perfect guy for the job. Everyone knows about my wreck. They came after me at my weakest and where I'm always the most scared. They knew you wouldn't be in the car with me. You drive so much better than I do. I'm still always so nervous. He knew all of that." Her voice faltered as she shook her head and blinked back tears. It seemed she finally allowed herself to feel and think about everything that had happened as well.

CHAPTER 34

INTENTION

Rainer's chest unfettered slightly. The realizations seemed to bring both peace and disgust in equal parts.

"I'm so sorry." Emily wrapped her arms around him.

After swallowing down another round of emotion, Rainer forced himself to ask what had been brewing in his mind without rest since he'd thrown the heat shield and electric cast.

"I killed him." He choked as tears fell from his eyes. He couldn't stop them.

"I know." Emily held him in her tender embrace. His gut clenched. He shuddered as pain spread from deep inside of his soul and flooded his body.

"I killed him, and I knew when I added the heat to my shield that the engine would explode, and then I had to make certain, so I shot electricity into it." He trembled as Emily held him. She nodded her understanding.

He pulled away and scrubbed his face with his hands. He needed to look into her eyes. Tears pierced their emerald depths as she gazed at him with adoration. He closed his eyes momentarily, but then shook his head. He forced them back open. He had to know.

"So…" he convulsed as she ran her hand tenderly across his cheek to wipe away more tears. Her cast moved through his face, and he forced himself to continue. "So do I..." he choked again. He clenched his jaw and attempted feebly to blink back another round of tears. "Do I feel different to you now?" he managed before his body shook uncontrollably, and he broke down again.

"No," Emily stated firmly. She kept her eyes locked on his. Intense relief washed through Rainer as he finally allowed himself to draw a full breath. "No, you feel just like you always have, since the first time I felt it when you kissed me when I was seven," she pled fervently.

After drawing a haggard breath, Rainer nodded. "You felt it then?"

Emily smiled. "Yeah. I think because I'm a Receiver and we develop our receptors before we can summon and cast, but I felt it, and even then I thought it was magical and wonderful and pure and good. It still feels just like that." She begged him to believe her. His head fell in his shame.

She placed her hands on his jaw tenderly and lifted his head back up. "I've never felt it when I'm around Vindico or Garrett. I never felt it when Cal would come back from Russia. You see, sweetheart, your intention is what sets your energy. It's not all black, or white, or whatever. Your mind, and your heart, and your soul matter so much more than the extra energy in your cells."

Rainer recalled Garrett unloading a pistol in Roberto Vasquez's chest, but that had seemed so justified. Vasquez had attempted to kill Mrs. Haydenshire and the new baby and then he'd taken Keaton.

Men like that didn't deserve to live. Rainer had decided as soon as Garrett had pulled the trigger, but it just wasn't that simple. He knew now. Rainer let her words baptize his wounded heart and his restless mind.

Murder had always seemed like something concrete. It was almost mundane in its blatant immorality. As he sat there on her parents' sofa clinging to her for dear life, Rainer realized that there was very little in the world that was concrete. Nothing was set in stone. People were never all good or all evil. They were capable of both, and his uncle's decision to let greed and jealousy drive him had ultimately been his undoing.

"Wretchkinsides didn't know that Garrett would be following us.

He thought it would just be the two of us with the twins. That's why he sent three drivers," Emily whispered.

She was trying desperately to make the distorted picture clearer in Rainer's mind. He let air escape his lungs in a pained hiss as he gave a slight nod.

"Are you okay?" Emily brushed a kiss across Rainer's jaw before tucking her head under his chin. His tears eventually dried.

"Yeah." Rainer finally felt like that might just be the truth.

That Sunday, his nerves came back in full force as he loaded his and Emily's bags into the back of the black sedan Governor Haydenshire had sent for them. It was nearing midnight. They'd waited in hopes that the press wouldn't be out in full force at the late hour.

Though she'd repeatedly insisted that she was fine, Rainer knew Emily was getting stir crazy locked away in the beach house with very little to do. Rainer felt whole again. She was there. She would always be there. That was all he would ever need.

The press began arriving in droves as soon as the car had pulled in the driveway. A photo had emerged from a bystander that showed Rainer's Mustang and Emily's Hummer at the scene of the accident. The press had eaten it up.

Vindico and Governor Haydenshire insisted that Rainer had been called to the scene, but as soon as Emily's Hummer had been identified it had been all the more difficult to explain away.

"Let's just go," Emily demanded as soon as she locked the house up tight. Rainer held the door for her and instructed the driver to stay in the car. He scooted in beside her, and they moved to the center of the backseat, shielded from view by the deeply tinted windows.

The driver backed out of the driveway as dozens of flash bulbs went off. They were followed and met at the airport by more reporters and cameras everywhere.

He grabbed their bags and shielded Emily as best he could as they raced to the private plane Rainer had booked.

"This way, Mr. Lawson." Rainer's head shot upwards. He

recognized the voice. Pete Namphis, the man who'd flown them to Paris, his father's pilot, smiled at Rainer kindly.

"Thank you." Rainer fought the urge to throw his arms around Captain Namphis.

"Anytime, son. It's the least I can do." He gestured to an exit door off of the gate as he helped Rainer block Emily from the onslaught of cameras.

"Governor Haydenshire phoned. He said you'd be calling in a private plane. I have a King Air. Now, it's not gonna be quite like those planes you fly in with the Angels, Miss Haydenshire, but I'll get you home. We'll see if we can't get you out of the camera lenses for a little while, anyway."

Emily beamed at him as they reached the tarmac. She threw her arms around him. "It's perfect. Thank you."

A broad grin spread across Captain Namphis's face.

"Really, you don't know what this means to me." Rainer followed Pete up the stairs to the cockpit of the small plane. Namphis crawled in his seat and gestured for Emily and Rainer to buckle themselves into the seats behind him.

"Your dad and his brother never did seem to see eye to eye. Joseph used to worry over him terribly," Captain Namphis commented as he summoned and spoke into his hand to get confirmation for takeoff from the tower. Rainer swallowed hard. "I remember your father saying that his brother would do just about anything but work for a dollar." Namphis chuckled. All of the blood in Rainer's body slithered quickly toward his feet. "I would never have said it to your old man, but I used to think to myself—those are probably the most dangerous men on the face of the earth. You know?"

Rainer nodded. Namphis was a brilliant man indeed.

They soon landed in DC.

"Do you need a ride back to the farm?" Captain Namphis offered as soon as the wheels touched the runway.

"No, sir. My brother's picking us up," Emily explained. "Thank you again for this."

"It's been my pleasure, and like I said, I'm gonna get my feelings hurt if I hear of some other pilots flying you to your honeymoon getaway."

"No, sir, it'll be you. Trust me," Rainer vowed.

"So, we are flying somewhere?" she quizzed.

"Maybe." Rainer and Namphis chuckled.

Emily seemed pleased Rainer was able to tease her again.

"Are you ready?" she asked as they took in the throngs of press in the airport.

"I don't guess I have much choice."

"Good luck, Rainer." Namphis shook his head as he took in the scene before them.

"Thanks," Rainer sighed.

CHAPTER 35
RELATIVE TRUTH

"Rainer, Rainer, Rainer..." The screeches began as soon as he and Emily set foot inside the airport.

"Emily, did Rainer force you to hide away with him?" called a frantic reporter from the *Inquisitor*.

Emily rolled her eyes and refused to answer. Rainer had instructed Logan to meet them in the parking deck, and he began working his way through the crowds, trying to get Emily out of there quickly.

"Rainer, why were you at the scene of your uncle's accident? Can you tell us what happened? Was your uncle working for the Interfeci? Were you the officer that took him down? Rainer, did you kill your uncle?" finally spilled from the mouths of the masses. Rainer and Emily calmly walked out to Logan's car.

"Hey man, welcome home." Logan gave his signature wry smile. He was leaning on the trunk of the Accord. He was being photographed constantly as he slapped Rainer on the back and helped him load the luggage into the car.

~

The story eventually spun to partial truths. Vindico confirmed that Stan Lawson was working with the Interfeci and had accepted a deal to be the hit for Emily. He'd gotten solid confessions from the other two drivers.

Governor Haydenshire confirmed that Rainer had been in pursuit of his uncle, but he'd bent the truth slightly by stating that it was under orders of Iodex. Everyone had insisted that Stan Lawson had lost control of his car and wrecked it of his own accord.

By Friday, most of the questions screeched at Rainer everywhere he went were along the lines of what his father would think of his only brother working for a criminal organization. Rainer offered little to no response. He often wondered what he could say as the answers seemed fairly obvious.

Governor Haydenshire had been out of town for several days. He'd concluded most of his campaigning all week and was keeping everything close to DC for the last few days before the election.

Mrs. Haydenshire was so pleased he was home and that his excessive traveling was over that she insisted they have their usual Sunday Haydenshire family dinner. The governor was due home around three.

Emily and Adeline had insisted that she let other people do the cooking, so everyone was pitching in. Levi was manning the grill for steaks, and everyone was bringing a side. Levi was an Occamy Predilect just like his mother, and his cooking was always outstanding.

The election was Thursday, and Governor Haydenshire was expected to win solidly with the latest polls showing him with seventy-eight percent of the vote. The governor's campaign managers were planning a huge costume ball in his honor Friday night, on Halloween.

Emily was to leave bright and early Saturday morning for Brazil. Rainer's stomach churned every time he thought about it. He'd spent the past week trying not to think about it except when he was forced to. He'd taken Emily to Georgetown the day before, and Adeline had given her the immunizations she was required to receive.

Throughout most of the day Sunday, while Emily was preparing large batches of her mother's twice-baked potatoes, she would tear up suddenly, and Rainer would wrap her up in his arms and continually reassure her that everything would be fine.

"The two worst weeks of my entire life were while you were in London, and yes, that includes the two I spent in the hospital." She shuddered. Every time she pointed this out, it cut Rainer to the core, but he refused to ask her to stop.

He'd broken up with her and left. He deserved the pain.

"I know, but that was entirely different. First of all, I was a seventeen-year-old, idiotic prick, and we'll be able to talk and text, which we couldn't do then. And we won't be broken up." He still found the memory repulsive.

"I know." She laid her head in the crook of his neck and let him soothe her.

By the time they carried the platters of potatoes into her mother's kitchen, Emily was overwrought.

"Emily, sweetheart, you will both be okay. I promise." Her mother pulled her in for a hug as soon as she saw Emily blink back tears.

Nana took in the situation and headed in to help. She unzipped a garment bag to distract Emily with the first of several bridesmaids' dresses that she'd completed, so that Mrs. Haydenshire wouldn't have to sew them.

"Oh, Nana, that's perfect. Thank you." She threw her arms around her grandmother. Mrs. Anderson was holding up a deep purple, strapless dress with a low neckline. It would fit tightly to the waist and then had a loose chiffon draping skirt that would hit above the knee.

Rainer was thrilled that something had brought a smile to Emily's face.

Nana Anderson put her arm around Adeline. "Now I just need to try it on you and make sure I got all the measurements correct, sweetheart. And I'll need all of the other girls as well," Nana reminded Emily.

"I know. I just have to pick them." Emily bit her lip.

"It's almost November, sweetheart. If we're getting married in April, we have to get everything done." Her reminder that it was almost November had Emily's smile fading fast.

"My sweet Emily…" Nana placed her hands on Emily's shoulders. "Don't waste the time while you're here wishing you didn't have to leave. You know, right after Paps and I got married, he had to go to Fort Rucker for six weeks." She fixed Emily a cup of tea and handed it to her. She guided her down at the kitchen table. "I was nineteen years old, living in a one-bedroom apartment by myself in Washington, DC, and my husband was eight hundred and fifty miles away. I didn't know another soul in the entire city, and Paps was only allowed to call on Sunday afternoons, for fifteen minutes." Emily looked both appalled and fascinated.

"What did you do?" She drew a long sip of tea. Rainer smiled and listened in as well.

"I sat myself down on the only chair that we owned at the time, and I made myself a cup of the same tea we're drinking, my sweet Emily Anne." She touched the rim of Emily's mug. "And I had myself one good cry. And then I got up and figured out how to walk myself to the market. I took in some extra sewing for something to do. When Paps sent his paychecks home on Friday, I took the $48.76 stipend that he earned and made us a home." She smiled at the recollection.

"Wow." Emily seemed shocked at the very small income Paps made in his Gifted Army days. Nana beamed at Paps.

"And I'll tell you this, my sweet girl," Nana drawled, "your mama was born nine months to the day that Paps got home from his training." Nana and Emily both laughed. Mrs. Haydenshire shook her head, and the governor grimaced.

"I think we could skip over that part of the story, Anne."

"But that's the very best part."

Emily and Rainer laughed harder. "So,"—Nana squeezed Emily's hand—"you enjoy Rainer while you're home, and you miss him real good when you're gone. Then it'll make your coming back sweeter than ever." She winked at Emily, who nodded and wrapped her arms around Rainer's waist. He cuddled her close and kissed her forehead.

Levi did indeed provide the family with some of the most delicious steaks Rainer had ever tasted, and the side dishes everyone brought were devoured. The Haydenshires seemed very pleased, but Rainer noted them holding hands under the table. He suspected that since the governor hadn't been home in almost two weeks, they were also looking forward to all of their grown children heading to their own houses.

Nana provided several apple pies from apples off of the trees in Paps's small orchard, and the governor pulled two of the homemade vanilla ice creams made over the summer from the freezer. He helped his mother-in-law serve bowl after bowl of dessert.

CHAPTER 36

WORTH A THOUSAND WORDS

A knock sounded firmly on the door as everyone began dessert. Garrett, Logan, and Rainer shared ominous glances as they all stood to answer. Garrett made it to the door ahead of Logan and Rainer.

"Who's there?" he called.

"It's Stella. I'm sorry to interrupt, but I really need to speak to the governor. We have a problem."

Garrett pulled open the door to reveal Stella McKesnick, the governor's press secretary, and Judy Young, the governor's campaign manager. Mrs. Haydenshire smiled kindly as she and the governor stood.

"Judy, Stella, come in and have some pie," Mrs. Haydenshire urged.

"Oh, Mrs. Haydenshire, I don't know what happened, but *this* didn't happen." Judy looked pale and horrified by whatever she'd come to tell the governor.

"What didn't happen?" Governor Haydenshire demanded.

"Mrs. Haydenshire, I would never...and he would never ever..." She gestured to the governor.

"Okay..." Mrs. Haydenshire now looked extremely concerned. Stella was carrying a wide, manila file folder. She stared at it as if it were a bomb set to detonate at any moment.

The governor seized the folder. "May I?"

Stella nodded, and Governor Haydenshire flipped it open. He gasped as his eyes bugged and his mouth fell open in shock.

"What is it?" Emily edged closer.

"But how? This never? When did?" The governor couldn't seem to make a coherent statement. Mrs. Haydenshire pulled the folder from her husband's hands. She looked equally stunned.

"Would you care to explain this?" she demanded of her husband and then of Judy. Emily became impatient and took the folder from her mother. She showed it to Rainer and her brothers.

Everyone stared in utter disbelief at the newspaper headline—"Governor Stephen Haydenshire says his wife handles everything with grace and dignity. Wonder how she'll handle this?" The full-page, color picture was of the governor leaning out of what appeared to be a hotel room door. He was in boxers and a bathrobe, and Judy looked quite pleased as she walked toward him in what appeared to be very short silk shorts and a very skimpy tank top. Judy began to sob in earnest.

"Mrs. Haydenshire, you have to believe me. I would never ever cheat on Darren, and he would never ever cheat on you." She gestured to Governor Haydenshire.

"That was taken while we were in Portland." The governor shook his head in utter disgust. "Judy came to my room late that night. Something had happened?" He furrowed his brow.

Judy nodded. "That was the night I got that call from Warren that something was wrong with one of the campaign accounts. I had to get one of the security codes from you to get the banners printed for the rally the next morning."

The governor nodded his agreement. He still looked utterly disgusted.

"His room was just down the hall from mine, and I was exhausted. I just ran across to get the codes. I tried calling, but he'd turned the ringer off on his cell."

"I was exhausted. I was trying to sleep."

"But Mrs. Haydenshire, Darren went with us to Portland. He was in my hotel room. You have to believe me," Judy begged.

"I do," Mrs. Haydenshire agreed, but the pain etched on her face wounded everyone in the room. She was waging war against tears. Her emotions appeared to be winning out over her repose. She shook her head, spun quickly, and flew up the stairs. Everyone was silent for the length of one heartbeat as they heard the master bedroom door close firmly and the lock turn.

"Lillian," Governor Haydenshire pled. Abhorrent pain cast his entire being as he raced up the stairs after her.

Everyone sat in stunned silence as Henry's sweet face turned terrified. His bottom lip protruded heavily as tears formed in his eyes. Emily began to cry as well, and Rainer wasn't certain what to do.

"Here, you hold her. I've got him." Garrett scooped Henry from his highchair. He casted his shield firmly around Henry, and he calmed.

"Maybe you all should go on," Nana Anderson soothed. "Rainer, would you and Emily mind keeping the boys at the guesthouse tonight?" she asked. Rainer agreed, but Will stood and shook his head.

"No, Nana, we're not walking out," he commanded firmly. "Dad didn't do anything, and he would never have done what they're accusing him of. So, we're all going to stay right here and fight this because this entire damn election has gone far enough. They've both always been there for all of us no matter what we've ever done. They've never walked away, and we're standing beside him now."

"Well, you can stay here if you want," Garrett argued. "But we're"— he gestured his head to Logan and Rainer—"flying to Portland. We'll be back in just a little while."

Logan furrowed his brow. "Why are we going to Portland?"

"Look at those pictures," Garrett commanded. He gestured his head to the offending folder that was now in the middle of the dining room table.

"I'd rather not, if it's all the same to you," Logan came right back with a disgusted shudder.

Garrett rolled his eyes. "Stop thinking like a bratty kid, and start thinking like an Elite Iodex officer," he demanded of Logan. "Someone had to take the photos, right?" He turned to Judy who was sobbing quietly in the corner of the vast Haydenshire dining room. "I'm betting there wasn't a photographer in the hallway."

Judy shook her head and tried to wipe away her tears. "No, but I wouldn't have cared if there was. Like I said, I would never even think of that." She gestured to the folder. She seemed incapable of keeping her chin from trembling.

Garrett nodded as he picked up the folder. "Look, the photos were taken from overhead. That means the camera is hidden either on top of a door, or in an exit sign, or something like that," he explained as everyone began considering who had done this. "I'd bet my next several paychecks on the fact that someone cloned Buffett's phone and called you to inform you of a problem that didn't actually exist. They knew you'd probably have to go talk to Dad about it as soon as you hung up. A rapid camera probably took pictures constantly until they caught one they could use, but setting up a camera with that kind of capability takes a little finesse. I'm betting they haven't retrieved the camera. This was too well executed. They waited a full week and a half to release this. I doubt they planned to get caught and blow the whole thing by removing the camera. They wanted it out just before the election."

Rainer felt hopefulness permeate the space where battered pain had just occupied. He knew how Emily and all of her brothers must feel. His world fractured like someone was trying to forcefully remove a part of his very being as he listened to Governor Haydenshire plead with his wife to let him in their room to let him comfort her. The door had remained locked.

In Rainer's mind and in all of their children's view, the Haydenshires had been an unshakable rock, a strong foundation. Trying to chip away at the very house that had raised them cut deeply in a place where wounds may heal but scars remained forever.

"This is tomorrow's front page?" Garrett interrogated Stella. She nodded and looked horrified. She was probably already trying to determine the best way to combat something like this with photographic evidence.

"Lillian, please!" they all heard the governor beg, and Emily sobbed. She knotted Rainer's shirt in her fists. She could feel her father's pain and her mother's horrifying fear.

With a determined nod, Garrett moved away from the table.

236

"Then we have all night." He pulled his phone from his pocket.

Rainer forced himself to think logistically. Thinking with any emotion at all was simply too painful. "Okay, but if the camera is still working, then as soon as we enter they'll know," he pointed out.

"Yeah," Logan agreed. "And I'm not really looking to take on half of the Interfeci. We need to get that camera out unharmed and prove what Peterson's done."

Garrett nodded as he scrolled down the contact list of his phone. "Yeah, Dan's going with us, and we could probably get most of Elite as well. I'm not sure if you've ever seen Danny fight"—Garrett chuckled—"but I'd say he's a little better than decent."

Everyone forced a chuckle at the understatement.

"Rainer, you have to go. You have to prove Daddy didn't do this." Emily pulled Rainer away from the rest of her family.

"Do you think you can really prove that?" Judy's voice shook with desperate hope.

"I sure as hell am gonna try," Garrett assured her. He grabbed his holster and his jacket after dialing Portwood's number. Vindico was meeting them at the Senate after he scrambled a jet.

Rainer nodded his agreement as Emily pulled him toward her and whispered, "She knows Daddy didn't do that." She gestured back to the folder on the table. "She's hurt because he made her have to think about something like that, and I know exactly what that feels like."

Rainer really didn't want to think about him going to a strip club or about how many things he'd kept from Emily that week. He had a job to do, and he was going to do it. He'd learned his lessons.

A moment later he was kissing Emily goodbye and climbing into the recently repaired Highlander as Garrett drove like a bat out of hell all the way to the Senate.

Rainer had been given a list of numbers of papers and news organizations from Stella. He was to phone as soon as they located something. If they were going to beat the trumped-up, infidelity charges to the papers, the press would have to be alerted instantly.

CHAPTER 37

DEEDS NEVER DONE

lite Iodex boarded a plane. They were all sporting the same signature military drive and scowl. Garrett handed the folder to Vindico.

After flipping it open, he shook his head. "He's a sick bastard." He shut the folder quickly.

Ericcson picked it up. "Who would believe this? Anyone who's ever met the governor would know he'd never cheat. I doubt he even fantasizes about other women."

"Uh, dude, that's my dad." Logan's shudder made everyone laugh. The plane, with a full battery of pilots and coolant officers, took off, and an hour and a half later they were exiting and loading into SUVs that Vindico had arranged.

The airport was relatively quiet. Vindico had called Mr. Buffett's house phone to inform him that they suspected his cell had been cloned. He'd assured Vindico that he'd never phoned Judy, and that to his knowledge, there had been no problems with the governor's campaign accounts. He was standing by, ready to be interviewed by the press.

Judy's husband, Darren, had shown up at the farmhouse while they were in the air. Emily had texted Rainer. He'd told anyone that would listen that Judy had only been gone from their room a few minutes and had immediately returned and phoned what she'd thought was Buffett's cell to give him the numbers he'd requested.

There was some worry over whether or not money had been stolen from the account via the passing of security codes, but Vindico called it when he explained that if they'd removed money from the account before they broke the scandal, it would have alerted someone.

Timing, in this case, was everything. He and Buffett had already decided to remove the money in the account. Vindico pointed out that those responsible probably intended to take the money while the Haydenshires reeled from the scandal.

"All right, when we enter, keep a close watch on anyone who tries to make a quick escape," Vindico ordered. "Someone in that hotel knows what took place, and we can't have anyone tampering with the camera. The way to prove the governor's innocence is to use the time stamp on Mrs. Young's cell phone and the time stamp on the photos," Vindico explained.

With that, the large black Escalade pulled into the parking lot of the mid-range hotel in downtown Portland.

"Turn off the ringers on your phones. No distractions," Vindico ordered. Everyone followed suit. As it was three hours earlier in Portland, the streets were more crowded than the ones in Arlington had been when they'd left.

Vindico threw open the double doors in the entryway of the hotel. Badges were held high by every Elite Iodex officer as they entered.

"Police! I just need everyone to stay right where they are," Vindico menaced.

There was a man dressed in a polyester suit standing near the front desk. His hotel name tag declared him to be Steve, and it encouraged guests to ask him if they needed any assistance. He moved toward the hallway that led to the elevators. Vindico had him by the scruff of his collar in a moment's notice.

"Steve," Vindico sneered. "Just the man I was looking for." He spun him so he was staring into his infuriated eyes. He drove his index finger into Steve's badge. Steve winced as the metal bludgeoned his skin. Vindico pretended to read the badge.

"As a matter of fact, I do require your assistance. It's so nice to get good service these days." Rainer watched all of the blood slither rapidly from Steve's face as Vindico plunged the nametag harder and farther into his chest. Rainer cringed. He knew the sheer strength of Vindico's arm and how badly that had to hurt.

Though Judy, who Rainer had to admit had been an excellent campaign manager, had provided Garrett with both her and Darren's room number and the governor's, Vindico demanded that Steve lead him to the camera.

As most men who were less than six feet tall and didn't look like they could lift a tank with one hand did not refuse Dan Vindico, Steve nodded hesitantly but refused to speak. He cowered as he loped toward the elevators.

As soon as they all entered one elevator together, Vindico began his threats. "You know I'm going to arrest you, and I've been a little bored lately, so I'm really hoping that the camera might still be running. I would love for Nic's boys to show up to help you out, but if you want to go ahead and spill the shit before I knock it out of you, then I'll see if we can't cut you a little slack."

Steve glanced around nervously at the infuriated, scowling men that surrounded him. Each and every one of them worked out regularly and would take a great deal of pride in snapping Steve limb from limb. He began to shake his head.

"I was just supposed to call if the police showed up. I don't know anything," he pled.

Vindico chuckled as the elevator opened on the fourth floor. "Oh, I don't know, Steve. Everybody knows something. Now, why don't we play nice, and you show me where they put the camera."

Garrett stepped in as bad cop. "Trust me, Steve. You don't want us to play dirty," he threatened as Steve took in the ominous tattoos that were rippling down Garrett's bicep.

"You can't threaten me. I have rights," Steve demanded impotently.

"Threaten you?" Vindico huffed with a wry grin. "Anybody here heard me threaten anyone?" he asked the officers that surrounded him. "Yet?"

Rainer joined in the no sirs that immediately spilled from everyone's lips.

"So, how much and who paid you, Steve?" Vindico demanded as they walked down the hallway toward room 415 which had been the governor's.

"I told them they couldn't put cameras in the rooms," Steve vowed.

Vindico rolled his eyes. "I love how criminals on their way to Felsink want to tell me about all of their good deeds, but listen up, Steve. Recording people on private property and publishing their pictures without their permission is against the law, be it in a hallway, or in the bedroom, or hell, even in the john. So, I'm going to ask you once more. Where is the camera? And this time you're going to tell me." Vindico's eyes flashed in fury as Steve nodded.

"There." He pointed to a small fire alarm box. It was mounted approximately eight feet up one of the walls, just before room 407, which had been Darren and Judy's room.

"Very good. You're not quite as stupid as you look." Vindico reached and pulled a black walkie-talkie off of Steve's belt.

"Hey, you can't use that. It's for employees only," Steve gasped.

Vindico laughed as he shook his head. "Now look who doesn't want to break rules."

After casting the walkie-talkie, Vindico spat. "Uh, yeah, this is Steve. I need a screwdriver and a ladder on the fourth floor." He rolled his eyes as he mocked Steve's voice.

A few minutes later, two men from maintenance arrived with a ladder and a tool chest.

"The service here really is impeccable," Vindico sneered. "Don't worry. I will be filling out my comment card."

Logan immediately set up the ladder, and Rainer grabbed a Phillips head out of the tool chest. He handed it up to Logan.

"Careful, Haydenshire," Vindico urged. Logan nodded and began unscrewing the box.

"Now, what was the number you were supposed to call when we showed up?" Vindico spun so Steve was between him and a wall. He was literally backing him into a corner.

"If I tell you that, they'll kill me." Steve sounded truly terrified.

"Yeah, life's a bitch and then you die." Vindico gave a flippant shrug. "So, like I said, if you help me out, we'll see if we can't put the guys you took the money off of for doing this away for longer than you'll be in yourself. Maybe their days in Felsink will make them reflect on their misgivings? Maybe it will piss them the hell off and they'll spend the entire time thinking of ways to do you in? I don't really give a shit, Steve, but I can tell you this—if you don't tell me everything I want to know, I'll mention your name so often to the press when I give interview after interview after interview about this fiasco...." He pointed to Logan who was delicately pulling the face off of the fire alarm box. "You'll be so damn famous people will be asking for your autograph. So, if you want to live past noon tomorrow, I'd start talking."

"Uh," Steve seemed to consider all of his options. He calculated the distance between himself and the elevator, and Vindico laughed. He summoned instantly and held the brilliant green glow of his double-banded shield in his hand. He waggled his eyebrows.

"Oh, run, Steve. It would make my whole day."

"Here." Logan hesitantly lifted a tiny camera out of the hole in the wall that had been covered with the alarm box.

"You know, I'm pretty sure the fire inspector would be interested in this as well." Logan glared at Steve. Rainer immediately pulled his phone and called the numbers for the press.

With that, Steve handed a card to Vindico who handed the card to Garrett.

"Ah, Barton, of course. He's Wretchkinsides's go-to camera guy, isn't he?" Garrett pulled his cell from his pocket with a wry grin. He dialed the number as Steve's eyes goggled, and he shook his head spastically.

With a defiant chuckle, Garrett moved the phone from his mouth just slightly and disguised his voice.

"Yeah, man, it's Steve at the Greenfield. Iodex just showed. They're everywhere. What should I do?" Garrett feigned terror. Vindico laughed silently as a broad grin lit his face.

"Okay, yeah, yeah, I'll hold 'em off and keep them busy in the manager's office," Garrett promised and then ended the call as everyone moved to different positions near the elevators to await the arrival of Wretchkinsides's men.

"Oh, here." Vindico pulled a pair of handcuffs from his belt loop and cuffed Steve. "Don't want them to think you helped us out, after all." He casted the cuffs and sealed Steve in. Then he shoved him to a seated position on the floor.

As they waited, Rainer let his mind travel back to Arlington to Mrs. Haydenshire. He shook his head as he considered what the election had meant for her.

Her husband, who was also her best friend, had been denounced and mocked. Her youngest son had been taken. Her unborn daughter had been poisoned. She herself had nearly been killed. Her daughter and her twin sons had nearly been run off the road. Then she'd been forced to stay home and away from the governor. Through it all, she'd remained steadfast and strong. It seemed too much to ask of one woman, of one mother.

Rainer's heart ached as he prayed that there would be something on the video that would prove to her that the governor would never cheat, even though Rainer believed that deep down she knew that.

He wanted her to be forever certain and forever sure of the governor as her rock. Rainer knew that Governor Haydenshire would remain faithful until he drew his last breath just like Rainer would be for Emily.

A moment later, the bell on the elevator gave a foreboding chime as the doors opened. Gildev Barton and Clive Mastiff stepped off of the elevator frantically.

Vindico had Barton down almost as quickly as Logan took out Mastiff. Rainer gave Logan an impressed smile.

He shrugged. "I'm not just a bratty kid," he quipped to Garrett who laughed and nodded his approval. There was plenty of press waiting outside the hotel when Vindico and Garrett escorted Barton out and Logan and Rainer followed with Mastiff. They were both scowling angrily. Portwood and Ericcson led Steve out, who'd begun crying like a baby.

They loaded Wretchkinsides's men into a local Iodex car, and Vindico signed the papers to have them flown to DC. Everyone loaded into the Escalade as Vindico turned on his laptop and wired the camera in. He shook his head as soon as he began studying the camera.

"There's not going to be anything on this," he lamented.

"How do you know?" Logan asked.

"It had a two-way feed. They accessed what they wanted, and then deleted the video once they had the shot." He sighed as his computer booted and instantly loaded the digital data on the video. There was nothing but black and white fuzz on the entire drive.

Rainer didn't know what he was going to tell Emily or what he was going to tell the Haydenshires. Vindico phoned Stella and explained what had happened. She thought that the testimony from Buffett and the video of the arrests would be helpful, but they'd been too late. The story of the governor's cheating on his wife of over thirty years would run as expected in papers across the Realm the following day.

The rebuttals and the evidence of the setup wouldn't make it in the papers until Tuesday, only two days before the election. Stella had already had numerous reporters out to the farmhouse taking interviews from Judy and Darren, and Mrs. Haydenshire had still not emerged from their bedroom.

Vindico visibly shuddered as he listened. No one spoke on the plane ride back to DC.

"Wait." Vindico, who'd been absolutely silent the entire trip, stood suddenly and paced down the center aisle of the plane.

"What?" Rainer urged hopefully.

"This isn't much, but it just might be something." He phoned Stella again.

"Yeah, read me the time stamps on Judy's phone from the call she thought was from Buffett until she called him back," he demanded.

He was silent as all of Elite Iodex watched him closely. A wry grin spread across his face.

"Three and a half minutes, huh?" He chuckled. "Yeah, if he was that quick, I don't think he'd have been given the opportunity to make eleven children. Rush photos of the time log to my office. I'll add it to the confessions from the arrests tonight, and we'll plaster that all over the papers Tuesday. It's not as good as video, but it'll have to do."

Rainer felt a slight glimmer of relief, but he knew doubters would say that the timing of the phone calls proved nothing. The fact that Judy's husband was on the trip would be more pertinent.

Rainer knew all of that, but he hoped against hope that with everything they had proven, Mrs. Haydenshire would at least be reassured.

CHAPTER 38

WHAT YOU KNOW AND WHAT YOU SEE

It was well after midnight when Vindico, Rainer, Logan, and Garrett headed back inside the farmhouse. Governor Haydenshire still looked sick as he sat on the couch.

Stella, Judy, and Darren had gone home after talking with Vindico on the phone. All of the Haydenshire children were still there sitting with their father.

Emily moved to Rainer. "She came down for just a minute. Dad begged her to believe him, but she didn't even speak. She just took the twins and went back upstairs. She put them to bed, and then she locked herself back in." Tears leaked down Emily's face as she explained what had happened. "She wouldn't even talk to me or to Nana."

"I'm so sorry, Governor. I did everything I could." Vindico looked like he'd been thoroughly defeated.

"This is not your fault, Dan." Weary desperation etched each word that egressed the governor's mouth. "I don't know what I could have done differently." He shook his head in utter defeat. "She knocked on my door. I threw on my robe and answered. I've attempted to sleep in hotels all over this entire country. I'm exhausted. She asked me a question. I went to my briefcase. I gave her the number, and I went back to bed. How could that possibly have shattered through the past thirty-two years? That's what I don't understand."

Terror coursed through Rainer's veins. He'd never heard the governor sound so desperate.

"She'll come around, Dad. It's been a really rough couple of months," Will soothed.

"Son, in the past thirty-two years, this is the first night I've ever been locked out of that bedroom." Governor Haydenshire tried to make his son see the magnitude of the situation.

Emily moved to her father. She seated herself beside him on the couch and let her cast work through his hand. "I think Mom just needs a little time. Will's right. Everything that's happened, even if it wasn't done directly to Mom, it was done to one of us or to you. That hurts her so much. She's so worried about the baby, but she doesn't want to tell us that. It consumes her. She's so worried about you and all of us. It's just too much. She's been through so much and she needs some time to process it all." Emily's entire body trembled in her effort to blink back tears. She seemed to have realized the gravity of her mother's adoring love.

"I would never, ever cheat on your mother." The governor stood and began pacing. "I couldn't. I don't know how men do that. How do you crawl into bed with a woman who isn't your wife, and then look your wife in the eye the next day, and then look your children in the eye? The thought makes me physically ill."

"I know that, Stephen." Everyone's head whirled as stunned silence filled the room. They took in Mrs. Haydenshire standing in her bathrobe with her pregnant stomach protruding much more than Rainer had noticed at dinner. Her eyes were red and bloodshot. They were badly swollen, but Governor Haydenshire looked at her like he'd never seen anything more beautiful.

"Lillian, please." He moved to her but halted himself before he reached her. He wasn't going to touch her until he knew that was what she wanted. Rainer knew the feeling only too well. "Please, please listen to me. You are my whole entire world. I would never ever jeopardize what we have."

Everyone looked away from them. The moment was too tender,

too raw, too intimate. It wasn't meant for anyone else's eyes. The pain between them was palpable and almost obscene in what it had robbed from them.

Mrs. Haydenshire convulsed slightly as Vindico slipped out the back door without even saying goodbye.

"I know." Mrs. Haydenshire fought sobs but her repose continued to elude her. The governor didn't seem to care that most of his children were present and privy to their display.

"Lillian, please baby, please don't cry. I don't know how, but I swear to you I will make this right." Mrs. Haydenshire nodded and reached for a tissue to wipe away the tears that fell in sheets from her exhausted eyes.

"Can I hold you, please? Please," Governor Haydenshire pled, on the brink of tears himself. Rainer shut his eyes and prayed she would allow him. His heart ached for the governor.

She nodded hesitantly, and the governor wrapped his arms around her tightly as she began sobbing into his shoulder in convulsive fits of emotion.

Everything had finally gotten to her. She broke down in his arms, and he held her up. Rainer knew he always would.

Rainer took Emily's hand and gestured to the door. She was wiping away tears of her own as she followed all of her brothers out the back door.

They all agreed to meet there early the next morning. Whatever the governor was planning, they all planned to stand firmly with the man who had raised them. No one deserved what they'd been dealt, and there was no finer man in the entire Realm than Stephen Haydenshire.

CHAPTER 39

THE FURY, THE AUDACITY, AND THE END

The next morning, Rainer stood in a navy blue blazer and a blue and red striped tie right beside Emily. Governor and Mrs. Haydenshire—whom Emily, Brooke, Sarah, and Adeline had worked on tirelessly to make it appear that she hadn't cried for hours the evening before—stood in the center, behind a podium. Their children were surrounding them.

Vindico, Buffett, and Governor Carrington stood ready to speak as well. The director nodded to Governor Haydenshire as dozens of cameras began rolling.

"I didn't write a speech for this event. I didn't have my press secretary or my campaign manager go over the things I needed to say this morning. So, I'm going to speak to the Realm, and I'm just going to say the things that need to be said. Ultimately, the decision of what you're going to believe and whom you're going to vote for is yours entirely, but I've put my family through enough, so here goes." Governor Haydenshire drew a steadying breath.

"Several months ago, three of my sons, and yes, for anyone who's marking my words today, I do already consider Rainer Lawson one of my own, and no, he has not yet married my daughter..." he added quickly. "Three of my sons were called from their beds in the middle of the night to go out and put their lives on the line to rescue Serena

Portescue. She'd been kidnapped by the Interfeci in hopes of gaining a monetary ransom from Crown Governor Carrington.

"My sons, along with the rest of our esteemed Iodex protection units, were able to rescue Serena, but the terror and the job were more than Regis wanted to deal with anymore, and he asked me if I would run for Crown.

"If he'd been able to tell me what my family was going to be put through in the process of me running for Crown Governor, I'm not certain that I would've made the same decision, but here we stand." Fury and disdain poured from his mouth.

"Since that fateful night, my wife and I found out we were expecting our eleventh child. We were thrilled, of course, until the night of Governor Carrington and Serena Portescue's wedding. Upon learning of my bid for Crown, the Interfeci organization, via a man my opponent signed the release papers for that ended his time in Felsink seven months early, placed a deadly and nearly untraceable poison in my wife's drink. It most certainly would have killed her had it not been for my future daughter-in-law." He gestured to Adeline.

"Now, if that weren't enough, I'd pled with my opponent to allow our family their annual trip to the beach for Labor Day. While we were there, he hired not one but three private investigators to follow my children and myself. I believe Iodex has documentation to prove this. Do you not, Daniel?" the governor quizzed Vindico.

Vindico moved in front of the microphone.

"I have copies of the checks paid for out of former Governor Peterson's personal checking account in my possession," he informed the cameras before he stepped away.

"Then, one of my youngest sons was taken while on the boardwalk with his brothers and sister. Try to imagine, for just a moment, the hell that my wife and I went through when the same man who attempted to kill my wife had his hands on my little boy." The governor choked over the emotion of the memory.

"You can see them here today." He gestured to Henry who was in Emily's arms and Keaton who was in Patrick's. "It seems the Realm has taken everything else, so I figured you all might as well have pictures of them as well," the governor spat angrily before he continued.

"Then and there, I decided I wasn't putting Lillian and my children through that kind of horrendous abuse. I would just not run. But then it got so much worse." The governor shook his head in disbelief.

"Now, what I'm about to say, I'm not supposed to tell you. I'm not supposed to even know this, but I'm tired of the games and the lies and the nightmare that I've forced my wife and my family to live, so Dan, if you want to arrest me then go right ahead. Right here on national television, I'm going to tell the Realm that my opponent accepted a substantial cash donation to his campaign, the first of many, from the head of the Interfeci organization, Dominic Wretchkinsides." He dared anyone or anything to object.

"I couldn't do it. I couldn't turn the Realm that Joseph Lawson, Gavin Willow, Arthur Vindico, Regis Carrington, and I worked so hard to establish over to criminals. So, I decided to take Dan up on his offer of broad range protection for my family. I tried to convince myself that it was for the best for my family. You see, I don't want my wife or my children or my grandchildren"—he gestured to Will and Brooke, who was so full of Will's daughter she could hardly stand—"to live in a Realm governed by criminals.

"I was blasted by my opponent and by the press for the money it was costing to keep my family safe, but I forged on. Then my wife was rushed to a specialist a few weekends ago in tremendous pain." The governor shook his head at the memory.

"We found out that our child is different, special if you will, or will have a few special needs. We had no time to be with one another to process that information, or for me to be of any assurance to Lillian before we found out that my opponent had bribed a receptionist at the specialist's office. So, a few hours after we'd been given the information, the Realm also knew of our news." He shook his head in disbelief.

"So, I gave yet another speech, fighting and vying for the Realm to remember who I am and what I've done. I've dedicated the last thirty years of my life to being a governor for this Realm. I fought and worked desperately to ratify the Constitution that Joseph Lawson wrote and ultimately died to uphold. That was in the past, and it didn't seem to matter. The fact that my child might not be Gifted meant more," he lambasted the viewers.

"My child, my little girl..." Governor Haydenshire's eyes flashed furiously. "See, we'll never know why this happened—if it was the poison that my wife ingested or if it's our age that caused these complications. There are many reasons my little girl will be the way she will be, but until this moment I'd not pointed that out.

"Lillian didn't want me to place blame, but I will never believe that it's our age." He emphasized the word our. "My wife, the love of my life, has delivered me ten, beautiful, healthy children, and just two years ago she gave me our twins. So, no, I don't believe our age has anything to do with this. I will always believe that Roberto Vasquez, under orders of the man funding my opponent's campaign, not only hurt Lillian but hurt my child as well." The newscasters present reeled inaudibly from the governor's statements.

"But it continued..." the governor stated almost in disbelief. "My daughter, who was driving the twins, was nearly run off the road after a handgun was aimed at her from another vehicle. Then, last night, as the campaign is finally winding down, I thought I could give my wife one night to have her children surround her and for our lives to resemble something normal. I found out during dessert that my opponent has placed a camera in a hotel smoke detector and caught my campaign manager coming to my room to ask me a question in the middle of the night." He huffed indignantly. "I will be happy to stand up here and tell you that I have never and would never cheat on Lillian."

He reached and took Mrs. Haydenshire's hand. She smiled up at him sweetly.

"She is the love of my life, and I understand that the photos in the papers this morning look bad. I will tell you that Judy Young knocked on my door in the middle of the night, and I answered the door. She asked me a quick question regarding campaign fund accounts. I answered her question, and she returned to the room she was sharing with her husband," he vowed adamantly.

"But I've decided that the only people I need to believe me are standing on this stage with me right now. If you want to believe me, then I certainly appreciate it as I've spent most of my life trying desperately to fight for the good. I've tried to be a good, upstanding citizen, and in all my years as a governor of this Realm I have never lied to this Realm. So, it seems you should believe me now, but I also know that we tend to believe what we want to hear and see only what we want to see.

"So, I stand here today, and I'm not even going to ask you to vote for me. I'm simply going to ask you this..." The governor paused dramatically. "Do you want to vote for a man who is capable of doing all that has been done to my family and to myself? Do you want Lachland Peterson running this Realm?" he quizzed quietly, with the strength of a man who'd done nothing wrong and who'd decided he didn't have anything left to lose.

After the governor was done, Vindico explained what had happened in Portland the night before, and Buffett declared that he'd never made a phone call to Judy in the middle of the night.

Then the waiting began...

~

Thursday evening, Rainer and Emily paced with all of the Haydenshires in the governor's campaign headquarters. They watched as the numbers continued to roll in. Voting day was a Realm holiday, so no one had been in the Senate all day.

Everyone waited anxiously for the polls on the West Coast to close. Patrick and Will counted the votes as they were phoned in.

The photos of Governor Haydenshire and Judy had done a great deal of damage, but the testimonies of Vindico and the arrests had done some repair. It was anyone's guess at this point.

"They have to believe him," Emily whispered.

"They will." Rainer prayed he wasn't lying to her.

By 12:45 the twins were sound asleep in the portable cribs the Haydenshires had brought for the evening.

Will leapt onto a table and held up his laptop. "Dad won with sixty-eight percent of the vote!" he declared. Everyone cheered quietly as not to wake the twins.

Utter relief washed through Rainer as he lifted Emily off the ground in his exuberance. Governor Haydenshire shook his head in disbelief as Mrs. Haydenshire wrapped her arms around him.

Rainer smiled as he watched them. He knew he was in the presence of a true and lasting love. It was one he felt so blessed to be a small part of.

CHAPTER 40
A COLLECTIVE DISASTER

While Emily was in the shower the next day, Rainer phoned the Hotel Royale to make certain that all of the provisions he'd ordered were being taken care of.

He was assured that the roses and the wine had already been delivered, and that everything would be ready when he and Emily arrived that evening after the governor's inaugural ball.

Though he tried to focus on their evening together, Rainer's heart ached every time he thought of driving her to the arena the next morning and then of not seeing her for over three weeks.

Vindico had assured him that although Wretchkinsides had a setup in Rio several years before, that Alexi Pravus, the man who'd run the Rio branch of Interfeci, had been moved to Colombia and that operations had temporarily been shut down in Rio. He felt that Emily would be perfectly safe as long as Garrett went along, and Brazilian Iodex was aware the Angels were in the country working. Garrett was going with the Angels as their security and their contact with the orphanage.

Logan sank down at the kitchen table and poured himself a bowl of cereal though it was noon. They hadn't gotten home until nearly three in the morning after helping the governor's campaign staff clean up and clear away the remnants of the campaign.

"So," Logan quizzed with a wry smile. "About how much fun are you going to be for the next three weeks? Just so I can plan accordingly."

"Just shut up," Rainer quipped.

Logan rolled his eyes. "About that much, huh?"

"She'll be gone almost a month. That's a long time." Rainer knew he sounded like a whining child.

Emily emerged from the shower with her hair twisted up in a towel and was wearing her least attractive bathrobe. She marched to the table.

"What if some girl at the Senate has just been waiting on me to leave, and then she's going to ask you out?" Her eyes were spinning wildly as she fought tears.

Logan shook his head. "Okay, I'm going back in there to eat. You two are a collective disaster." He refilled his bowl and moved back to his and Adeline's room.

"Are you going to say yes?" Emily demanded insanely.

"Sweetheart," Rainer soothed. This was not the first time over the past week that she'd dreamed up something completely outlandish. He stood and wrapped her up in his arms. This was not an easy feat as her body and hair were swathed in terry cloth. He rubbed her back consolingly.

"No one is going to ask me out, and more importantly, my baby and my heart will be in Brazil, and I will be here missing them both terribly," he vowed. "Now, Miss Bacall, I believe that your grandmother will be here momentarily to do your hair, so perhaps you should get dressed."

He and Emily always went to costume parties as Bogie and Bacall. Every year they'd been at the academy, they'd gone as the famous couple for the Halloween dance.

Emily loved dressing up as the Hollywood bombshell, and when she'd read that Bogie always referred to Bacall as his baby, she'd fallen head over heels for playing the part.

Other than the sheer amount of hair grease he had to apply to pull off Humphrey Bogart, Rainer had to admit he enjoyed it as well. He loved that Emily got such a kick out of it. He loved the way her eyes danced and how her grins were unending when she got to pretend to be one of her favorite actresses of all time.

Nana Anderson had recreated Lauren Bacall's famous white, billowing, deep V-neck dress with the thin black empire waist, which Emily looked stunning in. Rainer rather liked Emily's hair coiffed in a tight wave. It was like she'd stepped right out of a bygone era and into his arms.

As the Senate Chamber Room was to be used for the inaugural ball, no matter who had won, Rainer wondered momentarily how the Petersons were handling their loss. They'd been invited to the event, of course, but Rainer was certain they wouldn't show.

When his father had been killed and Carrington had run unopposed to step in as Crown Governor, which had been his father's wishes, there had been no ball. There was no celebration at all. The Realm mourned the loss heavily, but everything about this night felt different.

The press, in its ever-vacillating temperament, seemed to have decided, for the first day of his reign, to stand behind Governor Haydenshire and herald his good deeds. The Realm seemed to be responding with goodwill and allowed their best to shine through. This evening was to be a celebration of all that had been established and all that had been fought and died for.

The very energy that pulsed around the Gifted people seemed to vibrate with elation and pride.

Emily unwound the towel from her hair, and Rainer smiled.

"See, now I can kiss you." He planted a kiss on her cheek. She giggled and then smirked.

"Yeah, but I bet Bogie never told Bacall to put clothes on."

With a hearty laugh, Rainer shook his head. "If you don't put the dress on, then I can't take it off of you, baby," he goaded in his best Humphrey Bogart impression.

Emily beamed and then raced to the back door to let her grandmother in.

"I haven't seen your mother so happy in weeks," Nana gushed as she nodded when Emily offered her tea. "All this stress, I'll tell you...

our new Crown Governor and his first lady deserve a year off." She shook her head. Rainer and Emily agreed.

Logan came to give his grandmother a hug and then began searching for more food. He and Adeline had many conversations over the past few weeks on what to wear for the ball. He'd made numerous dirty innuendos about them dressing as each other so that he could play medio. Adeline would generally blush and roll her eyes. They'd finally settled on Popeye and Olive Oyl.

Logan grabbed a Dr Pepper from the fridge then settled on the couch so that Adeline could draw his anchor tattoo with eyeliner.

"All right, Lauren, I'm headed to the shower, baby." Rainer winked at Emily.

"I just love it when he calls me that," Emily admitted as her grandmother laughed.

"Yes, dear, we've noticed."

"Remember not to shave," Emily called.

"Done," Rainer assured her. He generally didn't shave for a day or two before donning his long vintage tuxedo jacket to pull off Bogart's rougher appearance.

CHAPTER 41

BOGIE AND BACALL

With his mind full of Emily and the night he'd planned in the extremely romantic Hotel Royale, Rainer drew a deep breath and forced himself to focus on the hours of the evening and not think about what the morning would bring.

He could see her all dressed up, with her eyes alight from the excitement of the party. He could hold her in his arms and feel her luscious curves sway against him on the dance floor. Then he could take her to the suite he'd booked, give her a bath, feel her energy, take care of her, fill her with him, make love with her repeatedly, and will the morning light to stay away by getting lost in the two of them together.

Three and a half weeks in Brazil seared through his mind again, but he shut it down and filled his mind with thoughts of her instead.

Rainer waited in the living room. He was dressed in a vintage tux from the 1940s. His hair was slicked with black grease. As he retied his bow tie, Adeline and Logan appeared. Rainer laughed.

"Very nice."

"Ay-ga-ga-ga-ga," Logan added in a terrible Popeye impression.

261

"If you do that all night, I will hit you," Rainer warned, which effectively cracked Adeline up.

"And I'll let him," she added as Logan feigned insult.

"Is Em ready? The limos will be here soon." Logan checked out his white sailor's cap in the mirror over the mantel. Rainer moved to their bedroom door.

"Ms. Bacall, you're needed on set." He knocked lightly. Logan rolled his eyes as Adeline swooned.

"I'm coming," Emily called.

"How about I won't do my ay-ga-ga-ga-ga all night, if you won't hello baby her all night."

Rainer shook his head. "Sorry, man, it's part of our thing, and it generally leads to me getting lucky so..." he harrassed just to make Logan gag.

Emily emerged wearing the long, flowing, white gown with the black banded waist that put her cleavage on stunning display. Her hair was fixed in auburn coiffed waves, and her makeup was done to suit the part. Rainer gave her a sultry grin.

"Well, hello, baby." He watched the thrill dance in her eyes.

"Ah geez, do we have to ride with them?" Logan spat as Adeline giggled.

A limo that already contained Will, Brooke, Patrick, and Lucy pulled into their driveway.

Rainer helped Emily in and seated himself beside her. Patrick chuckled as Logan climbed in after Adeline.

"Did you forget your spinach?"

"Nah, spinach gives me gas, man," Logan explained wryly as everyone groaned. The exhaustive, stress-filled days of the past few weeks were finally behind them. Everyone seemed to settle in and decide to just have fun for a little while.

Patrick was dressed as a rather convincing James Dean, and Lucy was playing Marilyn Monroe, although Rainer overheard her whisper to Emily that she didn't think she had the chest to pull off Marilyn.

Patrick heard her as well and immediately began whispering in her ear how drop-dead gorgeous he thought she was. By the time they arrived at the Pentagon, Lucy was giving Patrick looks that said they probably wouldn't be staying at the ball all that long.

"Might have another niece or nephew here in about nine months," Rainer teased Emily and gestured to Patrick and Lucy as they headed into the Senate ahead of them. Patrick reached back at that moment and grabbed a handful of Lucy's backside that was wrapped, rather tightly, in the dress she was wearing. Emily giggled and nodded.

They moved through all of the security checks and entered the Chamber Room. Emily sighed contentedly. A broad smile lit her face.

"It's beautiful." The vast room was bedecked with thousands of tiny twinkle lights all casted to sparkle just right. The tables that surrounded the dance floor were dressed in white linen tablecloths, and the room held a dozen flowering dogwoods, Mrs. Haydenshire's favorite tree.

The Haydenshire lion crest banner hung from each of the walls and on the back of the draped seats of the tables. The archway to enter the dance floor was covered in hanging Crown Imperial flowers. Pear blossom bouquets, the sign of health and hope, were on the serving tables, which contained delectable spreads of more food than Rainer had ever seen in one location.

Each table was candlelit around huge centerpieces of lavender irises, the symbol of the Realm, which stood for faith and hope.

At the last minute, Judy had requested that tiny amaranth flowers, in a deep pink, be added to the centerpieces. They were the symbol of fidelity. The effect was stunning. The room itself seemed magical, and Rainer smiled as he watched Emily's eyes glittering as she took it all in.

An hour into the party, the Haydenshires made their grand entrance. Everyone applauded, and whistles rang through the vast crowd as the newly minted Crown Governor pulled Mrs. Haydenshire in for the first dance.

All of Iodex was there to show their support of the new Crown. Rainer was rather surprised that Vindico had invited Bridgette to the event. He and every other person in the room were not as surprised by that as they were that Bridgette was wearing a rather naughty nurse costume. It would have been vastly more appropriate in her bedroom than it was at a costume ball. Emily's eyes goggled.

"What, he didn't let her change from work before he brought her here?" she huffed furiously.

"Just ignore her." Rainer didn't want to think about Bridgette or what he knew was the only reason Vindico was dating her since it had nothing to do with liking her.

As far as Rainer could tell, Bridgette annoyed Vindico just as much as she annoyed Emily, but she was a key to Wretchkinsides and that was all Vindico wanted.

Grandpa Haydenshire had shown in a tux that appeared to have been crafted in the late seventies. When Mrs. Haydenshire had shaken her head and suggested that perhaps his son being elected Crown Governor of the Realm might've warranted a new tux, he'd informed her that he'd paid good money for the one he was wearing.

With a chuckle, Rainer moved to the punch table. He accepted two cups from the wait staff and greeted Tuttle and Vindico as they made their way over.

"What, you didn't want to play doctor to her nurse? No, wait, you should be her patient." Tuttle waggled his eyebrows and laughed at Vindico who was dressed in what appeared to be an extremely expensive tux.

Vindico rolled his eyes and held up two fingers as the woman pouring the punch filled two more goblets.

"That's not even a costume," Tuttle continued to chide as he pointed to Vindico's tux.

"Sure it is. I'm the Chief of Iodex, in a tux."

Bridgette's naughty nurse costume was not the most revealing costume of the evening by a long shot. Emily's mouth fell open as Lindley Vindico entered with her date. She was dressed as a Playboy Bunny, complete with the ears and bow tie, only her version of the black getup barely covered anything at all. Her date was wearing a red silk robe and black silk pajama pants. He was carrying an unlit pipe as he was playing Hugh Hefner.

"Is she fucking serious?" Vindico shook his head as Governor

Vindico's mouth fell open in horror. He spun to march over to Lindley. Vindico caught his father on his advance.

"She wants you to get mad and freak. That's why she does this," he reminded his father. Governor Vindico seemed appalled by his youngest daughter's display. Deep disappointment etched his entire being.

Rainer and Emily shook hand after hand. They were shocked to see the Fitzroys there, but he'd been invited along with the French Prime Minister. Many foreign heads of state were in attendance as well. Rainer smiled and was heartily greeted by the British Crown, the head of the British Realm, who'd been good friends with his father.

"Hey, do we know that guy?" Logan gestured to a man with deep black hair who was speaking to the Haydenshires.

Rainer racked his brain. "I think that's the Australian Premier and his sons. Uh, Ethan and Arlo, I believe." Rainer recalled having been introduced to the man and two of his grown sons a few minutes earlier. "But I don't think we've ever met them before tonight."

"Yeah, that's what I thought, but it was weird when I shook his hand—it was like I knew him or something." Logan looked extremely confused.

"Maybe he just reminded you of someone. Energy patterns can be similar," Emily commented.

"Yeah, Em, I'm not a Receiver. That doesn't happen to me."

"Well, not all of our energies are that different. Maybe you know someone he's related to or something?"

"Yeah, maybe." He was still studying one of the Australian Premier's sons.

Governor Haydenshire asked Emily to dance, and everyone applauded as he led his daughter out to the dance floor. Rainer smiled as he watched her father's pride swell as he twirled Emily around.

Fitzroy had cornered Rainer earlier in the evening to ask how long Vindico and Bridgette had been an item. Rainer's response seemed to disturb Fitz. "This kind of bullshit is why I followed you that day," he'd explained.

"Very convincing Bogart." Vindico smiled at Rainer as he,

Ericcson, and Ericcson's date, approached him. They'd been laughing at something just moments before.

"I look better with my Bacall."

Dan laughed.

"Yeah, and I'm betting you'll let her teach you how to whistle, as well." He recalled the famous movie line with a knowing grin.

"I'm hoping."

Ericcson smirked and gestured to his date. "This is Drew Marshall, Lawson," he introduced. "He already knows how to whistle." Everyone cracked up as Rainer shook Drew's hand.

"And what are you all laughing about?" Fionna Styler sauntered up on the arm of her date. She smiled broadly at Vindico. She was dressed as Audrey Hepburn. Her long chestnut locks were piled high on her head in a sophisticated twist, and she was wearing a near duplicate of the famous Givenchy, white, sleeveless dress with black flowers on the long billowing skirt and bodice. She completed the look with long, satin, elbow-length white gloves, to fit the part. Save her deep olive complexion, she pulled it off perfectly. Her date was attempting to be Spencer Tracy, but he looked nothing like him. He'd also been ignoring Fionna most of the evening. He talked nonsensically about running for one of the open seats on the governing board.

"You look lovely this evening, Miss Hepburn." Vindico ignored her question as he picked up Fionna's hand and kissed the glove. Fionna glowed.

"Why thank you, Chief Vindico. I heard you were going as Head of Iodex this evening," she teased.

"In a tux," Vindico quipped with mocking arrogance. Fionna laughed as she gazed at him. Rainer was astonished as he watched Vindico add a cocky wink to his declaration.

CHAPTER 42
THE DANCE

Emily returned to Rainer after the dance with her father. She was flushed from the lights and told Fionna how fabulous she looked.

"Why thank you, Lauren. You and Bogie look lovely this evening as well," Fionna teased. The ladies began giggling. Rainer and Vindico shook their heads. The Senate Band drawled the first notes of "I'll Be Seeing You" and Emily swooned.

"Oh, that's Nana and Paps's song." She bit her lip as Paps led Nana to the dance floor.

"Can I get a dance, baby?"

Emily nodded and let Rainer lead her to the dance floor. Many guests were wearing tuxes and ball gowns and had only added masquerade masks to go with their ensembles, but the evening air seemed to hold trilling magic as Rainer swayed Emily around the dance floor.

Everyone applauded as Governor Haydenshire moved to the band, after the song was over, to make a request. He smiled adoringly at his wife, as the first chords of "Can't Help Falling in Love" swelled from the band. Tears pricked Mrs. Haydenshire's eyes as she fell into her husband's arms to dance to the song they'd danced to at their wedding.

A man in a black masquerade mask stumbled into Emily as they returned to their seats. Rainer caught and steadied her.

"I'm sorry, Miss," the man apologized.

"That's all right." Emily shivered slightly.

"What's wrong, baby?" Rainer decided that playing Bogart wasn't very hard since he preferred to call Emily baby anyway.

"I don't know. That guy sort of felt weird." Her body gave an involuntary shudder as she tried to look back through the crowds to see the man again.

"Weird how?" Rainer quizzed.

"Not really bad, just maybe a devious thought or two. Everyone has them occasionally, but I mean, I picked up on him in a room full of Gifted people?"

"Security is pretty tight here tonight. You had to have the invite to get in and everyone was screened," he reminded her as they'd both had to summon and be read before even they were allowed in. Then everyone was patted down and casted to make certain they weren't carrying a weapon.

"I know." Emily forced a smile, but Rainer sensed that it was only to appease him.

As the night wore on, Rainer continued to twirl Emily around the dance floor. He let his mind drift to the hotel room that awaited them.

"Where are we staying tonight, Mr. Bogart?" Emily whispered seductively in his ear as they danced.

"That is for me to know and you to find out, baby."

"Okay," Emily conceded as she nestled her head on Rainer's shoulder. He pulled her tighter to him. "What are we going to do when we get there?" Her enchanting voice, hungry in her whispered breath, made Rainer ache.

He leaned his face to hers so he could whisper in her ear. Rainer began telling her just a few of his plans for their evening.

When he finished, she was panting. Her eyes begged him as the song ended. He hoped that the extremely posh hotel had followed his instructions to the letter.

Rainer couldn't wait to let Emily see the room. He'd gone all out, but his heart ached every time he remembered why the night was special and what the next day would bring. He followed Emily back to their table where Levi and Sarah were engaged in some rather heated kisses.

The band director magnified his voice and began to speak.

"Crown Governor and Mrs. Haydenshire would like to invite everyone to the last dance of the evening and…" the director drawled, "our new first lady has instructed me to tell you that this dance will be ladies' choice." He chuckled as everyone laughed.

Emily grinned at Rainer. "Who are you hoping might ask you to dance, Mr. Bogart?"

Rainer chuckled. "Well, I've been flirting with this really hot redhead all night, but she's way out of my league."

Emily laughed as she stood and took Rainer's hand. She pulled him back to the dance floor.

"When this dance is over, we can leave," she tempted him as he folded his arms around her.

"Mmmm. Then let's make it quick. Because I want to get you out of here and me into you." Her breaths quickened deliciously.

As Bridgette had been drinking the free champagne all evening, she was in no shape to ask Vindico to dance. Rainer shook his head slightly as Vindico offered her a cup of coffee but didn't really seem to care. Emily's eyes goggled, and Rainer furrowed his brow.

"I wish she wouldn't put herself through this." Emily gestured to her right. Rainer turned and saw Fionna offer her gloved hand to Vindico.

He nodded and gave her a flirtatious smile as he led her to the dance floor. A minute later, they seemed to have melted into one another. Vindico's hand was slipping lower and lower down the back of Fionna's dress with every note of the song.

As the rather long song reached its final verse, Rainer's cell phone gave its ominous alarm in his pocket. Logan's did the same as he stopped dancing with Adeline right beside Rainer and Emily. Every phone belonging to Iodex officers all over the room were ringing simultaneously.

With his stomach churning, Rainer answered. Vindico apologized to Fionna as he did the same. Fionna shook her head and told him it was fine and not to worry, as she and every Iodex officer's dance partner studied them. Everyone wondered what on earth was going on.

Terror tensed in Rainer's shield as he heard the State police call informing Iodex officers, either on call that evening or not, that there'd been a kidnapping. Vindico shook his head and ended the recorded call. He phoned the Iodex officers who were in the office on call that evening.

Rainer watched as Vindico went pale and began asking questions that Rainer couldn't hear. He and Logan edged closer as did Portwood, Ericcson, Tuttle, and Ramier.

Horror etched Vindico's chiseled features as Rainer heard him demand, "Do we have any idea where they've taken her?"

As his heart sunk, Rainer braced and waited to hear. After another minute, Vindico ended the call. He looked sick.

"What's going on, Daniel?" Governor Haydenshire moved toward Vindico as well. Guests and foreign diplomats all over the chamber room became very curious very quickly.

"Let's go," Vindico suggested as everyone followed him out of the chamber room and into the Iodex offices. All of the governors followed them out along with Fitzroy, Mrs. Haydenshire, Emily, and Adeline.

Vindico spun as soon as everyone entered the office space. Rainer's heart raced, but he wasn't yet certain why.

"Son, what happened?" Governor Vindico asked. The expression on his son's face seemed to deeply concern the governor.

"They've taken Samantha Peterson. They're, uh..."—he drew a steadying breath—"punishing the former governor for losing."

"Any idea where they are?" Garrett leapt.

Vindico shook his head. "No, and I'm not certain there will be a ransom call. Malicai told Wretchkinsides from prison that it was her fault he got arrested for bugging Lawson's room. Peterson agreed when Wretchkinsides offered to fund his campaign that if Wretchkinsides would guarantee him a win, he'd do anything Interfeci wanted. Needless to say, they weren't pleased he wasn't elected."

"You have to try and find her," Emily gasped.

"Baby girl." Governor Haydenshire shook his head as he tried to calm her. Terror washed through Rainer as he let Vindico's words reel through his mind coupled with the last few things he'd said to Samantha.

Deep, penetrating regret pierced through him. He'd said some terrible things, and he very seriously doubted that Samantha Peterson would remain alive long enough for him to apologize.

Fitzroy began pacing. "Do you know which team took her?" He choked over the words.

"Cascavel." Vindico shuddered as all of the blood in his face drained. Logan and Rainer shared a horrified expression. The Cascavel cobra was one of the most vicious, deadliest snakes in the world. The man who'd taken the nickname lived up to the description.

Vindico's phone rang again, and he answered instantly. A hush fell over the room. He casted the cell so everyone could hear the voice on the other end.

"Tell me we have something," he pled.

"Maybe," Officer Sorenson explained hesitantly. Rainer recognized the voice. Sorenson was the head of the Non-Gifted police, DC precinct. "Just on a whim, I sent a team with a liason out to those warehouses out in Springfield. He picked up on several people out there in one of the abandoned buildings, the ones by the river docks. They were all Gifted, Dan." Vile revulsion flooded through Vindico.

Emily convulsed violently as she felt his reaction. Fitzroy reached and steadied Vindico.

"I'm sorry, Dan. When I heard who took her, I just had a hunch. Tigers don't change their stripes. Don't guess snakes do either," Sorenson offered.

Suddenly Rainer understood as bile rose in his throat. Cascavel must've been who'd taken Amelia, and he must've taken Samantha to the same location.

"No, that's okay," Vindico forced. "We'll get out there right away."

"Call for backup when you head out. Don't do this on your own, Dan."

"Will do," Vindico agreed. His voice sounded distant and furious as he ended the call.

"Daniel," Governor Vindico stepped in immediately. "Let Fitz run this one for you. You don't need to go back there, son."

Vindico glared at his father. "This is my job and my team. I don't try to tell you how to be a governor. Don't tell me how to run Iodex." Governor Haydenshire and Garrett shared an ominous expression. Tears fell from Emily's eyes as she shook her head. Rainer squeezed her hand.

"You have to find her," she begged. Her eyes were swollen with terror and desperation in their depths. "You have to save her."

Rainer nodded, but Mrs. Haydenshire pulled her away from him.

"Emily, he's going to try, sweetheart," she soothed.

"Mom, I was so awful to her." Emily began her confession, but it drowned quickly.

"All right. Peterson realized something had happened about an hour ago, when Samantha didn't come home." Vindico seemed to cement himself in the task at hand, but the haunted look in his eye existed in a distant past. "One of Malicai's friends told her he wanted to see her, and she was headed to Felsink. Peterson told her not to go. Like I said, this isn't for money. Wretchkinsides doesn't like to lose, and he generally reacts rather violently.

"Cascavel took her to the docks on purpose. He's wanted another go with me for ten years now, so listen up," Vindico challenged as he narrowed his eyes, unable to keep the utter hatred from leaking into his voice. "He is mine," Vindico demanded. "I'm sure he's not alone. Take out anyone who gets in your way, but Cascavel is all mine."

Everyone nodded their understanding as the governors all shared extremely concerned expressions.

"This is the worst possible situation because Wretchkinsides doesn't want anything. He's probably ordered Cascavel to kill her as soon as they hear us coming, so I'll do my best, Crown Governor, but I don't know if I can get her out," Vindico pled to Governor Haydenshire.

"You always do, Daniel. Just please be careful," Governor Haydenshire urged.

At that moment, as tension and terror crackled through the room, Rainer spun. He heard someone sobbing.

CHAPTER 43

BITTER REGRET

The Petersons rushed into the room followed by the security guards. Rainer knew he would never be able to remove the harrowing sounds of Yvette Peterson's screaming sobs as they reverberated through his entire body.

"Dan, please, you have to help me. I know we haven't always seen eye to eye, but that's my little girl," Peterson choked.

Vindico shook his head in baffling frustration. "I will do my damndest, but I told you something like this would happen. You lie with dogs like Wretchkinsides, you don't just get bitten—you get eaten alive."

"I know. I should've listened. I just never imagined," Peterson pled feebly. He turned to Governor Haydenshire. "I never knew what they were capable of. He just said they would make you drop out of the race. I'm so sorry. I didn't know."

Governor Haydenshire drew a deep breath. He reached for Mrs. Haydenshire's hand.

"Lachland, there are things that are so much more important than winning. I sincerely hope that not winning this election is the biggest regret you have this evening and for the rest of your life. I will do everything in my power to see that Samantha is rescued. I do, however, know precisely what you're going through as several of my children were threatened in all of this insanity you decided to turn a blind eye to. I hurt for you, and I pray that this ends with us all being able to put our lives back together."

After shaking his head and drawing a steadying breath, Vindico dialed the precinct's number back. "We're heading out. Make certain you're not seen or heard. Elite Iodex will go in. Once we've secured them, you can move in and load up whoever survives."

With that, Adeline fell apart. She sobbed uncontrollably as she fell into Logan's arms. Logan glared furiously at Vindico.

"Geez! You think you could not say shit like that in front of her?"

"I didn't tell her to come back here, Haydenshire," Vindico snarled.

"Daniel." Governor Vindico narrowed his eyes. "I know what happened, and I know what you're doing. But you need to simmer down and get your head together, son, before you get someone hurt or worse."

Vindico drew another deep breath as he turned to Fitzroy. "You in?"

"Hell yeah," Fitzroy vowed. "I've waited my whole career to watch you spear the snake." An image flashed in Rainer's mind. Vindico's tattoo, the one on his left breastplate, sported a large snake with a spear through it numerous times. Blood dripped from the dying beast.

"Then let's do this." Vindico grabbed the keys to the Expeditions from his desk and directed everyone to a vehicle. Rainer wrapped Emily up tightly in his arms.

"Rainer." Emily shuddered and gasped as she knotted his shirt in her fists. "Please be careful, please."

Rainer kissed her heatedly and then choked over what he was forced to say next. "Baby, uh, if I'm not back when you leave, I love you, and I'll call you as soon as we're through. Okay?"

"No, I can't leave until I know you're okay. I won't. I won't. They can't make me." Emily clung fiercely to him.

Governor Haydenshire moved in. "Come here, baby girl. He's going to be just fine, and we'll get you to the airport if he gets held up." Governor Haydenshire forcefully pulled Emily's hands off of Rainer.

Rainer was certain he was being torn apart at the seams as Emily convulsed in her father's arms.

"No," she shouted and broke away from his grasp. "Wait!" She rushed back to Rainer. "Take the ring, please."

"Emily, no." Rainer refused. He wasn't taking the ring off of her, and he was certainly not going to risk her going to Brazil for three weeks without it if he didn't get back in time. He held Emily's shoulders and leaned until he was staring into her eyes.

"I will be fine, and I will either pick you up at the farmhouse, or I'll be at the arena to see you go. Okay? I promise, but I've got to go." Rainer willed her to understand as he tried to push calming energies into her, but she was frantic, and he had very little access to anything calming at the moment.

He brushed a kiss across her lips and felt her tears on his own face.

Rainer holstered the pistol Fitzroy handed him as he climbed into the Expedition that the Elite team was occupying. He quickly removed the jacket to his tux, as Logan pulled off everything but the red shirt and jeans he'd donned to play Popeye.

Vindico cranked the car and flew out of the parking deck.

Rainer glanced at the dashboard clock. It was after one in the morning. Emily's flight was at seven. She had to board the Angels jet at six. His stomach churned. He wouldn't break his promise to her. He'd find a way.

"Hey man, I'm sorry. I know you and Em had a big night planned," Logan whispered so that no one else in the car heard him. Rainer tried to remember what he'd been dreaming of all evening long until everything had fallen apart.

"I have to be at the arena at six. I can't let her go without seeing her," he pled in a terror-filled whisper.

Logan offered him a kind smile as he nodded. "I'll get you there. I won't let you let Em down." As the lights of DC faded in the distance, Rainer tried to push all of his fear and disappointment over Emily's leaving away and focus on saving Samantha.

State police cars met them as they neared the Potomac. The cars moved into position, behind the Expedition Vindico was driving.

Vindico turned the lights off on the SUV and every other car following them did the same. He turned down a long two-lane road that wound around the industrial buildings that preceded the shipping docks.

"Do you think we'll get her out?" Logan choked in a barely audible whisper. Revulsion washed over Rainer. He didn't want to think about it. It was too much. He couldn't imagine Peterson having to live with the fact that he'd caused his daughter's death.

"I hope." Doubt threatened to overwhelm him.

Vindico parked the car between two towering shipping crates as the other drivers tried to hide their vehicles as well. He moved his hands to the windshield and began scanning.

Rainer braced. If anyone in the building picked up on his energy in the scan, it might all be over before they'd even been given a chance to get Samantha out safely. Dan pulled his hand away and shook his head.

"There are only three guys. Like I said, they aren't planning on her surviving, and they don't have anything to lose, so there was no need for a full team. This is what Cascavel wanted. He just wants me," Vindico sneered.

"The feeling's been mutual for a while now," Fitzroy vowed. "Let's give him what he thinks he wants."

"Oh, I plan to."

Rainer and Logan shared a quick glance. Vindico sounded pleased to be where they were and to be doing what they were doing. He sounded like he'd been looking forward to this for some time.

"All right, there are two by the bay doors." Vindico pointed to the large sliding doors on the west side of the metal building. They were blocked from the moonlight.

"You cast your shield and chamber your pistol in the car. If they hear or see anything, they'll kill her. Mark my words. There must be a loft on the east side. Cascavel and Samantha appeared to be up there. So, be careful. If he's above you, he's got a distinct advantage," Vindico warned. "We need to take out the two by the doors without Cascavel knowing, so move silently and follow my lead." Vindico gave the final orders as Elite Iodex exited the car but didn't shut the doors. Vindico shook his head at the officers who began opening the doors on other SUVs and squad cars.

He reached for his phone. Vindico silenced it then texted his instructions for everyone to remain in their cars until he called for them, and that only the Elite squadron would be performing the rescue. Rainer lowered his chambered pistol between his legs as he moved in a crouch position behind Logan.

They edged silently and stayed in the shadow of the building. Rainer's heart hammered as he tried desperately not to make a sound. He tried to remember all of the training he had. This was when it mattered.

They neared the bay doors, and Garrett gave the signal to sink to the ground. Everyone followed suit and began low crawling along the cement blacktop.

The silence echoed with terror. Tension crackled through the line of Elite Iodex as they stood and backed silently up to the metal wall. They slid along the building and made certain to stay in the cover of darkness.

Vindico halted abruptly. He held up his pistol and shook his head. He summoned, inside of his shield, indicating that they were not to shoot the guards at the door. They were to take them down with energy in an effort to keep Cascavel from knowing they were there.

CHAPTER 44

THE HISS AND STRIKE OF THE SNAKE

The team gave a single, cadenced nod. Rainer could hear his heartbeat pound in his ears. He felt his blood pulse. It was filled with terrorizing fear as it coursed through his veins.

Suddenly, a bloodcurdling scream shattered through the night. It took Rainer a split second to realize it was Samantha. His heart flew as Vindico cursed.

"Move now," he shouted as Fitzroy and Garrett summoned and took down the guards.

Bullets flew from overhead. Rainer deflected two with his shield. He heard them ricochet against the metal building.

They advanced quickly, until Rainer heard Garrett's gasping string of curse words.

"Garrett!" Logan panicked. Rainer jerked to the left and saw blood pouring from Garrett's shoulder. He'd been hit when one of the guards had momentarily weakened his shield.

"I'm fine. Just get Samantha." Garrett kept his hand pressed firmly on his shoulder while blood oozed between his fingers.

"No." Logan shook his head. He wrapped his shield around his brother. Vile revulsion flooded through Rainer's body. Bullets continued to rain down over them constantly. The harrowing repercussions of the slugs shattered around the metal walls.

He was unable to think beyond what he'd been instructed to do. Rainer followed Fitzroy as they raced behind Vindico up a set of sheared metal stairs. They halted at the top. Samantha was slumped in the corner. She appeared to be breathing but not conscious.

"Vin-di-co," Cascavel hissed in a simpering Russian accent. "So nice of you to dress for our meeting." He gestured his pistol to Vindico's tux. Rainer tried to understand what he was seeing as he watched revulsion wash through Vindico.

Both men held guns, as did all of the men behind Vindico. They were all pointed at Cascavel. Vindico shook his head as Rainer tried to understand why Cascavel's jeans were unbuttoned and unzipped.

"You're a sick bastard," Vindico spat furiously. "I'm not letting you do this anymore. You're not walking away this time. It's over."

A harrowing, evil laugh echoed from Cascavel.

"You're weak. You didn't stop me last time, and you won't tonight," Cascavel stated pompously. Fitzroy edged to the side and attempted to cast a shield over Samantha, but Cascavel was faster. He shot a heat cast at Fitzroy, making Fitz use his shield for himself.

Still following Vindico's orders that no one was to take Cascavel down but him, Rainer and Portwood kept their shields up with Ericcsson and Tuttle behind them. Ramier had stayed below to keep the guards subdued. He'd called in a medio medevac team for Garrett.

"The last time we met..." Cascavel drawled hatefully. "Good times. You got the jump on me. I was tired. Been having fun fucking up your girl. What was her name?" Cascavel goaded evilly.

Vindico's eyes flashed, and Rainer's stomach clenched tighter. If Vindico hadn't pulled the trigger after a comment like that, he had more patience than Rainer could ever hope to have.

Vindico narrowed his eyes and shook his head. "That wasn't the last time we met." His words were almost haunted in their apathy. He edged closer to Cascavel.

As if his mind had created shield casts of its own, the horrific details of what had happened to Amelia began to slowly seep through Rainer's understanding in confusing, gruesome detail.

Like turning the dial on a kaleidoscope, abject hatred coursed through Rainer's veins. He understood that Amelia hadn't just been murdered on the night of her capture. Cascavel hadn't just been trying to get Vindico to pull the trigger. He'd been telling the truth, and he'd done the same thing to Samantha.

Bile rose violently in Rainer's throat as he watched the deadly tango that Vindico and Cascavel were engaged in. Cascavel refused to move more than a few inches from Samantha, and Vindico edged tediously closer with each passing moment.

"Come on, Dan. He's yours. Just end him." Fitzroy kept his gun pointed at Cascavel's chest, but Vindico continued the dance. Rainer knew he had no intention of making the first move. He was going to kill Cascavel in self-defense. He was trying to save Samantha first.

Suddenly Cascavel flinched slightly, and Rainer gasped as Cascavel threw his right arm to the side and pulled the trigger. He killed Samantha at point-blank range.

"NO!" Vindico shouted, but he wasn't fast enough. Cascavel turned and pulled the trigger again. This time Vindico deflected the bullet. He threw it with every ounce of strength and unmitigated hatred that coursed through his massive body. It lodged deep in Cascavel's thigh.

Fury flashed in Cascavel's eyes as Rainer watched Vindico drop his gun and summon a furious blue and green swirling orb. His Double-Predilected cast lit the blood-drowned loft. It churned and swirled with abject hatred and vengeance. Everything that had made Dan Vindico the man he was lit inside the ferocious storm of malice he held in his hand.

He let his eyes close for a split second and then he threw. Blood sprayed across Rainer's body as Vindico casted Cascavel.

He was able to get in through the bullet wound. He exploded every major artery in Cascavel's body starting at his groin, then his abdomen, and then moving to his heart. He burst the vein in his neck, and with a wave of his hand he severed the head from the snake. Brain matter mixed in an appalling swirl on the floor at Rainer's feet. Cascavel fell instantly as blood poured from what remained of his body.

Completely stunned by what he'd just seen, Rainer's mind

attempted to block out the horrific images. Samantha Peterson's body bloody, bruised, and mostly undressed and of Cascavel's corpse, limp and drowning in a pool of his own blood.

CHAPTER 45
REPULSED

Rainer wasn't certain how it had happened, but Iodex officers and state police were escorting him down the stairs. Fitzroy stuck close to Vindico. He refused to let anyone else get near him.

Rainer stumbled out of the warehouse into the inky blackness of abhorrent reality.

Logan rushed to him. "Garrett's okay," he assured Rainer. "They're not even taking him to the hospital. They're just sending him to Mom and Dad's. Ad's gonna, uh…take care of him."

Rainer couldn't understand what he was saying. His mind was still brimming with fired shots, spewing blood, rape, and murder.

It took Rainer a minute to understand that Logan was physically holding him up and helping him walk.

"What's wrong with me?" Rainer demanded suddenly. He tried to force his body to stand on its own.

"Nothing. You're okay. That was just a lot of blood. It was a lot to see. You kept stumbling. Let me help you," Logan soothed. "Look, there's Dad, okay?" He pointed to the governor's Suburban as it pulled in. All of the blue lights were flashing. They gave an odd glow to the horrifying night. Logan sounded utterly relieved to see his father.

Rainer assumed the governor had come because of Garrett. He

didn't care why he was there. In that moment, Rainer just wanted the man that had raised him to tell him everything was going to be all right.

He forced his feet to walk in the direction of the Suburban, but suddenly someone else's hands were on him. He wrapped his arms around Emily as she sprinted from the car and into his arms.

"What are you doing here?" He gasped as he felt air fill his lungs and his brain snap back into normal speed.

"They called when Garrett got shot. I made Dad bring me with him."

Rainer nodded his understanding. He clung to her until he realized that he was getting blood on her. He pulled away, disgusted and repulsed.

"Rainer, it's fine. I don't care. Let me help you. Let me calm you down. I want to take care of you," Emily pled, but Rainer shook his head combatively. He couldn't have any part of Cascavel on her. He swallowed down the vomit that flooded his mouth.

"Emily, don't touch him." Governor Haydenshire raced to them after making certain Garrett was all right. Emily spun to argue, but the look on her father's face had her mouth closing.

"Logan, go help your brother with the seatbelt." The governor gave Logan the next order. Logan nodded as he eyed Rainer carefully. He turned and sprinted to help Garrett get in the car.

"Emily, go get back in the car. We're going home," Governor Haydenshire commanded with all the authority of the new Crown Governor.

Utter confusion etched Emily's demeanor as she walked away.

"Are you okay, son?" Governor Haydenshire soothed as he embraced Rainer. For just a moment, Rainer allowed himself to be held tightly in Governor Haydenshire's strong, soothing arms. "Let's get you home, okay? We'll talk whenever you're ready."

The governor walked beside Rainer. He kept up a steady, soothing conversation, but Rainer was unable to offer any response.

He seemed to understand that his voice was calming and steadying. He was the rock Rainer so desperately needed as he guided him. He always had been.

Emily cried quiet tears all the way back to the farmhouse, but Rainer refused to touch her. He was simply unable. Mrs. Haydenshire met them in the yard.

"Emily, take him upstairs and let him take a shower. Throw his clothes away, and then you two go on to bed. Use your old room."

"I'm all right, mom." Garrett objected to his parent's attempts to help him from the car. His arm had been healed but was quite tender. The Medevac team agreed that Adeline could care for him for the rest of the evening, and that he could join the Angels in Brazil on Monday, as long as he was completely healed by then.

Governor Haydenshire made certain everyone was inside, safe, content, and being cared for, before he informed them that he was leaving.

"Where are you going?" Mrs. Haydenshire quizzed. Panic set in her eyes.

"To the Petersons'." He shuddered.

Mrs. Haydenshire nodded. "Please tell them how sorry I am."

With a slight nod, Governor Haydenshire waved.

"I'll be back before Emily has to leave. I'll take them to the arena."

It was after three when Rainer emerged from the shower. His skin throbbed and glowed an angry red from scrubbing away the horrors of the night. He finally allowed Emily to wrap her arms around him as he held her.

"Let's go to bed for a little while," she soothed.

Rainer followed her to her old room and crawled into the safe haven of her bed.

Exhaustion won out over his terror, and he fell into a deep sleep as Emily kept constant vigil over him and casted him in her steady soothing rhythms of all-encompassing love.

CHAPTER 46

LEFT BEHIND

A few hours later, Rainer awoke as Emily slipped from the bed. "Where are you going?" He panicked, and she moved back to him.

"I have to get ready to go. I called Chloe and Medio Sawyer and begged for them to let me come Monday with Garrett, but I have to go today. If you want me to stay, I will. I won't go." Her voice shook in her plea. After methodically denying every fiber of his being from begging her to stay, Rainer shook his head.

"No, it's fine. I just wasn't thinking." He forced himself to get up with her.

"No, you stay here and sleep. You don't have to take me to the arena."

"No." He pulled her back to him. He was desperate to feel her before he would have to go without her. He seated her in his lap and cradled her. He reveled in the feeling of her safe in his arms. The night Cascavel had tried to take her assaulted Rainer's consciousness constantly.

"I'm so sorry I couldn't save her." He choked as images of his horrifying night began to seep back into his conscience.

"Rainer, no." Emily shook her head and wrapped her arms around him. "You were so brave, and everything you saw…I can't imagine. I'm so sorry. I'm so sorry I asked you to do what couldn't be done. I can't believe I have to leave you after a night like that."

Rainer shook his head. He didn't want to add to her self-imposed guilt. "I'll be fine." He left out the word eventually. No amount of pleading or hoping was going to delay the sunrise, so Rainer sighed. "Let me go home and get some clothes."

"Logan and Adeline brought you some a few minutes ago. Didn't you hear them come in?"

Rainer tried to draw steadying breaths. He inhaled deeply of the scent of her hair. He was instantly soothed. She handed him a pair of jeans and a Venton sweatshirt.

They dressed and hurried out to the governor's car. He stopped and picked up breakfast on the way and then flew to the arena so Emily wouldn't be late.

By the time they met the crowd of Angels waiting to board their plane, Emily's chin was quivering constantly as she blinked back tears.

"Just tell me to stay," she pled, but Rainer knew she had to go. He wasn't allowing her to give up her career because his occasionally forced him to see the horrors of the world in harrowing detail.

"You go, baby. I'll miss you like crazy, but I'll be standing right here when you get back. A month isn't really that long." He felt nauseous as he tried desperately not to think about not having her near him.

Fionna made her way over. "I'll take good care of her. I promise," she assured Rainer. Deep concern and empathy broadcast from her entire body. "I heard you had a rough night last night."

"You could say that," Rainer agreed though he wasn't feeling like much of a conversationalist.

"Is, uh…" Fionna choked and then drew a deep breath. "Is Dan okay?"

After considering all that had happened, Rainer shook his head. "I kind of doubt it."

"Yeah," Fionna nodded. "I kind of figured."

The pilots, coolant officers, and flight attendants began loading the plane. Governor Haydenshire hugged Emily goodbye.

"I'll just wait on you in the car."

Rainer nodded his appreciation that the governor wasn't going to watch him tell Emily goodbye.

"I love you so much." He wrapped Emily up in his arms.

"I love you too." She shuddered as she waged a war against her tears that she was losing badly.

"Call me when you land. Okay?"

"I will," she promised.

"K." Rainer wiped away more tears that had escaped against her stubborn will. "Please, please be careful for me." His voice cracked in his plea.

"I will. I promise."

"Emily, come on," Chloe called. Emily angled her head upward, and Rainer wiped away another round of tears and then laved her with a kiss that he fervently hoped he would still be able to taste a month from then.

A long drawn minute later, Emily drew a deep breath and hugged Rainer tightly.

"I took all of your T-shirts to sleep in," she confessed.

Rainer found his chuckle to be cathartic. "Good, baby. I wanted you to."

"And I took your pillow." She continued her confessions.

"Okay." Rainer smiled at her adoringly.

"I can't sleep without you." She trembled as her tears began once again.

"You'll be fine." He willed himself not to break down as his exhaustion and the harrowing night coupled with his despair that she was leaving.

"Emily!" Chloe sounded annoyed now.

Emily kissed Rainer again, and he watched her disappear up the stairs to the plane. He blew her a kiss, which she returned, before he sauntered slowly out to the governor's minivan.

He had a physical, echoing pain in his chest. He felt hollow like a very large part of his heart was being left behind.

~

Rainer awoke several hours later. Logan was shaking him.

"Hey, man, I think Em's calling you." He handed Rainer his cell.

"Hey, baby." Rainer cleared the sleep from his throat.

"I'm here."

"Did you have a good flight?" He rubbed his eyes.

"I guess. I have to go get checked in. We just got to the orphanage."

"Okay, sweetheart. Be careful."

"I will, but Rainer…" she begged. The terrified, weary tone of her voice concerned him. "If I want to come home, will you come get me? If anything happens with Mom and the baby…" she pled.

"Of course. You just say the word. I'll be on the next flight." He knew perfectly well that she wouldn't leave when there was work to be done, but she needed to know that he would catch her if she felt like she was falling. She needed to hear that he would always pull her from the abyss when it threatened to capsize her. He would always be her Shield.

"Okay." She sounded much more certain of herself suddenly. "I'll call you tonight."

"I can't wait," Rainer agreed and then immediately told her he loved her as she did the same. A moment later, she hung up. Rainer's heart ached.

"Why didn't you get in the bed?" Logan gestured to the couch Rainer had been sleeping on as he tossed his cell on the coffee table. He refused to tell Logan he hadn't wanted to get in their bed without Emily, but Logan had his number.

He gave him a grin. "Hey, I slept in a car for a week, so believe me I get it, but I don't think you'll survive a month on that couch."

Rainer sat up and yawned. "I'll be fine." He stared out at the stale gray sky and willed the day to be over with. That would get him one day closer to Emily's return.

He glanced at the clock on the stove. It was almost five. The Angels jet had made the normally thirteen-hour flight in just over six. Then the girls had to be driven to Recife, one of the poorest cities in Brazil, which had taken another couple of hours.

"Vindico called a little while ago," Logan eased.

"Is he okay?" Rainer shuddered as images from the evening before seared through his brain once again.

"Not really, but he wanted to know if you and I would go get a beer with him tonight. He and Fitzroy, maybe Garrett too, if he's up to it."

Rainer furrowed his brow and tried to determine what he could do to help his boss. He figured if he wanted to go get a beer that was the least they could do after all he'd been through.

"Ad's gonna hang out with mom." Logan sounded like he'd much rather stay home with Adeline than go out for a beer, but Rainer knew he wanted to be there for Vindico as well. "We're supposed to meet them at Lesco's in an hour. Do you wanna drop Ad off and then maybe drive around a little before we go?" There were far too many pleading notes in his tone. Rainer studied him closely for a moment.

"Sure, just let me grab my keys." Rainer knew Logan needed to talk about what had happened the night before as much as he did. He moved to his and Emily's bedroom door. He hesitated momentarily before pushing it open. Loneliness settled on him as he began locating his keys and ran a brush through his hair. The room felt strangely cold.

For the thousandth time in just the past few minutes he'd been awake, Rainer wished he could talk to Emily about the harrowing experience. Since she wasn't available, Logan was definitely his second choice.

One of the many things Rainer had learned in his self-imposed exile to London was that when things happened that caused him to have to reorder the way his world worked, it was nearly impossible without Emily there. She was his center, and nothing would ever make sense to him without her, but if Logan needed him, he'd be there, just as Logan had always been there for him.

Another scene from the night before splayed across his mind. The one of Logan helping him out of the warehouse when Rainer hadn't even realized he'd needed help. Logan had been there instantly. Another thought occurred to Rainer, one he found almost odd in its desperation. Rainer fervently hoped that Fitzroy was to Vindico what Logan was to him.

They dropped Adeline at the farmhouse with plans for Mrs. Haydenshire to give her a sewing lesson. Logan walked her to the door, kissed her goodbye, and then fell back into the Mustang with a yawn.

Rainer tried to force his body to sync with the clock. After staying up most of the night, rising early to go with Emily to the arena, then sleeping most of the afternoon, time itself had Rainer addled.

"Tell me what happened after we went upstairs." Rainer still felt like the night before was somehow disjointed. He couldn't seem to make all the puzzle pieces fit. Logan considered for a moment.

"You were there when he got shot," Logan reminded him. Rainer nodded. He wanted to move past that particular part of the story. Garrett Haydenshire crumpling to the ground screeching curse words as bullets rained down over everyone would haunt Rainer for the rest of his life. Logan seemed to understand.

"So, I casted him and tried to calm him down. I tried to heal him. I guess I can only heal Adeline or something, but I made him a little better. I kept him from getting hit again. Then the Medevac team got there and took us out. They pulled the bullet out and healed him, and I went back in to try to find you. All I heard were shots fired on that loft thing, and then I saw blood fly everywhere. Then you were all coming back down the stairs. Garrett told me what that guy did to Amelia, why Vindico was so crazy, and I heard Portwood talking about how he killed him." Logan seemed to gauge Rainer as they turned toward Lesco's. Rainer was driving rather slowly.

"Do you think that was okay?" Logan finally asked the question he really wanted answered. "I mean, you know, for Vindico to be his judge, jury, and executioner."

Rainer considered for several minutes. Thoughts of Stan's car bursting into flames formed in his mind. Rainer had never been arrested or even brought before the governing board to be questioned about how his uncle had died.

Governor Vindico had signed the papers declaring that it was self-defense, and that had been the end of it. He shook his head and tried to forcibly remove the image of the hissing Cascavel, the rapist, from his mind.

"I don't really know. I thought about that this morning while your dad drove me back from the arena, and I just decided that I would've done the same thing. Right or wrong, that's exactly what I would've done." Rainer offered Logan the conclusion he'd come to that morning. His killing Stan was the only life experience he had that could compare to what Vindico had gone through and what he'd done in vindication.

His decision had brought him peace. It was one of the reasons he'd been able to sleep that afternoon.

"Yeah, that's what I thought too," Logan offered. "I kind of got the impression Mom and Dad don't think he should've killed him quite like that."

"They weren't there. They didn't see what I saw," erupted from Rainer's mouth.

Shock etched Logan's face momentarily as he nodded his understanding.

CHAPTER 47

THE PRESENT

A few minutes later, they entered Lesco's. Les smiled his kind smile. The smell of the burger joint, as well as the twinkle in Les's eyes, soothed Rainer in its tranquil familiarity.

"Garrett and some friends of his are in the back. Are you meeting them, or are you two still not cool enough to hang with Garrett?" Les teased.

Logan laughed. "Nah, he lets us eat with him now, occasionally anyway."

"As long as they don't talk." Garrett laughed. He'd come to the front of the pub to show Logan and Rainer where they were seated. Les chuckled as he followed them back and supplied the table with pitchers of beer and several baskets of appetizers.

Rainer and Logan greeted Vindico and Fitzroy. Rainer studied Vindico. His eyes were swollen and red. They were bloodshot. At some point in the very recent past, he'd sobbed for quite some time.

Rainer looked away. He couldn't bear it. He couldn't reconcile it in his head. Dan Vindico was the strongest Shield Rainer had ever seen. His rippling muscles and his height made him look untouchable. In Rainer's mind, he was rock steady and relentless when it came to getting his guy. He certainly didn't cry. It just couldn't be.

Rainer's heart ached as he forced himself to meet Vindico's gaze.

After what he'd been through, he deserved the opportunity to cry. He recalled Vindico's words to try to make him feel better when he'd killed Stan and couldn't seem to contain his emotions.

"...and sometimes they're just because life is just too damn much to deal with."

Life had definitely dealt Daniel Vindico more than anyone should have to deal with.

"How's your shoulder?" Rainer turned his gaze to Garrett. This was the first time he'd really seen Garrett since the night before when Emily had led him to bed while Adeline was changing Garrett's bandages.

"It hurt like hell when it happened. Just a little tender now." Garrett threw several onion rings in his mouth.

"Are you still leaving Monday for Brazil?" Vindico asked. His voice was rough and gravelly from his emotion.

"That's the plan unless you need me to stay here," Garrett offered.

"Nah, you go on. It's good you volunteer down there, and I promised your dad the Angels would have security. You always have more service hours than anyone."

Garrett offered no response to the commendation.

They continued to eat in silence for several long minutes. Vindico studied Rainer occasionally. Not certain what to say, Rainer sipped his beer and secretly wished Emily would call.

"Can I ask you something, Lawson?" Vindico finally choked.

"Sure." Rainer noted Fitzroy nodding his approval.

"How old were you when they executed Maredon?" He gave Rainer the impression he was being interrogated.

Timothy Maredon was the man who'd killed Rainer's father, and his name always made Rainer's stomach turn in ragged, jarring twists. He tried desperately never to think of him.

"Uh, I was sixteen." He wondered where this was going.

"Did you go to the execution?"

"No." Rainer shuddered. He remembered that day in great detail just like he remembered the day of his father's murder.

"When you knew he was dead," Vindico hemmed, "...or when you killed Stan..." He whispered quietly as Rainer set down his burger. He was no longer able to eat. "Were you happy?" Vindico asked quite sincerely.

"No. Not on either count." Rainer tried his best to explain to Dan how each incident made him feel. "I remember overhearing the Haydenshires talking about the execution, and they would never have let me go. Not that I wanted to, but I just remember thinking what was the point? It wasn't going to bring my dad back." Rainer discussed these feelings openly with the men at the table.

Before that moment, he'd never said any of this to anyone but Emily. Vindico seemed to let Rainer's words wash over him.

"Yeah," he agreed.

Rainer wasn't entirely certain what he was agreeing to, though, so he continued, "I guess a part of me was glad because I think I was always afraid of Maredon, and I certainly always believed my uncle would gladly do me in to get the estate. So, I think it was a little bit of a relief, like the terror was over, but I think both things really just made me miss my dad so much more." Rainer poured his heart out for his boss who he realized now was also his friend.

Vindico's eyes flashed with relief as a slight smile spread across his face. Rainer had struck a chord.

"Yeah, that's it exactly," Vindico agreed as Rainer watched his shoulders start to relax and his breaths come easier. "I guess that's what I was talking about. I thought it would feel better, but it just doesn't. Me killing him didn't undo what he'd done."

Rainer and Logan were too stunned to speak. They felt vastly unqualified to offer comfort of any kind.

Vindico seemed to equivocate momentarily over whether or not he should finish with his confession. After seeing that Rainer and Logan were both committed to the conversation and wanted to help, he drew a long sip of his beer before finishing.

"I mean I'm glad he's dead. Hell, I'm glad I killed him." He glanced around to make certain no one heard him. "But I just thought it would feel better. It doesn't. Nothing seems to make it better."

Fitzroy furrowed his brow. "It will, Dan. Just give it some more time. Maybe find a woman who isn't Bridgette, someone who's more than a distraction. It's been ten years, man."

Rainer watched to see how Vindico would respond to Fitzroy's directive. Vindico shrugged, but Rainer knew he wasn't planning on taking the advice.

Silence loomed again as everyone except Rainer resumed eating. Rainer's phone chirped, and he reached for it instantly.

> There is absolutely nowhere here that I can talk to you. There are people everywhere. We're going to have to text.

"Do you mind if I answer this? It's Em," Rainer asked the table at large. Everyone motioned for him to continue as they ate.

> I'm sorry, baby. We could text during the day and then talk at night, maybe.

> No, we thought we would only be sharing rooms with one or two other Angels, but we're all in one room in bunk beds.

Rainer grimaced. He could tell even via text that Emily was exhausted and that nothing was going to cheer her up until she got some sleep. Another text came through immediately.

> All of the kids here just break my heart. I've already cried like ten times just seeing how they live. I can feel how hungry they are and how scared. I can feel everything they feel. It's awful.

Rainer's heart ached. He'd known Emily would have a difficult time with the Gifted orphans, at least until she got to know them. Her ability to understand and receive what they were feeling was going to make her very emotional.

> I'm so sorry, baby. Try to get some sleep. I know you were up most of the night worried about me.

Rainer fervently hoped that Emily would find the experience fulfilling. If she were enjoying herself, it would ease the aching pain in his stomach.

He texted back and then returned his phone to his pocket.

"How's she doing?" Garrett quizzed. "Does she hate me yet?" He chuckled as he continued to eat.

"No." Rainer furrowed his brow in confusion. "She's just a little tired."

"Yeah, I was pretty floored when Mom told both of you to go get in her bed last night," Garrett chided.

This brought a genuine smile to Vindico's face as he chuckled. "So, does that mean the governor has deemed you worthy?"

Logan and Garrett laughed. "He'll never be worthy," Garrett assured Vindico. "He's just lucky."

Rainer nodded his adamant agreement with the assessment and raised his beer in acceptance.

Everyone laughed and seemed to settle in. No one really wanted to discuss the evening before, but they all found peace in being with the people who'd been through the harrowing ordeal with them.

"If Em doesn't hate me yet, I'm sure Chloe does." Garrett slid back to his earlier statement.

"Why would they hate you?" Logan asked.

With a wry smile, Garrett chuckled. "Well, I mean I'm not saying the Angels aren't all great, sweet, hard-working women, but let's be real—they're all a little spoiled. Just take Emily..." Garrett urged. "The Crown Governor's baby girl marrying Rainer Lawson."

Rainer furrowed his brow. He'd never really thought of Emily being any more spoiled than he or the rest of the Haydenshire children. None of them ever acted like they thought anyone owed them anything.

"Em will love the kids, and they'll love her. That's why I wanted them to go. They can really make a difference, and I kind of think Chloe at least could use a few weeks to see that a lot of people have a lot less than the Chief of Staff of Georgetown Hospital's daughter who also happens to be the captain and highest paid player of the Arlington Angels."

Rainer's jaw tensed in what it took him a moment to realize was anger.

"I don't really think Emily needed to go to Brazil for a month to understand that." He was suddenly furious with Garrett. "Your parents did a tremendous job of teaching us all that growing up."

Logan glanced at Rainer and gave him a look that said he was definitely overreacting. Logan turned back to Garrett.

"He, like the rest of us, kind of had a long night. Only he had huge plans with Emily and a suite booked at the Royale that they never even saw. So, now may not be the best time to tell him that it's your fault Emily's not going to be here for a month. Trust me, they're like rabbits. By the end of three weeks, he's going to be so hard up we may have to get him crutches," Logan concluded by eliciting the laughter he'd been after.

Rainer drained his beer. He was ready to leave, and he was still irritated with Garrett.

Though Vindico chuckled, he looked concerned. "Hey, Lawson, I'm sorry. I completely forgot she was leaving this morning, and I didn't know you had plans last night. Not that it would've changed anything, but I really am sorry."

"No, it's fine. That's my job," he stated earnestly. "I just think with everything that Em's been through in the past couple of months, and with the wedding, and the new baby, and all of the shit with the election, this may not have been the year for the Angels to head off to Brazil. There are plenty of people in need right here in America." He threw Garrett an infuriated glare.

Garrett shook his head with a slight eye roll that let Rainer know he'd just been chalked up to the same spoiled status as Chloe Sawyer.

After deciding he didn't care, Rainer gave a slight huff. He felt like being mad at someone, and Garrett was just as good as any.

As the tension he felt permeated the table, Logan seemed to understand that Rainer needed to blow off a little steam before he ended up saying or doing something he'd regret.

"Hey, I know it's cold, but we haven't played paintball in ages," Logan urged the table. Vindico rolled his eyes, but Rainer could tell he was intrigued. Fitzroy and Garrett seemed pleased that Vindico was interested in something that might get his mind off of Cascavel and Amelia.

Fitzroy gave Garrett a concerned glance. "Are you sure you're up to that? Most guys look to get shot only once a weekend. Maybe we should go easy on your shoulder."

Garrett scoffed. "I don't play with a handicap, and who says I'm going to get shot?" he goaded cockily. "Call Will and Levi. I'll call Patrick and Connor," Garrett instructed Logan.

Rainer wondered if going out in the Haydenshires' back field and shooting one another was a little too reminiscent of the evening before, but he'd been playing paintball with the Haydenshire boys since long before his father had been killed. It was exhausting, and fun, and a physical release, which is exactly what he needed.

The only time he'd ever not enjoyed playing paintball was the day, many years ago, when Levi had gotten mad that Rainer had taken him out.

He'd fired a shot at Emily and had left a welt on her shin. Rainer had come unglued. He threw his newly developed shield at Levi. He was only fourteen and had little to no control over his abilities. His fury drove him, and he ended up in a vicious fistfight with Levi, which Will and Governor Haydenshire had promptly broken up.

Rainer had been punished for starting the fight as Levi had for shooting Emily. They'd ended up having to weed the entire garden that hot, summer day but had made up quickly and actually ended up having fun.

After coming back to the present, Rainer stood and followed Logan out of the booth. He listened to him tell Will to meet them in the barn.

Garrett studied Vindico. "You sure you're up for this?"

"Sure, why not? Nothing else has worked. Might be fun to make the Haydenshire boys cry." He seemed desperate to do something to get his mind off of the events of the last twenty-four hours.

"You wish," Logan and Garrett chanted.

CHAPTER 48
CONSUMED
DAN VINDICO

"I'm, uh…I'm sorry I haven't been out here for a while." The crushing guilt set like a stone in his gut. He always felt so horrible for not going to the grave that had robbed him of everything good in his life, but when he did go, it never offered him any peace.

She wasn't there, and he needed desperately to let her go. He'd existed inside of that tomb for so long he wasn't certain he knew how to live anywhere else.

"Hey, Dan, I'm sorry. Just let me call a cab," Fitz eased softly beside Dan as they stared down at the marble representation of all that Dan had lost.

He shook his head and tried futilely to halt the downpour of tears that burned his face and strangled his throat like a jagged noose. They slowly beaded and trickled down the headstone.

"It's fine," he lied. "Let's just go." He scrubbed his hands over his face and halfheartedly laid the bouquet of pink camellias on the top of Amelia's grave.

"You stay. I'll just catch a later flight," Fitz offered kindly. Dan turned and directed his feet back to the Expedition he'd taken from the office. He tried to hear his footsteps as they crunched on the graveled ground. He heard nothing but the fire's vicious roar.

He didn't speak. He was unable. The relentless fire that burned so fiercely in his gut had seared his vocal cords. His body reignited with vengeance and fury.

He cranked the SUV and narrowed his eyes in on the road before him. The path away from that damning enclosure, from that grave, led straight to Wretchkinsides.

"Are you sure you're okay? I can stay another night." Fitz was bordering on panic.

"I'll be fine." His voice was distant and raw. It existed a lifetime ago. It had taken up residence with his heart that had been replaced with a hollow, empty wound.

"Oh yeah?" Fitz shook his head. "When?" It seemed he was losing patience with Dan's vengeance-fueled wrath.

"When I end every last fucking one of them."

ABOUT THE AUTHOR

J.E. Neal (aka Jillian) vastly prefers coffee to tea, guac to salsa, the beach over anywhere else, and the world inside her head over the one outside her front door. She also loves not having to choose.

Driven by the question 'what if,' J.E. Neal's world began to manifest. What if there were people with powers the rest of us couldn't see? What if the energy of our world could be summoned and used at their will? Characters with these amazing abilities took shape in her mind. She created—and continues to create—an endless number of stories full of delicious escape from our reality where emotions are visible, desire is palpable, and danger is universal.

Learn more about J.E. Neal at JillianNeal.com

facebook.com/jilliannealauthor
twitter.com/JillianNeal_
instagram.com/jilliannealauthor

ALSO BY J.E. NEAL

ENERGY OF MAGIC

Shield and Shattered Cages (Book 1)

Shield and Faltered Steps (Book 2)

Shield and Splintered Oaths (Book 3)

Shield and Humbled Crown (Book 4)

Shield and Vile Serpents (Book 5)

Shield and Coveted Splendor (Book 6)

Shield and Guarded Shadow (Book 7)

Shield and Worthy Sinner (Book 8)

Shield and Sacrificial Heirs (Book 9)